可恶，为什么我只会“哇塞”！
恭喜你发现宝藏！
这是古代诗人转世吧？
生活何尝不是诗？

## 第五辑
# 默

123 · 人
124 · 一件事
127 · 风的旅人
128 · 花
131 · 腐朽
132 · 太阳的赠礼
135 · 母亲的病
136 · 我不知道
138 · 凌晨一点加班回家有感
140 · 尽头
143 · 浪漫
144 · 沉默
147 · 缝布娃娃
149 · 其实
150 · 一座幸福的小岛
152 · 因果

# 第四辑
# 见

106 · 海鸥
108 · 妄想症
110 · 晚霞（一）
111 · 晚霞（二）
113 · 小窗
114 · 玻璃海
116 · 霞
119 · 痴心妄想

第三辑

# 戏


74 · 孤独
76 · 社会
78 · 踩影子
81 · 眼泪
83 · 价格
84 · 名字
86 · 月亮
88 · 太阳
91 · 光
92 · 老师，你要相信我啊
95 · 钟
97 · 不想上学
98 · 班主任
101 · 骗子
103 · 我也是妈妈的妈妈

## 第二辑
# 你

38 · 失眠
41 · 故人
43 · 墙头，马上
44 · 你的城市下起了雨
47 · 相拥
49 · 蚂蚁
50 · 忘记
52 · 一百岁与一万句关于你
55 · 关于月亮
57 · 我是一棵榆木
58 · 金华秋实
61 · 信
63 · 林深与海蓝
65 · 思念
67 · 代替
68 · 三行情诗（一）
69 · 三行情诗（二）
71 · 落日

# 目 录

第一辑
## 我

2 · 我
4 · 花事
6 · 文字
8 · 听不见
10 · 我的爱
12 · 无用
15 · 妄想
16 · 完美
18 · 捉迷藏
21 · 习惯
22 · 衡水
25 · 温柔
26 · 一个自卑者的爱
28 · 离职
31 · 暮晚
32 · 鸟
35 · 2021 年 10 月 5 日真的很适合睡觉

# 第一辑 我

我就做庄子的那棵树

什么也做不了

所以能只是一棵树

# 「我」

八云家の折扇

我又不是那干干净净的女孩子，

穿一条白素白素的裙子，

戴着一顶太阳帽，

满是青春电影般的气息。

身上混杂着泥点的，

地上翻捡着树枝的，

嘴里咀嚼着花果的，

那才是我。

3

# 花事

洛蝶酱

我从未奢望美好会降临

但我仍旧坚信埋葬我的地方

会是一片没有尽头的花海

我的血肉和皮囊会被凛冬庇护

我的灵魂会在春光里驻足

倘若你在六月来见我

会有一朵玫瑰

悄然绽放

# 文字

字沫夜

我所有的文字都躺在壁炉里，

美好的词是蓝色的火焰，

阴暗的词是紫色的火焰，

而那些关于想念你的，

都默不作声地死去。

# 「听不见」

有事也勿扰

我捂住耳朵

听不见世间的喧嚣

放开双手

却听不见心里的声音

# 「我的爱」

安达

我爱我啊

我舍弃不掉我的一切

衣服、鞋子、手表、唱片

都是我的爱

对，还有落日

那是供给我思考留念的东西

# 无用

潘哆啦A夢

为了有尽的人生，

想做一个无用的人。

不再把期望当肥料汲取，

疯长的枝叶已压得我沉重；

放任饥饿与疲劳蔓延，

凋落为别人开的花。

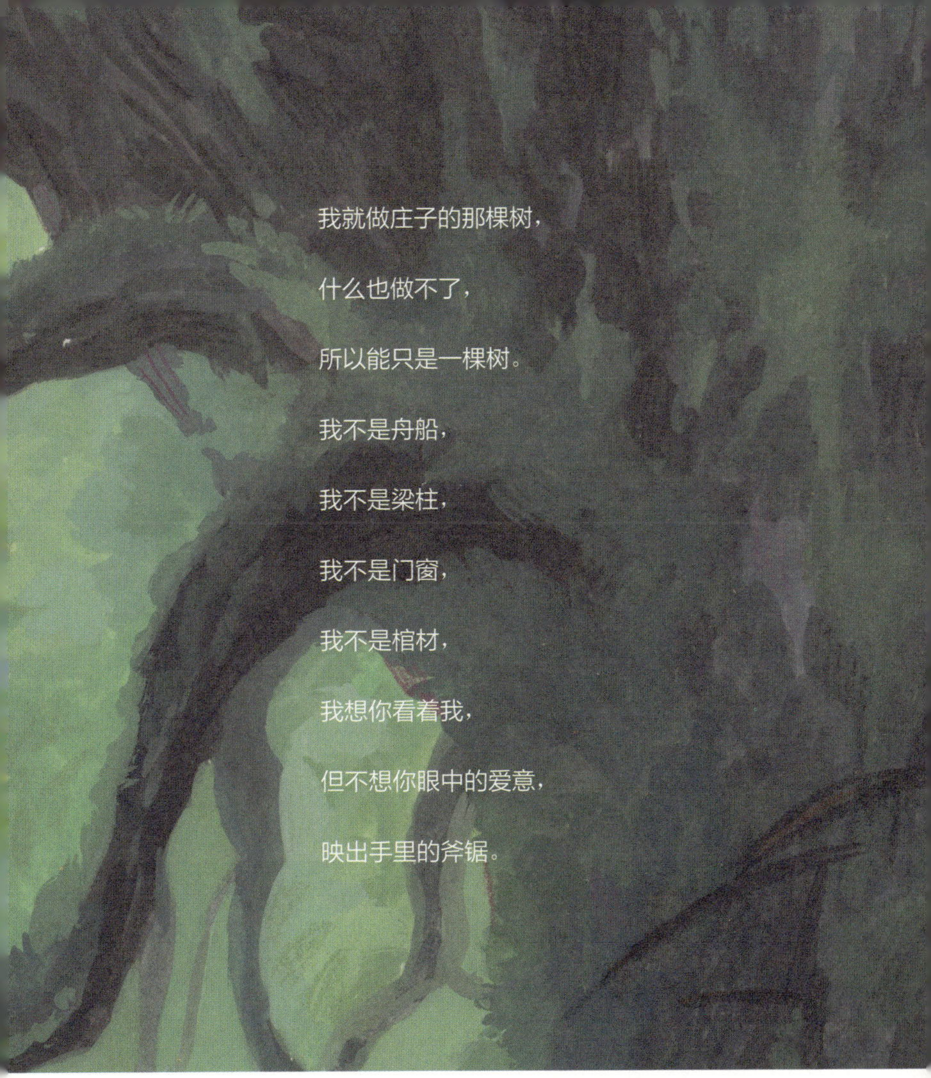

我就做庄子的那棵树，

什么也做不了，

所以能只是一棵树。

我不是舟船，

我不是梁柱，

我不是门窗，

我不是棺材，

我想你看着我，

但不想你眼中的爱意，

映出手里的斧锯。

# 「妄想」

没有新点子

我把太阳钉进我的脊骨

我要他永远和我连在一起

我要背着他走完我的宽广小路

我要他普照我的灵魂一生

# 「完美」

默久

丑陋的我，

在心里藏匿着。

一个近乎完美的你，

和一个不存在的，

近乎完美的我。

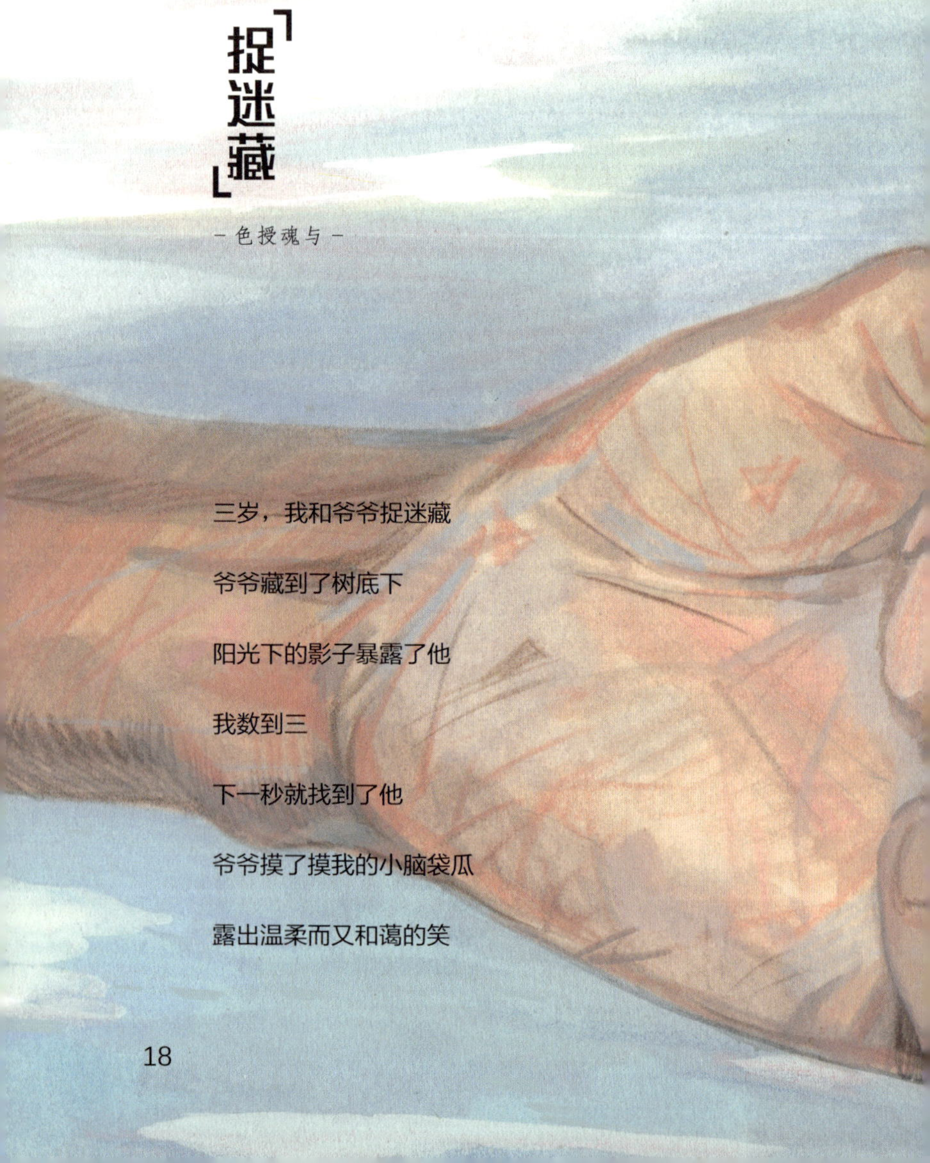

# 「捉迷藏」

— 色授魂与 —

三岁，我和爷爷捉迷藏

爷爷藏到了树底下

阳光下的影子暴露了他

我数到三

下一秒就找到了他

爷爷摸了摸我的小脑袋瓜

露出温柔而又和蔼的笑

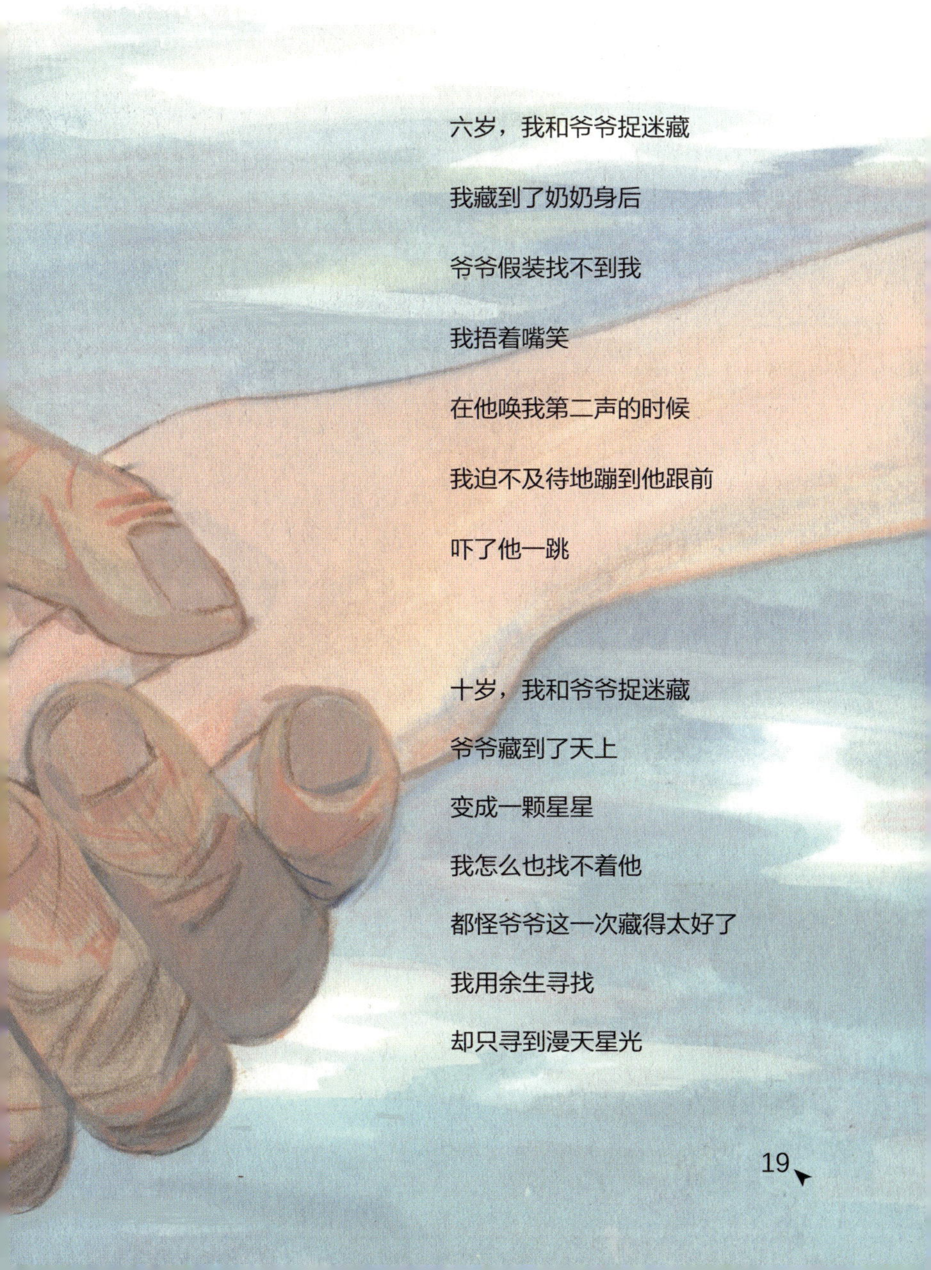

六岁，我和爷爷捉迷藏

我藏到了奶奶身后

爷爷假装找不到我

我捂着嘴笑

在他唤我第二声的时候

我迫不及待地蹦到他跟前

吓了他一跳

十岁，我和爷爷捉迷藏

爷爷藏到了天上

变成一颗星星

我怎么也找不着他

都怪爷爷这一次藏得太好了

我用余生寻找

却只寻到漫天星光

# 习惯

柳小怪哎

以前我习惯了孤独，

直到遇到你们，

现在我有点害怕孤独。

# 衡水

堕落在何时

绑手与笔的皮筋掉了

弯腰去捡

一抬头

窗外有火烧的云彩

有金黄的落叶

有飒爽的秋风

这是我在的世界吗

一根粉笔砸醒了我

连忙低头做起试卷

对嘛，这才是我的世界

# 温柔

凋零花

我总是小心顾虑他人的感受，

我并不是一个温柔的人，

只是比谁都更懂得难过。

# 「一个自卑者的爱」

绫波很零

我曾经爱上过一个姑娘

也曾发疯一般地着迷于她

她成了我的暴君

但我知道

暴君又怎会垂青一个庶民

# 离职

潘自力

边落残阳坠星河，

独望长空志不得。

我自挥手江湖去，

荆途易驱心难折。

# 暮晚

淦华

暮晚谁与我同游，时节早已别三秋。

我欲长歌不恋酒，今生思君未敢留。

# 鸟

弦心辰

我的脑子里有只鸟奇怪又体弱 *

它从来不曾飞翔，大概是不敢

于是我常带它去跑步

因为这世上复杂不受控制的事太多

而跑步只需左右脚交替向前

再勇敢一些去奔跑

就能听见风在林间的低语

它有时也会到心海里衔起一些石块

让我的心不会变得太坚硬

至少不会那么快

---

* 引用自法国著名小说家普鲁斯特的诗歌《我的脑子里有一只鸟奇怪又体弱》。

但更多时候

它只是长久地睡着

久得我都快忘了

我的脑子里有只鸟

奇怪又体弱

# 「2021年10月5日真的很适合睡觉」

elegant 福尔摩花

我的褥子是镇上最好的棉花

我的被子也是

今天下着雨只有 12℃

楼下一片水洼，无处下脚

恰好我也不愿出去

今天很适合睡觉

# 第二辑 你

我没什么要紧的事情

只好一直想你

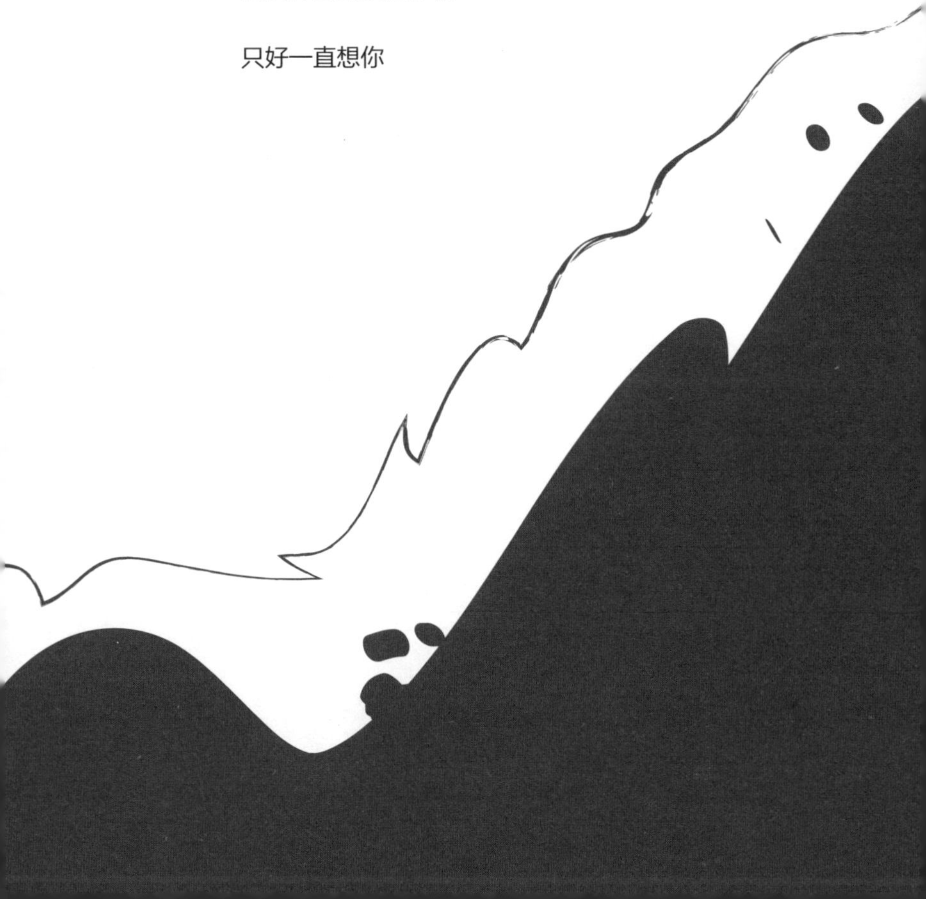

# 「失眠」

蒋阿 sir

我在每一个夜晚，

跟每一个月亮，

描述同一个你。

# 故人

溟邱

你笑我偷拿你的假牙，

我笑你皱纹翻成了浪花，

“哈哈哈哈……”

我在坟前弯起了月牙。

# 「墙头，马上」

目莲僧

或许是

三月的风流了浪，

春天的花开在了七月上，

那一天，我们远远相望。

你在墙头，我在马上。

# 「你的城市下起了雨」

目莲僧

想你的时候我就去晒太阳，

让阳光蒸发掉我对你的思念。

它们在天空中凝结，

变成云朵，

再飘到你的窗外。

于是，

你的城市下起了雨。

# 相拥

讲好一只机

我一定要在最凛冽的寒冬去见你，

那时风会把时钟吹到慵懒，

我们的相拥会变得很慢。

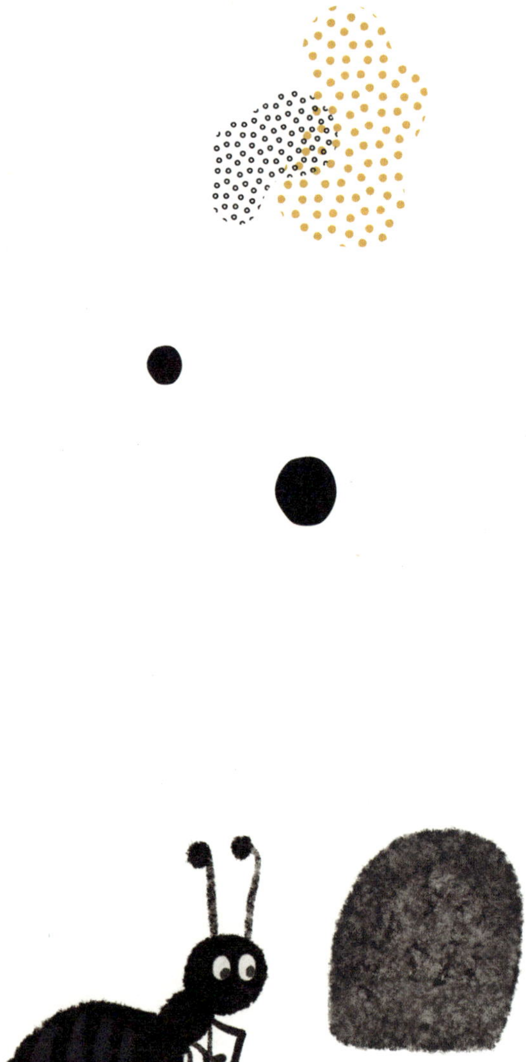

# 「蚂蚁」

贩懒

我像只小小的、黑黑的蚂蚁，

千方百计寻找有你的甜蜜。

你突然俯下身子问：

“蚂蚁啊蚂蚁，你有什么秘密？”

我疯了一样冲进巢穴。

你却以为，蚂蚁也不待见你。

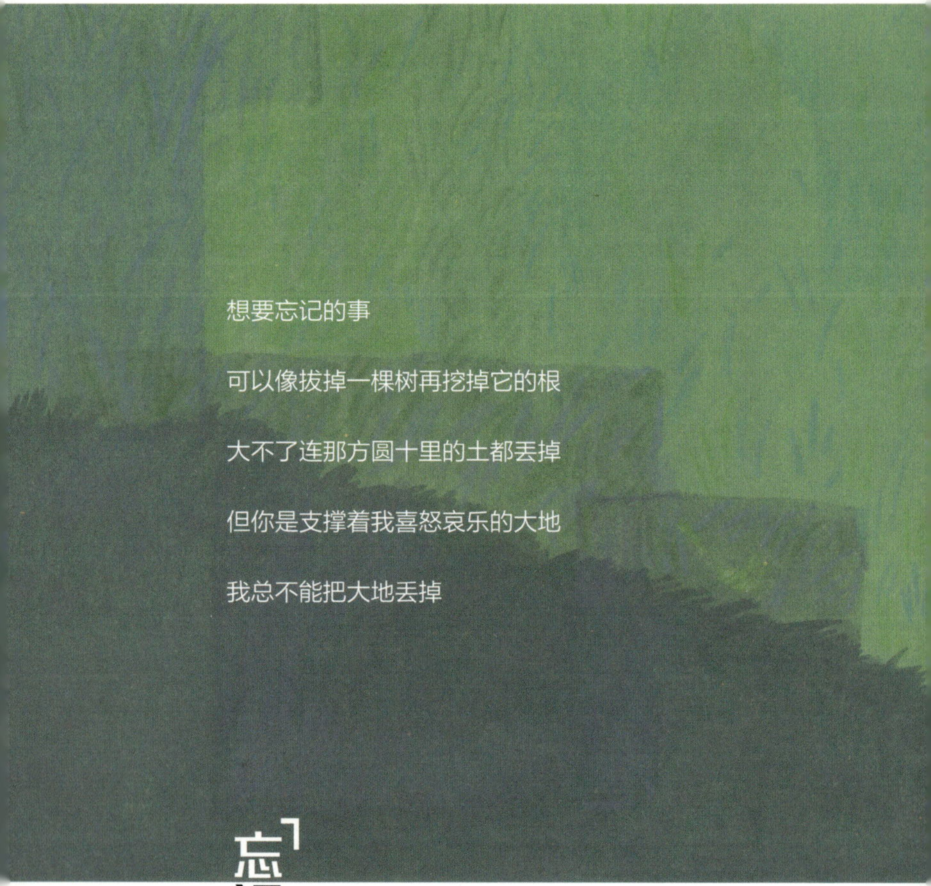

想要忘记的事

可以像拔掉一棵树再挖掉它的根

大不了连那方圆十里的土都丢掉

但你是支撑着我喜怒哀乐的大地

我总不能把大地丢掉

# 忘记

碎纸盒盒

# 「百岁与一万句关于你」

人性自走机

黄昏的光辉流淌出你眼眸

我挽你的手

云朵在街道停留

# 「关于月亮」

目莲僧

我没什么要紧的事情，只好一直想你。

想你一直晴朗，不下雨。

想你两小无猜疑，若即不若离。

想你千山隔不住，江海亦可平。

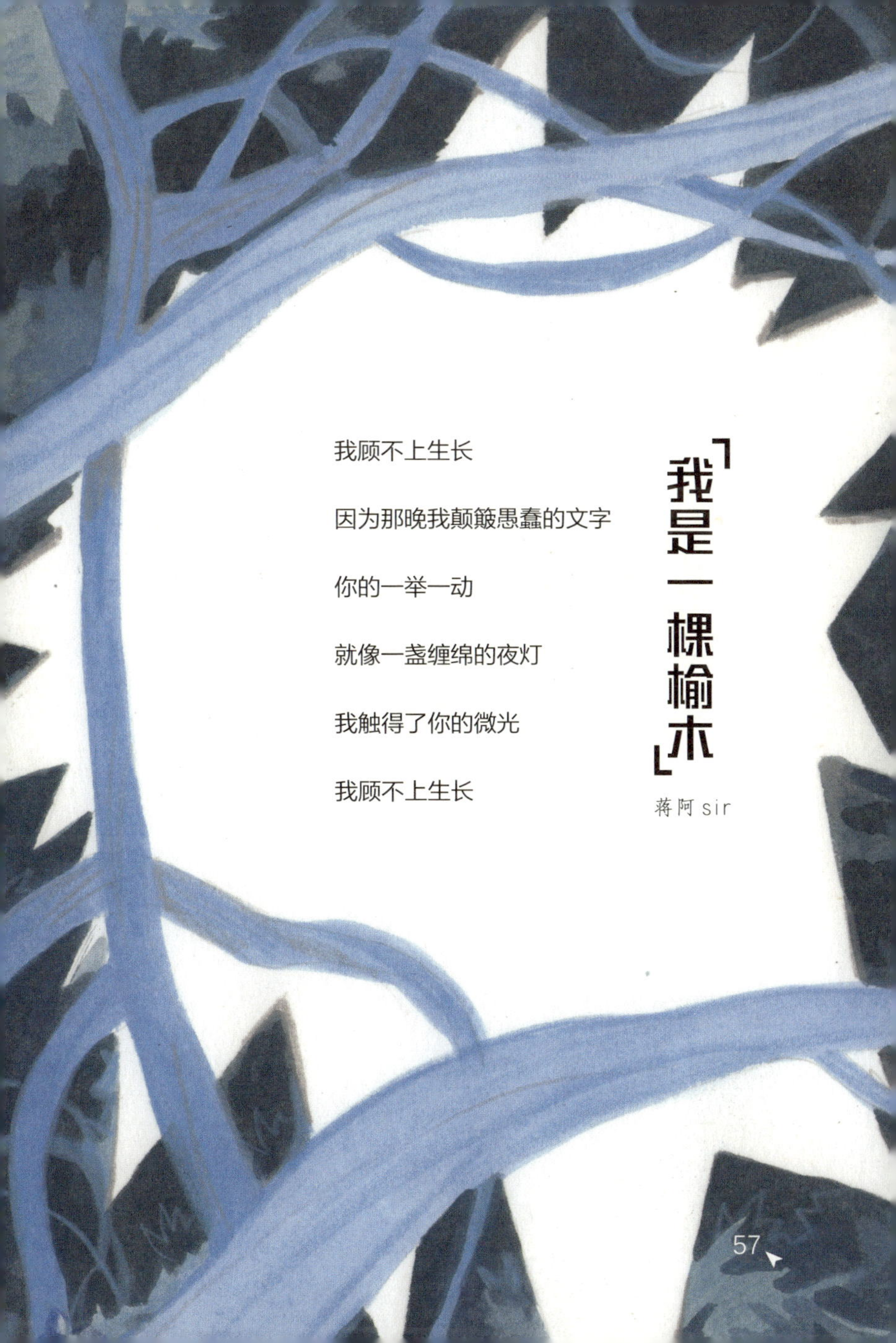

# 「我是一棵榆木」

蒋阿 sir

我顾不上生长

因为那晚我颠簸愚蠢的文字

你的一举一动

就像一盏缠绵的夜灯

我触得了你的微光

我顾不上生长

# 「金华秋实」

尾猫

想要带你去看铺满枫叶的路，

踩在上面作响的声音，

暖炉边上窝着的猫，

牵起你手时我的心跳。

# 信

高斯求不得

我写了封信，

却没贴邮票。

犹豫，

犹豫是否能准确寄到。

把信纸铺在空中，

我把欢快的鸟鸣，

清晨第一缕花香，

把粉红色的浅浅晚霞写进信里；

把这里的山、这里的云，

我把我的灵魂折得很小很小，

都写进了信里。

我把信写在了风里，

让风读给你。

我写了封信，

未贴邮票。

# 林深与海蓝

洛蝶酱

奥菲斯放逐了我

我仍旧寻觅你歌声里飞鸟般的翠绿

春天的寂静和你的眼眶一样

涌起窒息的旋涡

叶呼啸着狂奔

却怎么逃不出这片泡腾的竹林

她不是深处的牝鹿

而你是继承了波塞冬之名的猎人

# 思念

田C同学

我对你的思念

大抵是窗外的两片叶子

生于春，盛于夏

落于秋，藏于冬

# 代替

尾猫

人们用月亮去说喜欢，

赠送玫瑰表达爱意，

而我用蜡梅指认深冬，

将春天归咎于你。

## 三行情诗（一）

万叶今天吃什么 -

落日余晖

满天星河

你是世间第三种绝色 *

* 出自余光中的《绝色》。

# 「三行情诗」（二）

安达

与君书

花开十里

眉眼不相忘

# 落日

目莲僧

“我问你，这是啥？”

“酒啊。”

“错，这是流动的落日。‘玉碗盛来琥珀光’，太阳落下去的时候，神明把最美的晚霞酿进了瓶子里，让人醉的不是酒，是夕阳。”

“所以呢？”

“所以，我不是想找你喝酒，是想和你欣赏落日。”

# 第三辑 戏

我想看它

又不敢看它

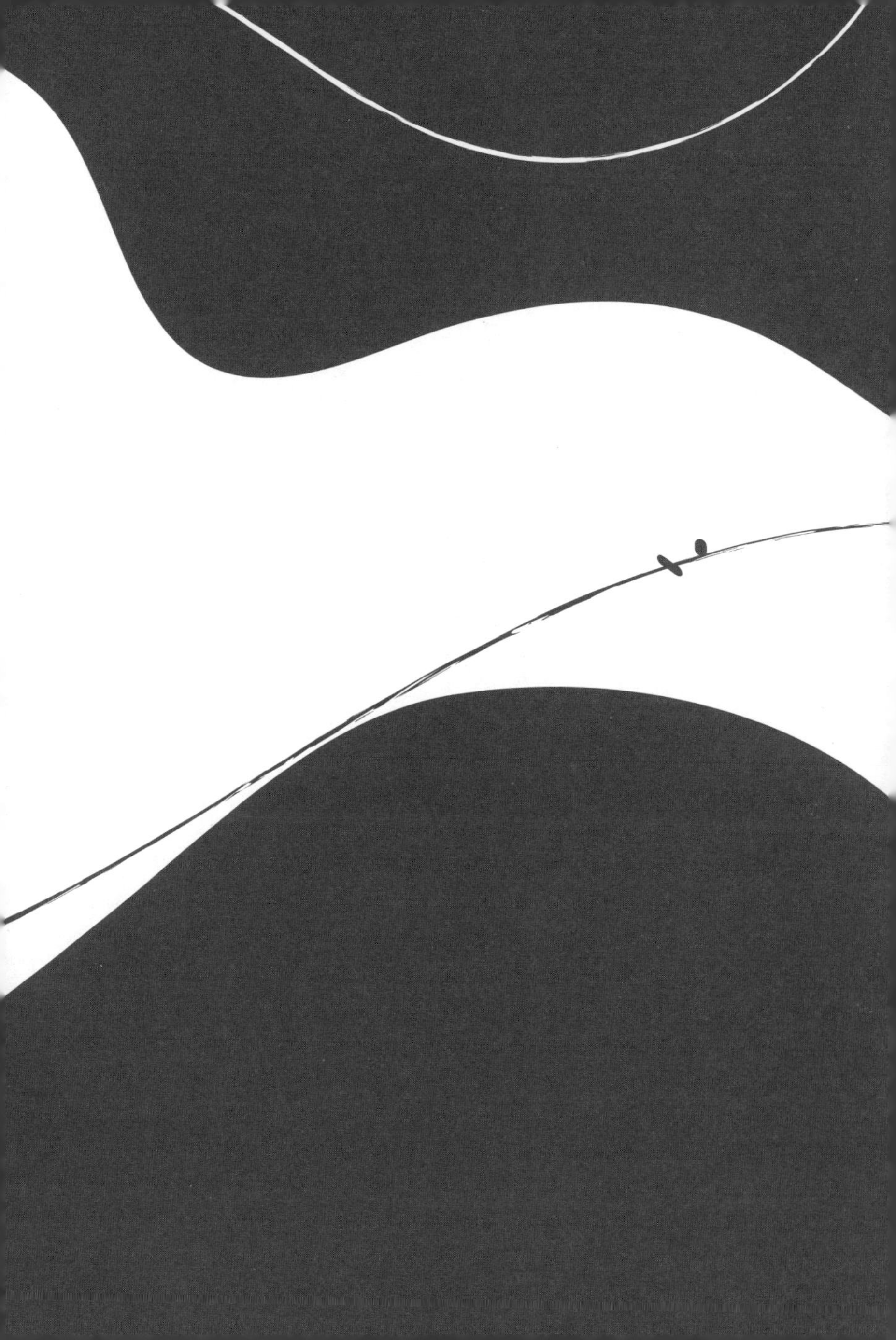

## 「孤独」

姜二嫚

我站在人群中

孤独得

就像 P 上去的

# 社会

聂昌

我毕业了，

他们说，社会是一头猛兽。

我很害怕，

我想着，猛兽恐怕要来吃我了！

抬头一看，

它根本没把我放在眼里。

# 踩影子

小逸

路上有个小孩在踩影子

我觉得好幼稚

所以绕开了

我怕他踩到我的影子

# 眼泪

碎纸盒盒

我的眼睛不漂亮了

因为流了太多的眼泪

眼泪是珍珠

我失去了很大一笔财富

# 价格

夏夏夏夏早安

她兴奋地拿起一件裙子

“也不是很好看嘛”

# 「名字」

木石轴心

我给孩子们起好了名字

男孩叫木石

女孩叫芸香

人人都说好

我欣喜自豪

孩子他妈一定也喜欢

我要去告诉她

可是

我还不知道她的名字

# 月亮

秋露重

医生说我散光，

我偷偷地笑了，

他又怎会知道，

乡下的我，拥有十二个月亮。

# 「太阳」

快乐的小奶昔

无论现在有多浑蛋，

小时候，

都会在纸角上留下一轮太阳。

# 光

姜二嫚

晚上

我打着手电筒散步

累了就拿它当拐杖

我拄着一束光

# 「老师，你要相信我啊」

不能被褒义词形容的人

我的上眼皮和下眼皮啊

你们为何如此地恩爱

就连上课时

都要在我眼前相会

# 「钟」

桑山 hples

我想看它

又不敢看它

我只好看向了老师

# 「不想上学」

小白脸_

电闪雷鸣间，风吹雨打天。

欲随庄周行，误到孔门前。

# 班主任

深海少女有点甜

她那一袭黑衣，

早已隐入了夜色中，

只留下一张苍白的脸，

幽灵一般，

从窗外望进来。

亲爱的妈妈收

# 骗子

山屿牧歌

如果，

有一天我死了，

请告诉我的妈妈，她的儿子——

是一个骗子。

# 「我也是妈妈的妈妈」

难悟兰因

他们吵架

我一定是站在妈妈这边

可能有失偏颇

但我相信这才是对的

小孩子被欺负了会找妈妈

爸爸也会给奶奶打电话

可是我的妈妈已经没有妈妈了

所以我就暂时做她的妈妈

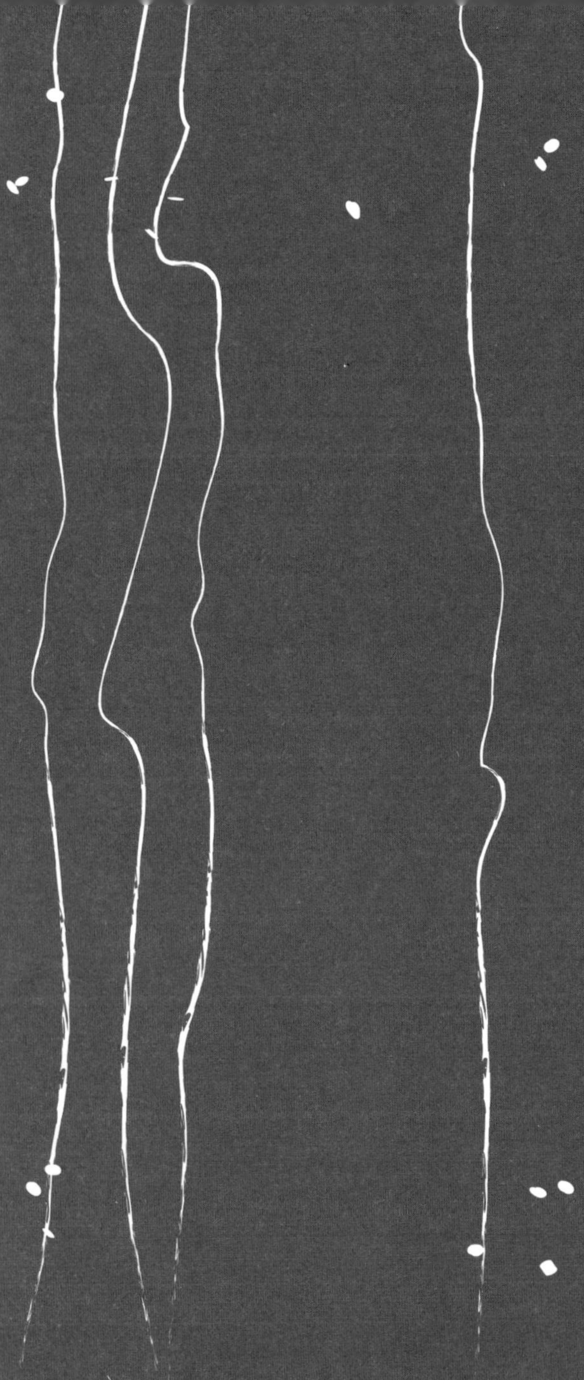

# 第四辑 见

世界是颠倒的

我脚踩着云

头上是清清绿水

# 海鸥

尾猫

我所见的除了云起海上，

浪拍礁石，

海鸥飞向遥远，

我所见的，

还有坐在身旁的你。

# 妄想症

小林川丶

我心深处，有一片大海，

那里没有海鸥的喧嚣，

只有微风的轻语和海浪的潮汐，

繁星在空中开着茶会，

光芒闪烁，

如此绚丽，

黑夜之中，

万籁俱寂。

# 晚霞（一）

之念爱学习

只有在学校里，

我们才会想起看窗外的晚霞。

# 晚霞（二）

反正不投币那就随便改

我觉得最好看的是高中的晚霞

可惜当时不能带手机，

也可能是当时不能带手机

它一直在我的记忆里被美化。

# 小窗

顾铭夕 xi

中学时代晚自习时候的天最好看了，

好像要把世间的绮丽全包进一个个小窗里，

顺便借着看彩霞的由头偷偷往后看他一眼。

# 玻璃海

画狐白御

玻璃般的海，

席卷着我，穿越时空，

从清澈的早晨到醉酒的黄昏。

# 霞

hc 只是无聊

黑夜亲吻白昼

她羞得红了脸

躲到群山后

小声呢喃着

明天见

# 「痴心妄想」

尾猫

世界是颠倒的，

我脚踩着云，

头上是清清绿水，

我拉着你，

往那彩虹上走去。

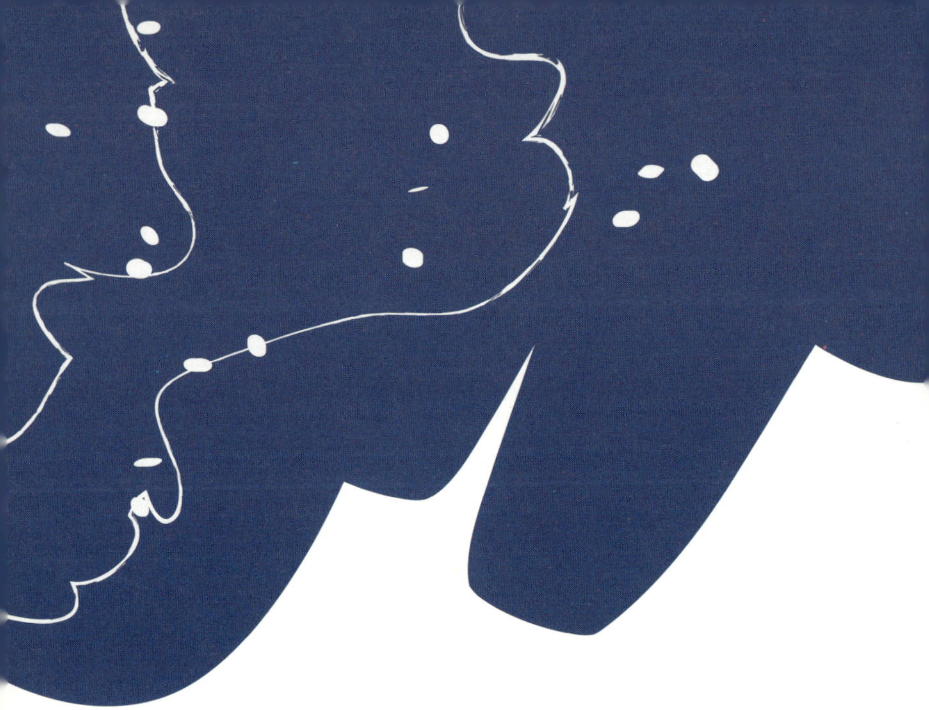

# 第五辑 默

如果某天要死

就要孤独地不为人知地死

# 人

七临厌酒

我问妹妹长大了想做什么，

她说她想做个桌子、椅子、门……

我问她为什么不做一个“人”，

她说在这个房间里，

没有人，

只有大人和小孩。

# 一件事

安达

如果某天要死，

就要孤独地不为人知地死。

不抱任何希冀与幻想，

只要静静地躺下，

一捧黄土掩面，

等待时间掩盖一切。

自此之前身上发生的一切都只能称为“一件事”，

包括这个孤独的死。

# 风的旅人

巨山精神病院院长

风中离去的旅人啊

请将无瑕的格桑带走

于人海中凋零

也会留下一路芬芳

风中归来的旅人啊

请把朱艳的琉璃带回

破碎于荒原

思念也会送达

风中逝去的旅人啊

请将格桑与琉璃同葬

诞生于风中

魂归于风中

## 「花」

予尔娇

女儿从没见过花

于是得来邻人的一枝花

我将它插在墓旁

好叫她来日识得此花

再不做盲婚哑嫁

# 「腐朽」

云上乘风

我的身体像是死去了

随后心也跟着死亡

像是找不到该跳动的地方

于是我躺下

便开始了真正的腐朽

# 「太阳的赠礼」

不爱笑的橘猫

落雪消逝于太阳的赠礼，

如同感情破灭于不问君意。

# 「母亲的病」

凌一流

她在疼痛与煎熬中

拿出铜墙铁壁的意志

面对生活

叫嚣的尘埃

听话地收起了落魄样

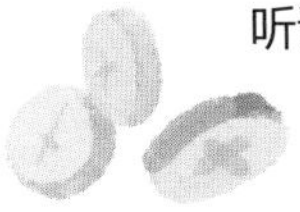

# 我不知道

elegant 福尔摩花

我不知道怎样的人生才算精彩

我的不算

你的也不算

只有那些我未曾谋面的才算

# 「凌晨一点加班回家有感」

我有一个梦想

黑夜淹没了灯光

大山埋葬了匆忙

地铁悠悠开回故乡

奶奶站在槐树下

驮着我指着槐花说

“这些能不能买你的时光”

# 尽头

贩懒

我相信思想是有尽头的，

在尽头我可能什么都不会再萌生出来，

但是对你的爱意，

早在这条让我一直溯源的时间线上，

不断挂念。

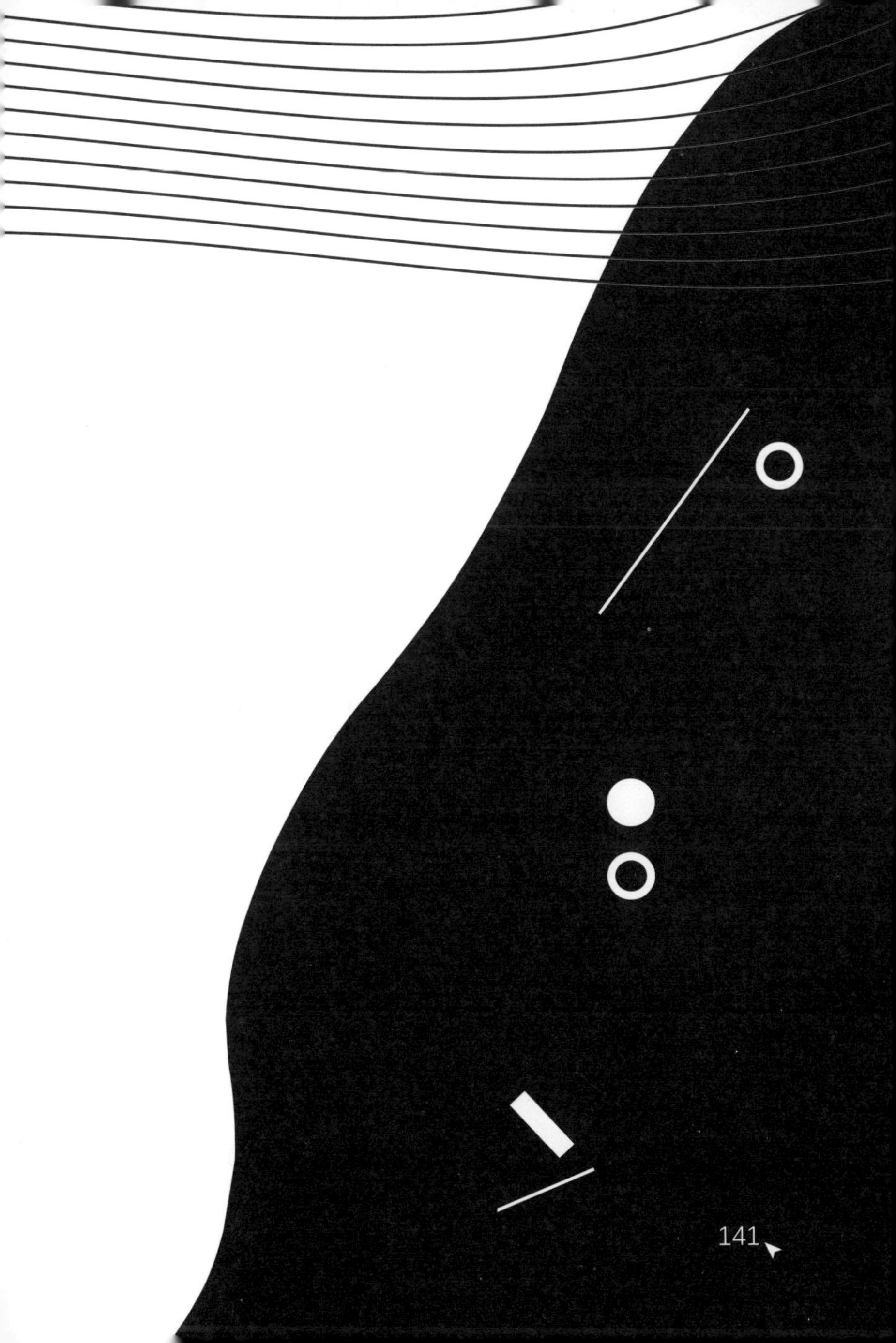

# 「浪漫」

Alex 纯洁

用你的生活来定义浪漫，

不要用浪漫来填充它。

# 沉默

无聊 bu 无聊

看啊！那是完美的！

一切都在这沉默中完美了。

沉默中的完美，

真的是完美吗？

我不能说，

因为我在沉默。

# 「缝布娃娃」

I_oY

剪刀裁去了我的爪牙

缝补进柔软的棉纱

摘掉我眼里的星星

针线与纽扣在黑暗中爬行

嘴角边悬吊着虚伪的微笑

眸子里流淌着漠然的死水

然后把我摆在橱窗上

说我很美

# 其实

土豪小乞丐

昨天我和爷爷聊天

他告诉我

鲜血，其实是红色的

男女，其实是有别的

人类，其实是会死的

世界，其实是有光的

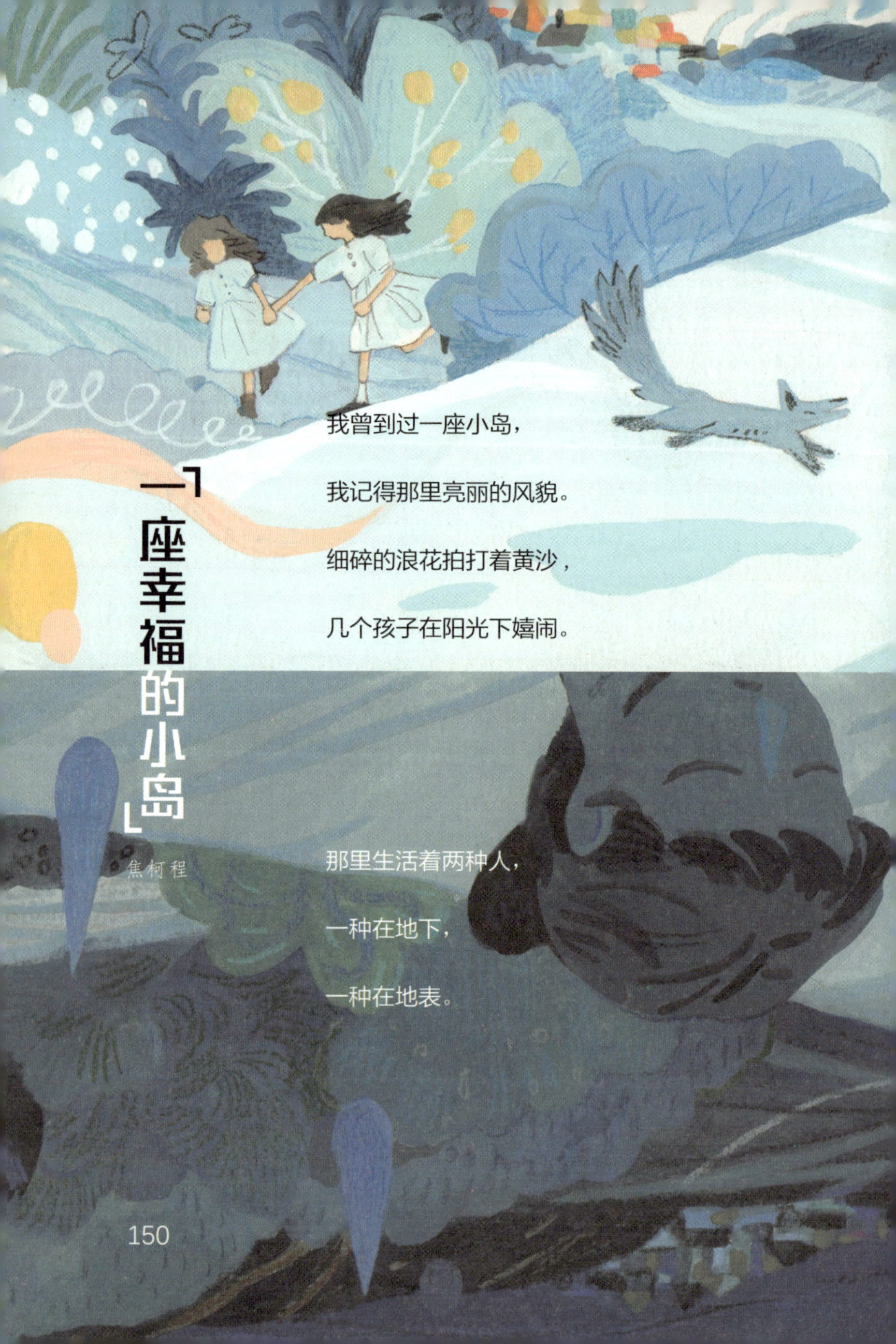

# 一座幸福的小岛

焦柯程

我曾到过一座小岛，

我记得那里亮丽的风貌。

细碎的浪花拍打着黄沙，

几个孩子在阳光下嬉闹。

那里生活着两种人，

一种在地下，

一种在地表。

活在地表的人们，

他们衣着光鲜，

谈吐优雅，

生活充满希望。

活在地下的人们，

他们无法言语，

但我猜测，

日子也不会太糟。

我相信，

这会是一个幸福的小岛。

因为，

岛上的每个人，

都说自己过得很好。

# 因果

杜小麦

一个馒头

两个馒头

三个馒头

嗝

一场大雨

两场大雨

三场大雨

阿嚏

一次争吵

两次争吵

三次争吵

请在这里留下你的诗歌

B站评论区

宝藏诗歌回收计划

拍照发送到新浪微博 @ 知音动漫图书，你的诗歌将会被更多人看到哦~

本页插图绘制：瓜里

## 图书在版编目（CIP）数据

B站评论区宝藏诗歌回收计划 / 阮俊霖编. -- 北京 : 中国致公出版社, 2023 (2023.8重印)
ISBN 978-7-5145-1999-0

Ⅰ. ①B… Ⅱ. ①阮… Ⅲ. ①诗集－中国－当代 Ⅳ. ①I227

中国版本图书馆CIP数据核字(2022)第120895号

B站评论区宝藏诗歌回收计划　　阮俊霖 编
B ZHAN PINGLUN QU BAOZANG SHIGE HUISHOU JIHUA

| | |
|---|---|
| 出　　版 | 中国致公出版社<br>（北京市朝阳区八里庄西里100号住邦2000大厦1号楼西区21层） |
| 出　　品 | 湖北知音动漫有限公司<br>（武汉市东湖路179号） |
| 发　　行 | 中国致公出版社（010-66121708） |
| 作品企划 | 知音动漫图书・时代坊 |
| 责任编辑 | 付　阳 邓　苗 |
| 责任校对 | 吕冬钰 |
| 插图绘制 | 一三菌落 |
| 装帧设计 | 王　钰 |
| 责任印制 | 程　磊 |
| 印　　刷 | 武汉精一佳印刷有限公司 |
| 版　　次 | 2023年3月第1版 |
| 印　　次 | 2023年8月第3次印刷 |
| 开　　本 | 787mm × 1092mm　1/32 |
| 印　　张 | 5.25 |
| 字　　数 | 45千字 |
| 书　　号 | ISBN 978-7-5145-1999-0 |
| 定　　价 | 48.00元 |

国家出版基金项目
NATIONAL PUBLICATION FOUNDATION

文物与文化遗产篇
Cultural Artifacts and Heritage

汉英对照

# 中国关键词

# KEYWORDS TO UNDERSTAND CHINA

## Dunhuang

## 敦煌


中国外文出版发行事业局（CICG）
敦煌研究院（DHA）
当代中国与世界研究院（ACCWS）
中国翻译研究院（CATL）



朝華出版社
BLOSSOM PRESS

## 《中国关键词：文物与文化遗产篇——敦煌》<br>图书编委会

# Editorial Committee

# 前言

文物与文化遗产是人类文明和智慧的产物，是连接过去与未来的桥梁，承载着各种文明的记忆，诉说着时代的辉煌与变迁。在历史的长河中，中华文明以其深厚的底蕴和独特的魅力，共同构成了人类丰富多彩的文明宝库。其文物与文化遗产数量众多，灿若星辰，是中华民族几千年未曾中断的文化历史的积淀和精华，不仅构筑了中华民族的文化自信，更是全球文明传承与创新的重要力量，为世界文化的多样性和人类文明的交流互鉴提供了宝贵的资源。

为讲好中华文物与文化遗产的故事，集中展示丝绸之路上的文明互鉴精神与文化交流成果，增进国内外读者对数千年来沟通中外的敦煌文化的了解，“中国关键词”多语对外传播平台组织策划了《中国关键词：文物与文化遗产篇——敦煌》。本书按照走进敦煌、历史人物、敦煌文物、敦煌石窟、守望敦煌和互鉴共进的编写逻辑，综合借鉴“中华思想文化术语传播工程”等有关成果，选取 80 条关键词进行重点介绍和解读，向国内外读者呈现丰富多彩、生动立体的丝绸之路上的敦煌文化形象，推动中华文化更好走向世界。本书为中外对照版，由于能力及时间所限，在遴选编写中文词条时，难免挂一漏万。为使译文更符合目标语读者的阅读习惯，我们对翻译表达进行了创新探索，旨在提升读者的阅读体验。

“中国关键词”多语对外传播平台是中国外文出版发行事业局、当代中国与世界研究院、中国翻译研究院共同打造的国际传播品牌，主要围绕新时代中国特色社会主义的理念与实践，进行中文词条专题编写、解读和多语种编译，通过平面、网络、移动端等多媒体、多渠道、多形态持续对外发布，旨在以外国受众易于阅读和理解的方式，阐释中国思想，解读中国理念，传递中国方案，分享中国智慧。

讲故事需要关键词，讲好中国故事需要中国关键词。让我们用“中国关键词”点击中国、沟通世界，促进中外文明交流互鉴。

# PREFACE

Relics and cultural heritage are the products of human civilization and wisdom, serving as a bridge that connects the past with the future. They preserve the memories of various civilizations and narrate the glories and changes of different eras. Throughout its long history, the profound heritage and unique charm of Chinese civilization has contributed greatly to the rich and colorful treasury of human civilization. Its numerous relics and cultural heritage shine like stars, radiating the accumulation and essence of thousands of years of uninterrupted cultural history of the Chinese nation. Chinese cultural heritage has not only built cultural confidence among the Chinese people but also served as an important force for the inheritance and innovation of global civilization, providing valuable resources for reinforcing the diversity of world cultures and promoting exchanges and mutual learning among human civilizations.

*Keywords to Understand China: Cultural Artifacts and Heritage—Dunhuang* emerged from the China Keywords program, a multi-language platform to promote international communication and tell stories of Chinese relics and cultural heritage with focus on showcasing the spirit of mutual learning and cultural exchanges along the Silk Road.

The project seeks to foster better understanding among domestic and international readers regarding Dunhuang culture, which has linked China with other parts of the world for thousands of years. Drawing on the outcome of the Project on the Translation and Communication of the Key Concepts in Chinese Thought and Culture, it selected

80 keywords to present a vibrant, multi-dimensional image of Dunhuang culture along the Silk Road and promote improved global dissemination of Chinese culture. A formula was developed to introduce humanity's heritage in Dunhuang, historical figures, Dunhuang relics, Dunhuang caves, efforts to safeguard Dunhuang, and the expansion of mutual learning and progress. The book is bilingual. Due to limited time and space, it is by no means an exhaustive list. We have endeavored to make translation of these keywords easy to understand and idiomatic for readers.

The China Keywords program is an international communication brand organized by the China International Communications Group, the Academy of Contemporary China and World Studies, and the China Academy of Translation. Driven by the concepts and practices of socialism with Chinese characteristics in the new era, program participants edit and translate special Chinese concepts into different languages and release them through multiple printed and online media platforms and channels to explain and interpret Chinese thoughts and ideas, offer China's vision, and share wisdom.

Telling a story requires keywords; telling China's story well demands keywords intrinsically associated with China. China Keywords are intended to connect China with the rest of the world to promote mutual learning between Chinese and other civilizations.

# 敦煌概览

在中国的大西北，今甘肃省河西走廊西端的敦煌，地处陆上丝绸之路的咽喉要冲，自古以来被誉为东西方文明交汇的十字路口。如果说，有一个地方 2000 年来证明了伟大丝绸之路真实存在的话，那一定是敦煌；如果说，有一个地方能够图文并茂生动记录西汉以来中华民族与世界联动的每一刻历史脉搏的话，那也是敦煌；如果说，有一个地方能让人一眼千年、倾心交付的话，那依然是敦煌。

丝绸之路是连接古代东西方世界的大通道，敦煌作为丝路重镇，往来和居住在敦煌的各族人民在这片共生之地留下了丰厚的文化遗产，其中以敦煌汉简、敦煌石窟和敦煌藏经洞最为著名。敦煌汉简总数约 4 万枚，不仅把宏观的丝绸之路概念落实到极为具体的交通路线上，更详细地记录了早期丝绸之路上中原王朝与广大西域地区的频繁交往。敦煌石窟，包括莫高窟、榆林窟、西千佛洞等，共 800 多个洞窟，其中有 5 万多平方米壁画和

2000多身彩塑，以其内容丰富、数量巨大，不仅成为中国中古艺术史的资料宝库，更以图像的形式记录了1600多年的丝路历史。莫高窟第17窟藏经洞的开启，则是20世纪初的重大考古发现，其中出土的7万余件古代文献文物，为中华民族对人类文明的贡献提供了有力的实物证据。这些敦煌宝藏，共同图文并茂地讲述了中国与世界各文明间交往交流的历程。

2013年，中国提出共同建设“丝绸之路经济带”和“21世纪海上丝绸之路”的重大倡议，古老的丝绸之路被唤醒并焕发出新的生机。敦煌作为新丝绸之路上历史悠久的文化名城，仍然发挥着文化桥梁的纽带作用。作为中国拥有世界文化遗产数量最多、跨区域范围最广的文博管理机构和全世界最大的敦煌学研究实体，敦煌研究院将继续在这片土地上守护传承敦煌文化遗产。新时代新敦煌，敦煌也将继续承担连接古今、沟通世界的历史使命。

# DUNHUANG: HUMANITY'S HERITAGE

Dunhuang is located at the western end of the Hexi Corridor in Gansu Province in China's northwestern region, where it was a strategic hub along the ancient Silk Road. It has long been recognized as a crossroads hosting the convergence of Eastern and Western civilizations. No other place testifies to the influence of the magnificent Silk Road over the past two millennia more than Dunhuang. Nowhere else so vividly recorded interactions between the Chinese nation and the Western world since the Western Han Dynasty (206 BC-AD 24) through a rich tapestry of text and imagery. Dunhuang is a locale with the power to evoke a thousand years of history at a glance and capture the heart of anyone who encounters it.

A major thoroughfare connecting the ancient worlds of East and West, the Silk Road left a rich cultural heritage in Dunhuang, a vital hub on the ancient Silk Road where various ethnic groups interacted and coexisted. The most renowned heritage items are Dunhuang Han-dynasty bamboo slips, the Dunhuang Caves, and the Library Cave. The Dunhuang Han-dynasty bamboo slips number some 40,000 in total. The slips not only solidify the historicity of the grand concept of the Silk Road with specific documented transportation routes, but also detail heavy exchanges between the Central Plains dynasties and the vast Western Regions along the early Silk Road. The Dunhuang Caves, including the Mogao Caves, Yulin Caves, and Western Thousand-Buddha Caves, are composed of over 800 caves featuring more than 50,000 square meters of murals and over 2,000 colored sculptures. The rich content and immense quantity have made it a treasure trove of materials for the study of medieval Chinese art as well as a visual record of the 1,600-plus years of history of the Silk Road. The discovery of the Library Cave, a cave that collects Buddhist scriptures in Mogao Caves' Cave 17, marked a significant archaeological breakthrough in the early 20th Century. The excavation yielded more than 70,000 ancient documents and artifacts, providing compelling physical evidence of the contributions of the Chinese nation to human civilization. Together, these Dunhuang treasures vividly testify to the history of cultural exchanges between China and various world civilizations through text and images.

In 2013, China proposed the significant initiative of jointly building the Silk Road Economic Belt and the 21st-century Maritime Silk Road to revive the ancient Silk Road and infuse it with new vitality. The Dunhuang Academy, the largest Dunhuang cultural protection institution and Dunhuang studies entity in the world, will continue to guard and pass on Dunhuang cultural heritage from its original tract of land. In the new era, the new Dunhuang will continue its historical mission of connecting the world.

# 目录

CONTENTS

一

走进敦煌 —— 002
About Dunhuang

大盛敦煌 —— 004
Prosperous Dunhuang

丝绸之路与丝路精神 —— 006
Silk Road and Its Spirit

民族融合之地 —— 008
Hub of Ethnic Integration

多元文化圣殿 —— 010
Temple of Multiculturalism

敦煌的世界文化遗产 —— 012
World Cultural Heritage

敦煌学 —— 016
Dunhuang Studies

莫高精神 —— 018
Mogao Spirit

二

## 历史人物 Historical Figures — 020

张芝 Zhang Zhi — 022

竺法护 Zhu Fahu — 026

莫高窟的创建者 Founders of Mogao Caves — 028

元荣 Yuan Rong — 032

张议潮 Zhang Yichao — 034

洪辩 Hong Bian — 038

王道士 Wang Yuanlu — 040

斯坦因 Marc Aurel Stein — 044

伯希和 Paul Pelliot — 048

三

## 敦煌文物 Relics of Dunhuang — 052

敦煌汉简 Dunhuang Han-Dynasty Bamboo Slips — 054

悬泉置汉简 — 056
Han-Dynasty Bamboo Slips, Xuanquan Posthouse Site

西汉生态环保墙书 — 058
Eco-Themed Wall Text of the Western Han Dynasty

《案验康居王使者献驼册》 — 060
*The Official Document Regarding the Investigation of the Camels Presented by the Kangju Envoy*

《驿使图》 — 064
*The Courier*

《新修本草》 — 066
*The Newly-Compiled Materia Medica*

敦煌星图 — 070
Dunhuang Star Maps

《金刚经》 — 074
*The Diamond Sutra*

《秦妇吟》 — 078
*Lament of the Lady of Qin*

印度制糖法文献 — 082
Literature on Indian Sugar Production Methods

北宋敦煌官府的酒账 — 084
*Wine Accounts of the Dunhuang Government During the Northern Song Dynasty*

《叶净能诗》 — 088
*The Stories of Ye Jingneng*

《降魔变文》 — 092
*The Transformation Text of Subjugation of Demons*

《行脚僧图》 — 096
*The Traveling Monk*

四

## 敦煌石窟 — 100
## The Dunhuang Caves

敦煌石窟群 — 102
The Dunhuang Caves Complex

敦煌莫高窟 — 106
The Mogao Caves at Dunhuang

敦煌藏经洞 — 110
The Library Cave

敦煌壁画 — 114
Dunhuang Murals

音乐窟 — 118
The Music Cave

室内第一大佛 — 120
Largest Indoor Buddha

九层楼 — 122
Nine-Story Building

唐代彩塑群像 — 124
Tang-Dynasty Painted Statues Group

飞天 — 128
Apsaras

九色鹿 — 132
Nine-Colored Deer

反弹琵琶 — 136
*Playing the* Pipa *from the Back*

胡旋舞 — 140
Sogdian Whirl Dance

美人菩萨 — 144
*Beauty Bodhisattva*

睒子本生 — 148
Śyāmaka Jātaka

《张骞出使西域图》 — 152
*Zhang Qian's Diplomatic Missions to the Western Regions*

丝路各民族群像 — 156
Portrait of Ethnic Groups Along the Silk Road

胡商 — 160
Hu Merchants

《五台山图》 — 164
*Map of Mount Wutai*

《唐僧取经图》 — 168
*Xuanzang Going on a Pilgrimage for Buddhist Scriptures*

五

## 守望敦煌 — 172
## Guarding Dunhuang

敦煌研究院 — 174
Dunhuang Academy

敦煌研究院文物保护利用群体 — 176
Dunhuang Academy's Relics Protection and Utilization Team

敦煌研究院文物保护团队 — 178
Academy's Team for Relics Protection and Utilization

兰州大学敦煌学研究所 — 182
Institute of Dunhuang Studies, Lanzhou University

《敦煌劫余录》 — 186
*An Analytical List of the Tun-Huang Manuscripts in the National Library of Peiping*

敦煌遗书与《敦煌文献全集》 — 190
Dunhuang Documents and *Complete Collection of Dunhuang Manuscripts*

《敦煌石窟全集：莫高窟考古报告》 — 192
*The General Collection of the Dunhuang Caves: Archaeological Report of the Mogao Caves*

《敦煌学大辞典》 — 196
*Dictionary of Dunhuang Studies*

《敦煌艺术大辞典》 — 198
*Dictionary of Dunhuang Art*

《中国石窟：敦煌莫高窟》 — 202
*Chinese Grottoes: The Mogao Caves in Dunhuang*

《敦煌石窟全集》 — 204
*Complete Collection of the Dunhuang Caves*

井上靖《敦煌》 — 206
Inoue Yasushi's *Dunhuang*

《敦煌岁时节令》 — 210
*Time and Seasons of Dunhuang*

敦煌仙子莫伽瑶 —— 214
Dunhuang Fairy Mo Jiayao

敦煌画派 —— 216
Dunhuang School of Painting

六

## 互鉴共进 —— 218
## Mutual Learning and Common Progress

敦煌文博会 —— 220
Dunhuang Cultural Expo

《敦煌宣言》 —— 222
*Dunhuang Declaration*

敦煌论坛 —— 224
Dunhuang Forum

敦煌奖 —— 228
Dunhuang Award

敦煌纪录片 —— 230
Dunhuang Documentaries

《丝路花雨》 —— 234
*Along the Silk Road*

中国敦煌吐鲁番学会 —— 236
Institute of Dunhuang and Turfan Studies of China

东京艺术大学敦煌项目 —— 240
The Dunhuang Project by Tokyo University of the Arts

美国盖蒂保护研究所敦煌保护项目 —— 244
Getty Conservation Institute: Dunhuang Preservation Project

法国远东学院与敦煌学 — 246
École Française d'Extrême-Orient

中国敦煌石窟保护研究基金会 — 250
China Dunhuang Grottoes Conservation Research Foundation

香港敦煌之友基金会 — 252
Friends of Dunhuang (Hong Kong) Limited

国际敦煌项目 — 254
International Dunhuang Project

数字敦煌 — 256
Digital Dunhuang

敦煌遗书数据库 — 258
Dunhuang Documents Database

云游敦煌 — 260
Cloud Tour of Dunhuang

敦煌历史纪年表 — 262
CHRONOLOGY OF DUNHUANG

词条音序排列表 — 266
ALPHABETICAL INDEX

一

# 走进敦煌

敦煌，位于中国河西走廊的西端，地处丝绸之路的咽喉要冲，自古以来就是多民族交往、交流与聚居的地区。各民族在这片共生之地留下了丰厚的文化遗产，既见证了中国悠久的历史是各民族共同书写的事实，也见证了丝路各民族共同繁荣发展的轨迹。本章以敦煌为立足点，主要介绍其在中国历史、丝路交通、民族融合、文化交流上的重要地位和作用，还有留给我们的世界文化遗产、国际性显学敦煌学等丰厚宝藏。

# ABOUT DUNHUANG

Dunhuang, located at the western terminus of China's Hexi Corridor, serves as a critical node along the Silk Road. Historically, it was a region fostering communication and exchanges as well as a gathering place for multiple ethnic groups. These diverse cultures left behind a rich cultural heritage in a space of coexistence, which not only testifies to China's long history being jointly authored by various ethnic groups, but also points to a trajectory of mutual prosperity and development of the peoples along the Silk Road. This chapter focuses on Dunhuang's significant role and impact on Chinese history, regional transportation, ethnic integration, and cultural exchanges. It also highlights the inheritance of precious deposits through World Cultural Heritage sites and the internationally recognized field of Dunhuang studies.

## 大盛敦煌

敦煌，位于今中国甘肃省西部，河西走廊的西端，是古代中原进入西域的门户。古敦煌的地域范围包括党河流域和疏勒河流域的广大地区，即今天的敦煌市、瓜州县、玉门市、肃北蒙古族自治县和阿克塞哈萨克族自治县。这里曾经是陆上丝绸之路的重要中转站，被誉为“东西方文明交汇的十字路口”。敦煌的历史更是源远流长，早在新石器时代晚期这里已有人类生活。

“敦煌”一名，最早见于《史记》。东汉应劭解释说“敦，大也。煌，盛也”，就是指又大又繁华的地方。唐李吉甫说“敦，大也，以其开广西域，故以盛名”，认为此地对于开辟西域有重要作用。这些都是按字面意思解释的，也有很多学者认为“敦煌”一词，应是早期当地少数民族所呼地名的音译。汉文史籍将“敦煌”解释成“大盛”，足以说明其在历史上的繁华程度和在连通东西方世界时起到的重要作用。

元狩二年（前121），西汉在河西走廊设武威、酒泉二郡，敦煌地区归酒泉郡管辖。元鼎六年（前111），从酒泉郡中分出独立的敦煌郡。从西汉设敦煌郡至今已有2000多年的历史，敦煌持续见证了2000年来陆上丝绸之路不同时期的历史风貌。

## Prosperous Dunhuang

Dunhuang, located in the west of today's Gansu Province, China, is situated at the western end of the Hexi Corridor, making it a gateway from the ancient Central Plains to the Western Regions. The historical territory of Dunhuang encompassed a vast area including the regions of the Danghe and Shule rivers, which corresponds to today's Dunhuang City, Guazhou County, Yumen City, Subei Mongolian Autonomous County and Aksay Kazak Autonomous County. This region was once a crucial transfer station along the overland Silk Road, earning it the title of "crossroads of Eastern and Western civilizations". Dunhuang has a profound, long-standing history: Evidence of human habitation dates back to the late Neolithic period.

The name "Dunhuang" first appeared in *Records of the Historian* (*Shiji*). Eastern Han-dynasty (25-220 AD) scholar Ying Shao interpreted it as "Dun, meaning large; Huang, meaning flourishing", referring to a place that is both vast and prosperous. "Dun is large," stated Tang-dynasty scholar Li Jifu, "and because it opens up a vast western region, it has a great reputation," emphasizing the area's significant role in the development of the Western Regions. These interpretations are largely literal; however, many scholars believe that the term "Dunhuang" may be a transliteration of the place name used by early local ethnic minorities. Regardless, the interpretation of "Dunhuang" as "great prosperity" in Han-dynasty historical texts underscores its historical significance and the crucial role it played in connecting the Eastern and Western worlds.

In 121 BC, the Western Han Dynasty established Wuwei and Jiuquan prefectures in the Hexi Corridor, placing the Dunhuang region under the jurisdiction of Jiuquan. In 111 BC, Dunhuang became an independent prefecture. Since its establishment as a prefecture over 2,000 years ago, Dunhuang has nourished the historical landscape of the overland Silk Road for two millennia.

## 丝绸之路与丝路精神

丝绸之路，最初指陆上丝绸之路，是古代连接东西方世界的重要通道。传统意义上的丝绸之路起始于古代中国的长安（今陕西省西安市）或洛阳（今河南省洛阳市），通过甘肃河西走廊和今天的新疆地区，越过帕尔米高原，进入中亚、伊朗等地，连接起亚洲和欧洲的广大地区。1877 年，德国地质地理学家李希霍芬在《中国》一书中第一次将这条道路命名为“丝绸之路”，这一概念从此广泛传播。作为丝绸之路的重镇，敦煌是中国中原通往西域的门户，其境内的悬泉置、阳关、玉门关都见证着这条道路的真实存在。

丝路精神即丝绸之路精神的简称。丝绸之路作为人文社会的交往平台，多民族、多种族、多宗教、多文化在此交汇融合。在长期交往过程中，各个国家之间形成了“团结互信、平等互利、包容互鉴、合作共赢，不同种族、不同信仰、不同文化背景的国家可以共享和平，共同发展”的丝路精神。

2013 年，中国提出共同建设“丝绸之路经济带”和“21 世纪海上丝绸之路”的重大倡议，古老的丝绸之路被唤醒并焕发出新的生机。在新的历史条件下，继承和发扬以和平合作、开放包容、互学互鉴、互利共赢为特征的丝绸之路精神，把中国发展同沿线国家发展结合起来，将中国梦同沿线各国人民的梦想结合起来，赋予古代丝绸之路以全新的时代内涵。

## Silk Road and Its Spirit

"Silk Road", originally referring to the overland Silk Road, was an important passage connecting the Eastern and Western worlds in ancient times. Traditionally, the Silk Road is considered to have started from the ancient Chinese capitals of Chang'an (now Xi'an City in Shaanxi Province) or Luoyang (now in Henan Province), traversing the Hexi Corridor in today's Gansu Province and Xinjiang Uygur Autonomous Region, crossing the Pamir Plateau to reach Central Asia, Iran, and other areas, thus linking vast regions of Asia and Europe. In 1877, German geologist and geographer Ferdinand von Richthofen (1833-1905) first coined the term "Silk Road" in his book *China*, and the concept spread widely thereafter. As a location of strategic importance on the Silk Road, Dunhuang served as the gateway from Central China to the Western Regions, with landmarks such as Xuanquan Posthouse and Yangguan and Yumen passes remaining to testify to the specifics of this ancient trade route.

What is Silk Road Spirit? As a platform for cultural and social interaction, the Silk Road facilitated a convergence and integration of multiple ethnicities, races, religions, and cultures. Throughout a long process of interaction, various countries developed the Silk Road Spirit characterized by "unity and mutual trust, equality and mutual benefits, inclusiveness and mutual learning, and win-win cooperation". This spirit emphasizes that nations with different ethnic backgrounds, beliefs, and cultural heritages can share peace and pursue common development together.

In 2013, China proposed the significant initiative to jointly build the Silk Road Economic Belt and the 21st-century Maritime Silk Road to revive the ancient Silk Road and infuse it with new vitality. In new historical conditions, the aim is to inherit and revive the Silk Road Spirit characterized by peaceful cooperation, openness and inclusiveness, mutual learning, and win-win collaboration. This initiative seeks to integrate China's development with the development of countries along the route and align the Chinese Dream with the aspirations of people from these nations, thus endowing the ancient Silk Road with fresh significance in the new era.

## 民族融合之地

中国的河西走廊自古就是多民族聚居之地，地处河西走廊西端、丝绸之路咽喉的敦煌更是如此，史称“华戎所交一都会”。历史上，曾经有汉、羌、乌孙、月氏、匈奴、鲜卑、吐谷浑、粟特、吐蕃、回鹘、党项、蒙古等各民族在这里杂居生活，见证了各民族共同书写中国悠久历史的事实。这些民族不断创造和传承灿烂辉煌、各具特色的民族文化，并最终汇流到中华民族优秀传统文化的海洋。

在敦煌留存下来的古代文献中，不仅有汉文文献，还有大量用其他民族文字书写的文献，如古藏文、回鹘文、粟特文、于阗文、西夏文、蒙古文（含八思巴文）等，记录了丝绸之路上各民族交往、交流、融合的历史；在敦煌壁画中，不仅有汉族人物，还有鲜卑、粟特、吐蕃、回鹘、党项、蒙古等民族人物，生动地反映了敦煌古代各民族共同生活的情景。这些资料证明了敦煌自古以来就是多民族共同建立和发展的，真实地印证了中华文明的统一性特征。

## Hub of Ethnic Integration

The Hexi Corridor in China has long been a region of diverse ethnic habitation, and Dunhuang, located at the western end of the Corridor, made it an unavoidable waypoint of the Silk Road through which people originating from all places passed. Historically described as “the intersection of China and the Rong tribes, a hub for all”, Dunhuang has been home to various ethnic groups including the Han, Qiang, Wusun, Yuezhi, Xiongnu, Xianbei, Tuyuhun, Sogdian, Tubo, Uighur, Tangut, Mongolian, and others. Co-existing and laterally contributing to the rich tapestry of China’s long history, these ethnic groups continually nurtured and passed on individually vibrant, distinctive cultures, which eventually merged into the ocean of outstanding traditional culture embraced by the Chinese nation.

The ancient documents preserved in Dunhuang include not only a wealth of Han Chinese literature but also a significant volume of texts in other ethnic scripts such as ancient Tibetan, Uighur, Sogdian, Khotanese, Tangut, and Mongolian (including Phags-pa script). These texts record a history of interaction, exchanges, and integration among various ethnic groups along the Silk Road. Moreover, the murals in Dunhuang depict not only Han figures but also individuals from ethnic groups such as the Xianbei, Sogdian, Tubote, Uighur, Tangut, and Mongolian, vividly illustrating scenes of communal life involving different ethnicities. These materials prove that Dunhuang has historically been a site of shared establishment and development by multiple ethnic groups, authentically reflecting the unifying characteristics of Chinese civilization.

## 多元文化圣殿

敦煌作为中国古代各民族各地区以及东西方文化汇聚、融合的窗口，其本身就是一座多元文化交融的圣殿。中国的国学大师季羡林称：“世界上历史悠久、地域广阔、自成体系、影响深远的文化体系只有四个：中国、印度、希腊、伊斯兰，再没有第五个，而这四个文化体系汇流的地方只有一个，就是中国的敦煌和新疆地区，再没有第二个。”

敦煌文化是各种文明长期交流融汇的结晶，敦煌始终以中华文明为根基，不断吸收来自其他地域和民族多元文化成果。在留存于敦煌的古代文献当中，不仅有佛教典籍，还包括道教、景教、摩尼教典籍和祆教的记录，反映了多元宗教文化交流共存的面貌。在敦煌石窟当中，也可以看到来自希腊、印度、波斯、粟特等的多元艺术与中国本土艺术交流融合的实例。

由于敦煌地区多个民族、多种宗教、多样文化长期并存，其社会生活的各个方面都体现出多元融合的文化特点。如特定地理条件下发达的商业经济生活形态、汉胡兼顾的城市居住布局、农牧结合的饮食结构、华美多姿的服饰、不弃传统善融新俗的嫁娶丧葬等。世界上的四大文化体系能在敦煌互融共生，最根本的原因在于中国文化的包容性，这也是中华文明能长期繁荣发展的重要基石。

## Temple of Multiculturalism

As a window through which various ethnic groups, regions, and Eastern and Western cultures converged and blended in ancient China, Dunhuang itself serves as a temple of multicultural integration. Renowned Chinese scholar Ji Xianlin (1911-2009) claimed that only four, rather than five, cultural systems in the world were ancient, extensive, self-contained, and far-reaching: Chinese, Indian, Greek, and Islamic. The only place where all four converged was the regions of Dunhuang and Xinjiang in China. Nowhere else shows evidence of the presence of all of them.

Dunhuang culture is the crystallization of long-term exchanges and integration among various civilizations. Rooted in Chinese civilization, Dunhuang has never stopped absorbing the diverse cultural achievements of other regions and ethnic groups. Ancient texts preserved in Dunhuang include not only Buddhist scriptures but also records of Daoism, Nestorianism, Manichaeism, and Zoroastrianism, reflecting the coexistence and exchanges of diverse religious cultures. The Dunhuang caves have preserved examples of interaction of various arts from Greece, India, Persia, and Sogdiana as they fused with indigenous Chinese art.

Due to the long-term coexistence of multiple ethnic groups, religions, and cultures there, various aspects of Dunhuang's social life reflect characteristics of multicultural integration. These include commercial activities shaped by specific geographical conditions, an urban residential layout accommodating both Han and non-Han communities, dietary structure and practices combining agriculture and pastoralism, gorgeous and varied clothing styles, and the traditional yet adaptable customs surrounding marriage and funerals. The fundamental reason the four major cultural systems of the world were able to coexist and integrate in Dunhuang was the inclusiveness of Chinese culture, which has also been a crucial cornerstone of Chinese civilization's longevity.

## 敦煌的世界文化遗产

甘肃省敦煌市和瓜州县属于古代敦煌地域范围，现存 3 处世界文化遗产，即莫高窟、玉门关遗址和悬泉置遗址。

莫高窟位于甘肃省敦煌市区东南 25 千米鸣沙山东麓的断崖上，与山西大同云冈石窟、河南洛阳龙门石窟并称“中国三大石窟”。莫高窟现存 735 个洞窟、45000 平方米壁画、2400 多尊彩塑，被誉为“全世界最大的画廊”“东方的卢浮宫”。世界遗产委员会对莫高窟的评价是 :“莫高窟地处丝绸之路的一个战略要点。它不仅是东西方贸易的中转站，同时也是宗教、文化和知识的交汇处。莫高窟的 492 个小石窟和洞穴庙宇，以其塑像和壁画闻名于世，展示了延续千年的佛教艺术。”

玉门关设于西汉元鼎六年（前 111），位于距今敦煌市西北 90 千米的疏勒河边。汉玉门关遗址区包括小方盘城、大方盘

## World Cultural Heritage

Dunhuang City and Guazhou County in northwest China's Gansu Province are parts of the ancient Dunhuang region and home to two existing World Cultural Heritage sites: the Mogao Caves, the Yumen Pass ruins and the Xuanquan Posthouse Site.

The Mogao Caves, located 25 kilometers southeast of Dunhuang City at the eastern foot of Mingsha (Sounding Sand) Hill, are numbered among the "Three Great Grottoes of China" alongside the Yungang Grottoes in Datong, Shanxi Province, and the Longmen Grottoes in Luoyang, Henan Province. The 735 caves, 45,000 square meters of murals, and more than 2,400 painted statues have collectively earned titles such as "the largest gallery in the world" and "the Louvre on the Orient". The UNESCO World Heritage Committee evaluated the Mogao Caves as such: "Situated at a strategic point along the Silk Route, at the crossroads of trade as well as religious, cultural and intellectual influences, the 492 cells and cave sanctuaries in Mogao are famous for their statues and wall paintings, spanning 1,000 years of Buddhist art."

Yumen Pass, established in 111 BC during the Western Han Dynasty, is located approximately 90 kilometers northwest of today's Dunhuang City along the Shule River. Its ruins encompass the remains of Xiaofangpan Fort, Dafangpan Fort, sections of the Han-dynasty Great Wall, and beacon towers. The site includes 20 beacon towers and 18 segments of the Han-era frontier wall stretching from Cangting Beacon in the east to Xianming Beacon in the west. These structures are distributed linearly across a corridor measuring 45 kilometers long and 0.5 kilometers wide centered

城、汉长城边墙及烽燧遗址，包括 20 座烽燧、18 段长城边墙遗址，东起仓亭燧，西至显明燧，在长约 45 千米、宽约 0.5 千米的区域内以小方盘城遗址为中心呈线性分布。作为“丝绸之路：长安—天山廊道的路网”上的重要关隘，玉门关遗址确定了小方盘城和大方盘城遗存年代、性质，以及古驿道具体位置和走向，是古代中原通往西域的重要门户。

悬泉置遗址位于敦煌市与瓜州县交界处，是中国汉代邮驿系统中级别最高的驿站。其主要职责有二：一是接待过往人员，提供饮食、住宿、车马；二是传递政令和邮书。悬泉置遗址的发现，重点标注了丝绸之路在这一路段的具体走向，作为“丝绸之路：长安—天山廊道的路网”真实存在的驿站，第一次确证了丝绸之路这条交通线在历史上的存在。悬泉置出土的汉简，从机构、人员、运作到往来，详细地记录了汉晋时期如何经营丝绸之路，展现了中原王朝与广大西域地区频繁交往的史实。

around the Xiaofangpan Fort ruins. As a strategic pass in the routes network of the Chang'an-Tianshan corridor along the Silk Road, the Yumen Pass ruins provide critical archaeological evidence to date and determine the function of Xiaofangpan and Dafangpan Forts and map the precise route and direction of the ancient post road, and served as a vital gateway between the Central Plains and the Western Regions.

Located at the boundary between Dunhuang City and Guazhou County, the Xuanquan Posthouse Site is the highest-ranking post station of the Han-dynasty postal system. Its main responsibilities were twofold: first, to accommodate travelers by providing food, lodging, and transportation; second, to relay government orders and mail. Discovery of the Xuanquan Posthouse Site pinpointed the specific route of the Silk Road across the area. Remains of a real post station along the Silk Road pointed to a network of routes from Chang'an to the Tianshan Mountain Corridor and provided confirmation of the historicity of this transportation route. The Han-dynasty bamboo slips unearthed there meticulously document the operations of the Silk Road during the Han and Jin (265-420) dynasties, detailing how it was managed and showcasing the frequent interactions between the Central Plains dynasties and the vast Western Regions.

## 敦煌学

1900年，收存于敦煌藏经洞中的7万余件古代文献文物被意外发现，因为历史原因，这些藏经洞出土品流散于全世界各地，并由此产生了一门世界性的显学——敦煌学。中国学者陈寅恪在《敦煌劫余录·序》首次使用“敦煌学”一词，并被学界沿用至今。

敦煌学最初是以藏经洞出土文献为研究对象的一门学问，之后扩展到敦煌石窟乃至敦煌历史文化等相关研究领域。今天，广义上的敦煌学包括了以古代敦煌为中心的一切学术研究和敦煌遗产的现代科技保护工作，成为一种容纳了文、理、工的综合性研究。

由于敦煌和吐鲁番位于中国西北，同属古代丝绸之路的重镇，因此基于吐鲁番地区出土资料发展起来的吐鲁番学，经常会与敦煌学合称为“敦煌吐鲁番学”。敦煌吐鲁番学内容丰富，其研究对中国文化史和世界文化交流史有极其重要的作用。主要表现在如下几个方面：第一，以其出土的第一手档案资料，纠正正史记载的疏误、补充正史记录的细节。第二，以其保存的历史上失传的典籍，填补中国文学史、语言学、科技史、医药学史记录的多处空白。第三，因其大量非汉文文献，丰富了民族交往和中外交流的历史记录。第四，以其保存的丰富艺术品，为中国艺术史和丝绸之路交流史提供最形象的图像史料。

## Dunhuang Studies

In 1900, over 70,000 ancient documents and artifacts enshrined in the Library Cave in Dunhuang happened to be discovered. Due to historical conditions, the relics were scattered across the globe, giving rise to a significant global academic discipline known as Dunhuang Studies. Chen Yinke (1890-1969), a prominent Chinese historian, philosopher, and scholar, was first to use the term "Dunhuang Studies" in print in the preface of *Dunhuang jieyu lu* (*An Analytical List of the Tun-Huang Manuscripts in the National Library of Peiping*), and this realm is still recognized in academic circles to this day.

Dunhuang Studies initially focused on research of manuscripts excavated from the Library Cave, but it has since expanded to include the study of Dunhuang grottoes and the history and culture of Dunhuang. Today, the broader concept of Dunhuang Studies encompasses all academic research centered on ancient Dunhuang as well as modern technological conservation efforts for Dunhuang heritage. It has evolved into a comprehensive field of study that integrates the humanities, sciences, and engineering.

Due to similar locations in northwestern China and shared significance as nodes along the ancient Silk Road, Dunhuang Studies is often positioned alongside Turfan Studies, developed from materials excavated in the Turfan region. They are collectively referred to as "Dunhuang-Turfan Studies". This combined field is rich in content and plays an extremely important role in both Chinese cultural history and the history of cultural exchanges worldwide. Its significance can be summarized in several aspects: First, it provides first-hand archival materials that correct inaccuracies in official historical records and supplements existing details in the records. Second, it fills gaps in the history of Chinese literature, linguistics, the history of science and technology as well as that of medicine, with copies of historical texts that have been lost over time. Third, the wealth of non-Han Chinese literature enriches the historical record of ethnic interactions and exchanges between China and foreign countries. Fourth, the preservation of abundant artworks offers vivid visual documentation for the study of Chinese art history and the history of Silk Road exchanges.

## 莫高精神

“莫高精神”指从 1944 年国立敦煌艺术研究所成立开始，在以常书鸿、段文杰、樊锦诗为代表的几代莫高窟人身上积淀和凝结的代代相传的“择一事终一生”的可贵精神。2014 年，时任敦煌研究院院长的樊锦诗在敦煌研究院成立 70 周年座谈会上将这种精神明确命名为“莫高精神”。

2019 年 8 月，习近平在敦煌研究院座谈时指出：70 年来，一代又一代的敦煌人秉承“坚守大漠、甘于奉献、勇于担当、开拓进取”的莫高精神，在极其艰苦的物质生活条件下，在敦煌石窟资料整理和保护修复、敦煌文化艺术研究弘扬、文化旅游开发和遗址管理等方面做了大量工作，取得了不少重要研究成果。

如今，“莫高精神”既是中国文物工作者守护文化家园、传承中华文明、勇于改革创新的生动写照，更是推动文博事业不忘初心、牢记使命、继续前进的宝贵精神财富。

## Mogao Spirit

The term "Mogao Spirit" refers to the precious spirit of dedication embodied by several generations associated with the Mogao Caves directly, starting with the establishment of the Dunhuang Research Academy in 1944. This spirit, represented by figures such as Chang Shuhong (1904-1994), a prominent Chinese painter and art historian, Duan Wenjie (1917-2011), a distinguished scholar and expert in Dunhuang studies, and Fan Jinshi, a renowned archaeologist and scholar, emphasizes the idea of committing to a single endeavor throughout one's life. During the 2014 symposium celebrating the 70th anniversary of the founding of the Dunhuang Academy, Fan Jinshi, then president of the Academy, explicitly defined it as the "Mogao Spirit".

During a symposium at the Dunhuang Academy in August 2019, Chinese President Xi Jinping said that for 70 years, generations of Dunhuang scholars have upheld the Mogao Spirit of "staying committed to the desert, being willing to serve, courageously taking responsibility, and striving for progress". In challenging living conditions, many have made substantial contributions to data organization and protection and restoration of Dunhuang grotto materials as well as research and promotion of Dunhuang culture and art, cultural tourism development, and site management, achieving numerous important outcomes.

Today, the "Mogao Spirit" serves as not only a vivid representation of the dedication of Chinese cultural workers in safeguarding cultural heritage, inheriting Chinese civilization, and embracing reform and innovation, but also a valuable spiritual asset to drive the cultural heritage sector to stay true to its original mission while continuously advancing.

二

# 历史人物

敦煌自古文化积淀深厚、人杰地灵，历史上曾出现过许多硕学宿儒、名臣良将，在中华文明史上做出了突出的贡献。由于其拥有大量的历史遗存，近代也成为西方探险家涉足的重要地域。本章选取古代敦煌的文化名人书法家张芝、佛教高僧竺法护，石窟营建者的代表人物乐僔和法良、东阳王元荣，唐代名将敦煌英雄张议潮及其支持者高僧洪辩，以及近代敦煌藏经洞文物流散的关键人物王圆箓、英国探险家斯坦因和法国汉学家伯希和进行介绍，通过一位位真实存在过的历史人物窥探敦煌的历史脉络。

# HISTORICAL FIGURES

Dunhuang has a rich cultural heritage, and many exceptional individuals throughout history have called it home. A heavy flow of renowned scholars, statesmen, and military leaders have emerged from this region and made prominent contributions to the history of Chinese civilization. Due to its abundant historical relics, Dunhuang became an important area for Western explorers in modern times. This chapter highlights several cultural figures from ancient Dunhuang, including eminent Chinese calligrapher Zhang Zhi, prominent Buddhist monk Zhu Fahu, cave builders represented by Monk Yue Zun, Yuan Rong, a nobleman from Dongyang, and celebrated Tang-dynasty general Zhang Yichao and his supporter, eminent monk Hong Bian. Figures involved in the dispersion of manuscripts from the Dunhuang Caves in modern times included Wang Yuanlu, a Daoist priest and custodian of the Mogao Caves, British-Hungarian explorer and archaeologist Marc Aurel Stein, and French sinologist and scholar Paul Pelliot. The efforts of these historically significant individuals offer insight into the historical context of Dunhuang.

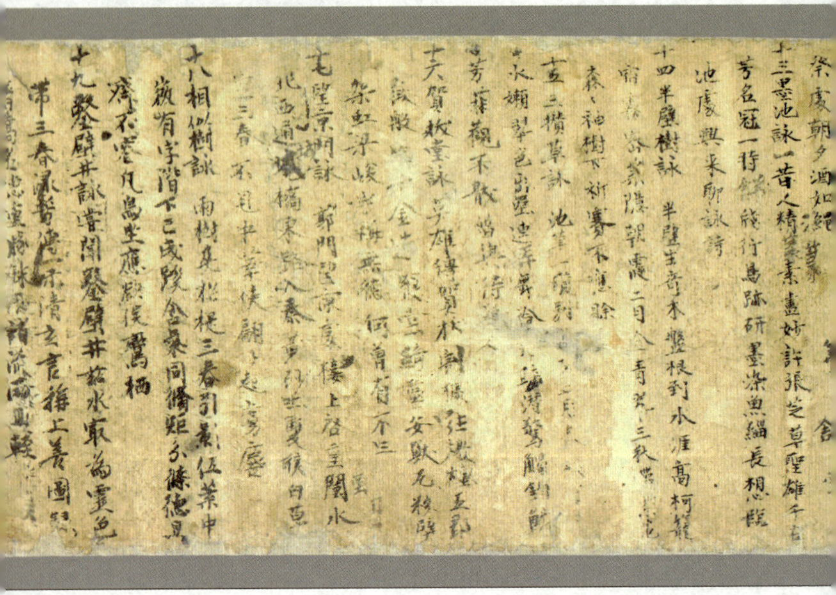

## 张芝

张芝（？—192），字伯英，敦煌渊泉人，东汉著名的书法家，因其草书造诣极高，在中国书法史上被尊称为“草圣”。东汉时期，敦煌地区学习书法的风气浓厚。其父张奂为方便张芝、张昶兄弟练习书法，派人锻造石桌、石凳于水池边。从此，张芝兄弟以帛为纸，临池学书，先练写而后漂洗再用。日复一日，年复一年，水为之黑，后世称之为张芝墨池。

## Zhang Zhi

Zhang Zhi (?-192 AD), also known by his courtesy name Boying, was a native of Yuanquan, Dunhuang, and a renowned calligrapher during the Eastern Han Dynasty. He is highly regarded in Chinese calligraphy as the "Sage of Running Script" for his exceptional skills in this form.

During the Eastern Han period, calligraphy was popular throughout the Dunhuang region. At Zhang's young age, his father, in order to facilitate calligraphic practice for Zhang Zhi and his brother, commissioned the construction of stone tables and benches by a pond. The brothers used silk as paper and practiced calligraphy by the water, writing, rinsing, and reusing the silk day after day, year after year, until the water turned black with ink. This location later became known as Zhang Zhi's Ink Pool.

敦煌文献 P.2005《沙州都督府图经》记载，张芝墨池位于敦煌县东北一里处。敦煌文献 P.2748《敦煌廿咏》还写有一首《墨池咏》，表现出对张芝品行和书法的赞赏。

张芝学习前人书法的长处并加以创新，终于摆脱旧俗独创一体，其字之体势，一笔所成，偶有不连，而血脉不断，字迹气脉贯通，隔行不断。古人谓之“一笔飞白”，也被誉为“一笔书”，其书迹在《淳化阁帖》存有五帖。

According to the Dunhuang manuscript P.2005, *Patterned Guidelines of Shazhou*, Zhang Zhi's Ink Pool is located about 500 meters northeast of Dunhuang County. Additionally, the manuscript P.2748, *Twenty Poems About Dunhuang*, contains a poem titled *Ode to the Ink Pool*, expressing admiration for Zhang Zhi's character and calligraphy.

Zhang Zhi learned from the strengths of earlier calligraphers while innovating, ultimately breaking from old traditions to create a unique style of his own. His calligraphy displays a fluid form, where each stroke is a continuous motion, even if occasionally not connected perfectly; nonetheless, the essence remains uninterrupted. His characters feature a seamless flow with energy and rhythm connected across lines. Ancient scholars referred to this as "one-stroke flying white", and it is also celebrated as "one-stroke writing". Five pieces of his calligraphy are held in *Calligraphic Inscriptions in the Secret Chamber of the Chunhua Period*.

## 竺法护

竺法护，又名竺昙摩罗刹，西晋时期著名的僧人。他的先祖本是月氏人，本姓支氏，世代居住在敦煌。8 岁时他随西域竺姓高僧出家，依照习俗改姓竺。晋武帝时，竺法护随师父游历西域各国，学习并通晓西域各国的语言文字，同时搜集大量梵文经典带回中国。

太康五年（284），竺法护回到敦煌后就开始翻译佛经，在弟子竺法乘等僧俗信徒的帮助下，将《修行道地经》和《阿难越致遮经》译成汉文，并在敦煌形成了一个以他为中心的汉胡僧俗信徒团体。后来竺法护又曾到长安、洛阳等地传教，并将翻译梵文典籍视为自己毕生的事业。他一生共译佛经 165 部，译文忠实原文，为佛法在中国的流传做出了重要贡献。汉长安城宣平门外有"敦煌寺"，竺法护在此译经弘道 20 余载，德高望重，僧徒信众数千，被时人誉为"敦煌菩萨"。

## Zhu Fahu

Zhu Fahu, also known as Dharmarksa, was a prominent monk during the Western Jin Dynasty. His ancestors were originally Yuezhi people with the surname Zhi who resided in Dunhuang for generations. At the age of eight, he became a monk under a renowned monk surnamed Zhu from the Western Regions, adopting the surname Zhu as per custom. During the reign of Emperor Wudi of the Jin Dynasty, Zhu traveled with his master across various countries in the Western Regions, where he learned and mastered the languages and scripts of those nations, simultaneously collecting a large number of Sanskrit texts to bring back to China.

In 284, Zhu returned to Dunhuang and began translating Sanskrit texts. With the assistance of his disciples and lay followers including Zhu Fasheng, he translated *Yoga-cārya-bhūmi-sūtra* and *Avinivartanīya-sūtra* into Chinese. He established a community of monks and lay followers around him in Dunhuang. Later, Zhu traveled to Chang'an and Luoyang to teach Buddhism while dedicating his life to translating Sanskrit texts. Over his lifetime, he translated 165 Buddhist scriptures, producing faithful translations that contributed notably to the spread of Buddhism in China. Outside Xuanping Gate in Chang'an stands Dunhuang Temple, where Zhu Fahu spent over 20 years translating scriptures and promoting Buddhist teachings. He was highly respected and gained a following of thousands of monks and laypeople, earning him the title of "Bodhisattva of Dunhuang" in his time.

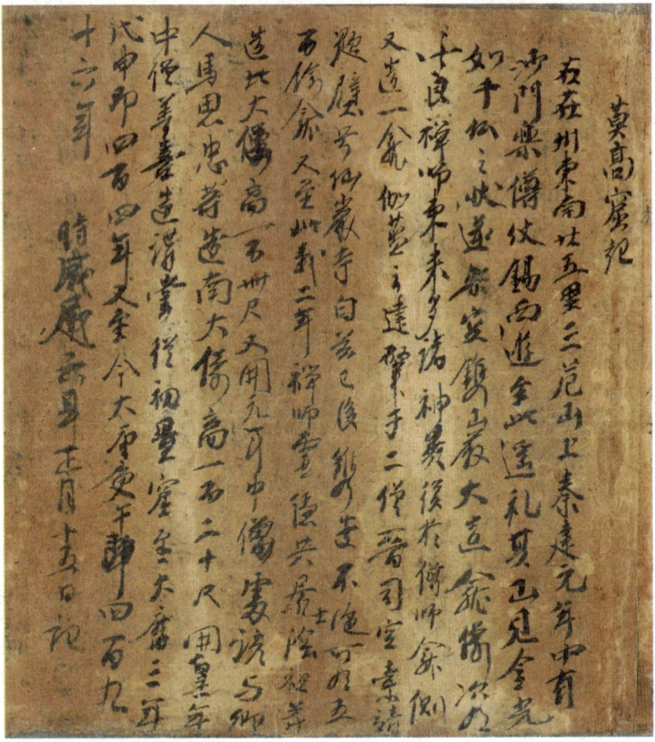
莫高窟记
右在州东南廿五里三危山上秦建元年中有
沙门乐僔仗锡西游至此遥礼其山见金光
如千佛之状遂架空镌岩大造龛像次有
法良禅师东来多诸神异复于僔师龛侧
又造一龛伽蓝之建肇于二僧晋司空索靖
题壁号仙岩寺自兹以后镌造不绝可有五
百余龛又至延载二年禅师灵隐共居士阴祖等
造北大像高一百卌尺又开元年中僧处谚与乡
人马思忠等造南大像高一百廿尺开皇年
中僧善喜造讲堂从初置窟至大历三年
戊申即四百四年又至今大唐庚午即四百九
十六年
时咸通六年正月十五日记

## 莫高窟的创建者

东晋十六国时期的前秦建元二年（366），一位名叫乐僔的和尚到达敦煌。他来到三危山前，身处隔河相望的三危山和鸣沙山之间，乐僔在这里禁不住遥拜大山，起身仰望时忽然看到金光千佛的神奇景象，就萌生了在这里开凿石窟的念头。于是，

## Founders of Mogao Caves

In 366 during the Sixteen Kingdoms period, a pilgrim-monk named Yue Zun arrived in Dunhuang. He wandered in between Sanwei Mountain and Sounding Sand Hill and gazed in awe at the majestic peaks. Looking up, he suddenly had a vision of a golden radiance in the form of a thousand Buddhas, which inspired him to carve caves in that location. Thus, Yue settled on the cliffs of Sounding Sand, where he practiced meditation while carefully excavating the steep rock face to construct the caves. Thanks to his relentless efforts, he ultimately completed the first cave on the mountain, marking the founding of the Mogao Caves.

乐僔在鸣沙山断崖前住了下来，一边坐禅修行，一边在峭壁上架空凿险，建造石窟。在乐僔的不懈努力下，多年以后，终于在山上凿建了第一个洞窟，莫高窟自此创建。

乐僔之后，又有法良禅师来到这里。他同样看到了在乐僔面前显现过的奇异景象，于是就在乐僔窟旁开凿了莫高窟的第二个洞窟。此后，这里的僧侣、香客、朝拜者络绎不绝，人们纷纷在这里修建寺院、开窟造像，规模越来越大。法良虽然不是第一个在此开窟的人，却与乐僔一同被认作莫高窟开窟的鼻祖，成为敦煌石窟的创建者。

After Yue Zun, another monk named Fa Liang arrived at the site. He too saw the extraordinary vision that had appeared to Yue and began to carve the second cave of Mogao next to Yue's. From that point on, monks, devotees, and pilgrims flocked to the area, building temples, caves, and Buddhist statues, hence expanding the scale of the site. Although Fa was not the first to carve caves there, he and Yue are both recognized as the founding figures of the Mogao Caves who played a crucial role in the establishment of the Dunhuang cave complex.

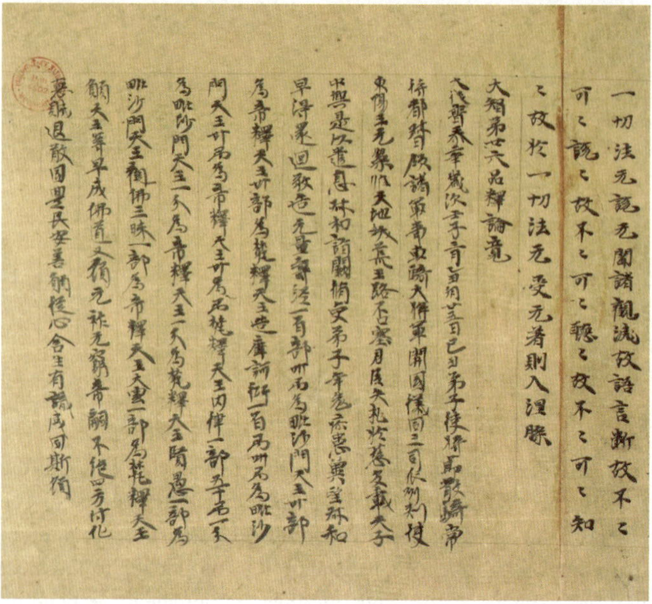

## 元荣

元荣（？—约 541），又名元太荣，北魏至西魏时期的瓜州刺史，为皇室宗亲。北魏为加强河西统治，孝昌元年（525）任命宗室元荣为瓜州刺史治理敦煌，永安二年（529）封元荣为东阳王。在北魏末年的乱世，元荣团结敦煌地方的豪强大族，保持了这里的社会安定。西魏时期，元荣继续管理敦煌。

永安至永熙（528—534）间，他曾出巨资写经 10 余部，包括现藏于中国国家图书馆的 BD.09525《仁王护国般若波罗蜜经》、法国国家图书馆 P.2143《大智度论》等。史载元荣还在莫高窟开凿了一个大窟，莫高窟第 285 窟洞窟规模宏大、绘塑精湛，被认为可能是元荣主持开凿的，因此也被称为“东阳王窟”。

## Yuan Rong

Yuan Rong (?-c. 541), also known as Yuan Tairong, was governor of Guazhou during the Northern Wei (386-534) and Western Wei (535-556) periods and a member of the imperial family. He was appointed governor of Guazhou in 525, in an effort to strengthen control over Hexi, and was granted the title of Prince of Dongyang in 529, to oversee Dunhuang. During the chaotic times at the end of the Northern Wei Dynasty, Yuan Rong united the local powers in Dunhuang to maintain social stability in the region. Throughout the Western Wei period, he continued to manage Dunhuang, ensuring its governance and prosperity amidst a turbulent political landscape.

From 528 to 534, Yuan Rong invested heavily in transcribing over 10 Buddhist sutras including *Karunikarāja prajñāpāramitā sūtra* (BD.09525), currently housed in the National Library of China, and *Mahāprajñāpāramitopadeśa* (P.2143), in Bibliothèque Nationale de France, the National Library of France. Historical records show that Yuan also excavated a large cave at Mogao, known as Cave 285, which features grand scale, exquisite paintings, and painted statues. This cave is believed to have been constructed under his direction and is therefore also referred to as the "Cave of the Prince of Dongyang".

## 张议潮

张议潮（799—872），沙州人，唐代著名的英雄人物。安史之乱后，吐蕃趁机攻占唐土，包括敦煌在内的河西广大地区陷入吐蕃之手。张议潮出生于陷蕃后的敦煌，早年就读于寺学，长大后担任吐蕃沙州刺史一职。

公元 842 年，吐蕃发生内乱，河西人民陷入了水深火热之中。河陇各地的吐蕃守将思想混乱，兵防空虚。唐王朝乘此时机，决心收复河湟。大中二年（848），张议潮率众起义，驱逐吐蕃统治者，一举收复瓜、沙二州，并派出多队使节设法赴长安向唐王朝报捷。与此同时，张议潮率领起义军继续收复河西其他地区。

## Zhang Yichao

Zhang Yichao (799-872), a native of Shazhou, was a renowned hero of the Tang Dynasty (618-907). After the An Lushan Rebellion (755-763), Tubo forces took advantage of the chaos to occupy Tang territory. The vast Hexi region, including Dunhuang, fell under Tubote control. Zhang was born in Dunhuang after it was occupied by the Tubotes. He studied in a monastic school in his early years and later served as the governor of Shazhou under Tubote rule.

In 842, civil strife erupted in Tubo, plunging the people of Hexi into turmoil. Tubote military commanders in various regions of Hexi had a poor grasp of the situation and left weak defenses. The Tang Dynasty was determined to reclaim Hexi as the window of opportunity emerged. In 848, Zhang Yichao led a rebellion to expel the Tubote rulers, successfully recovering Guazhou and Shazhou. He dispatched multiple delegations to Chang'an to report the victory to the Tang Dynasty while continuing to lead the rebel army in reclaiming other areas of Hexi.

大中五年（851），敦煌的使者终于抵达长安，献上瓜、沙、伊、西、甘、肃、兰、鄯、河、岷、廓等十一州图籍。唐宣宗接到报捷之后，特下诏表彰张议潮等人的忠勇和功勋。唐王朝于沙州建立归义军，统领瓜沙十一州，授张议潮归义军节度使、十一州观察使。河西归唐，张议潮领导的大中起义起到了主要作用。张议潮在河西重振了大唐声威，莫高窟第 94、98、85 窟均绘有他的供养像。莫高窟第 156 窟被认为是张议潮的功德窟，主室绘有长卷式《河西节度使张议潮统军出行图》。

In 851, the envoys from Dunhuang finally arrived in Chang'an, presenting maps and records of 11 regions including Guazhou, Shazhou, Yizhou, Xizhou, Ganzhou, Suzhou, Lanzhou, Shanzhou, Hezhou, Minzhou, and Kuozhou. Upon receiving the good news, Emperor Xuanzong of Tang issued an edict to commend Zhang and his men for their loyalty, bravery, and achievements. Royal Tang established the Guiyijun Regime in Shazhou to oversee the above-mentioned 11 regions, appointing Zhang as the military governor and supervisor of these regions. The uprising led by Zhang was a key turning point in the return of Hexi to the Tang regime, and Zhang then revitalized Tang's prestige in Hexi. His patron statues were enshrined in caves 94, 98, and 85 of the Mogao Caves. Cave 156 is regarded as the cave of his achievements and features a long scroll painting titled *Outing Scene of Zhang Yichao*.

## 洪辩

洪辩（？—862），因俗姓吴，又称吴僧统、吴和尚，晚唐时期敦煌的著名僧人。早在吐蕃时期，洪辩在担任大蕃沙州释门都法律兼摄副教授10多年后，晋升到沙州最高的僧官释门都教授。在公元832—834年间，于莫高窟开凿"七佛堂"，即现在的莫高窟第365窟，窟内西壁佛坛下功德文有其题名。

大中二年（848），张议潮起义时，洪辩作为沙州僧团的最高领袖，坚决支持张议潮起义。在张议潮向唐王朝派出报捷使团时，洪辩也派弟子悟真率僧人使团出使长安。唐王朝赐予洪辩多项殊荣，任命其继续担任河西最高的宗教领袖都僧统。

此后洪辩又在莫高窟开凿一座大窟，即现在的莫高窟第16窟，这个洞窟是莫高窟空间最大的洞窟。在这个洞窟甬道北壁，发现了举世闻名的藏经洞——莫高窟第17窟。莫高窟第17窟原为附设于第16窟的耳室，在洪辩离世后，他的族人、弟子将此室改为影堂，即洪辩的纪念堂，内塑洪辩的真身彩塑像，展现洪辩生前的生活。

## Hong Bian

Hong Bian (?-862), also known by the common surname Wu, and referred to as Wu Sengtong or Monk Wu, was a prominent monk in Dunhuang during the late Tang period.

As early as the Tubote regime, he served for over a decade as dean of Shazhou Overseeing all Political, Legal and Theological Master during the Tubote occupation before being promoted to the highest monk official position, professor of Monastic Law. Between 832 and 834, he excavated the Seven Buddhas' Cave in the Mogao Caves, which is now Cave 365. His name can be found inscribed in the merit text beneath the butsudan against the western wall of the cave.

During the 848 uprising led by Zhang Yichao, Hong, the highest leader of the monastic community in Shazhou, firmly supported the rebellion. When Zhang sent a delegation to report the victory to the Tang Dynasty, Hong dispatched his disciple Wu Zhen to lead a group of monks to Chang'an. The royal court bestowed numerous honors upon Hong, appointing him to continue as the highest religious leader in Hexi.

Later, Hong Bian excavated a large cave in the Mogao Caves, which is now known as Cave 16, the most spacious in the complex. Cave 17, the world-famous Library Cave, was discovered on the northern wall of the corridor in this cave. Originally an adjoining room to Cave 16, this chamber was transformed into a memorial hall after Hong's passing by his family and disciples, featuring a life-sized painted statue of Hong.

## 王道士

王道士（1849—1931），湖北麻城人，名圆箓，又作园禄。他是敦煌藏经洞的发现者，也是藏经洞文物流散的关键人物。王道士早年因家乡连年旱灾，四处逃荒。清光绪初，入肃州巡防营为兵勇，后离军，受戒成为道士，道号法真。

约光绪二十三年（1897）王道士来到敦煌莫高窟。他在莫高窟南区北段，清理积沙，供奉香火，收受布施，也外出募化，并以“莫高窟住持”

## Wang Yuanlu

Wang Yuanlu (1849-1931), or Wang Tao-shih, originally from Macheng in today's Hubei Province, was named Yuanlu ( 圆箓 ), also written " 园禄 " with the same pronunciation. He discovered the Library Cave in Dunhuang and became a key figure in the dispersal of the texts found there. In his early years, Wang faced repeated droughts in his hometown, leading him to wander about. In the early days of the reign of Emperor Guangxu of the Qing Dynasty (1644-1911), he joined the garrison in Suzhou as a soldier but eventually left the military to become a Taoist priest, taking the name Fazhen.

Wang arrived at the Mogao Caves in Dunhuang in 1897. He began clearing the accumulated sand in the northern section of the southern area of the caves, burning incense, receiving donations, and fundraising while adopting the title Abbot of the Mogao Caves. In June 1900, Wang and his team excavated a crack in the northern wall of the corridor in Cave 16, resulting in the discovery of a small cave filled with ancient texts and artifacts, now known as the Library Cave (Mogao Cave 17 today).

自居。1900年6月，王道士率人凿开莫高窟第16窟甬道北壁的一处裂隙，发现一个堆满古代文献文物的小窟“藏经洞”（今莫高窟第17窟）。

1904年，甘肃布政使司命敦煌知县汪宗翰对藏经洞文物就地封存，汪氏责令王道士对这批文物妥善保管、不许外流。1906年，王道士维修藏经洞所在的窟前建筑三层楼完工，并立功德碑记其事。从1907年开始，先后有斯坦因、伯希和、橘瑞超、吉川小一郎、奥登堡等外国探险者，从王道士手中骗购走了4万多件文献文物，占藏经洞文物的五分之三。

莫高窟二层楼对面的地面建筑，即王道士所建道观“三清宫”，也称“下寺”，现为敦煌研究院藏经洞陈列馆。1931年，王道士死后葬于莫高窟窟前大泉河东岸，其徒赵玉明等就其墓起塔，即“道士塔”，塔上嵌有其墓志铭。

In 1904, the governor of Gansu ordered Wang Zonghan, magistrate of Dunhuang, to seal the artifacts from the Library Cave. Wang Zonghan instructed Wang Yuanlu to ensure the proper preservation of these items and prohibited their dispersal. By 1906, Wang completed the construction of a three-story building in front of the Library Cave, and he erected a stele to commemorate this achievement. Starting in 1907, foreign explorers, including Marc Aurel Stein, Paul Pelliot, Zuichō Tachibana (1890-1968), a Japanese explorer and Buddhist monk associated with the Ōtani Expedition, a series of early 20th-century archaeological missions to Central Asia, and Koichiro Yoshikawa (1885-1978), a Japanese scholar and explorer, and Sergei Fedorovich Oldenburg (1863-1934), a Russian Orientalist and archaeologist, fraudulently purchased from Wang Yuanlu over 40,000 items of documents and artifacts, which accounted for three-fifths of the treasures enshrined in the Library Cave.

Opposite the three-story building at the Mogao Caves is the Taoist temple Three-Purity Palace, also known as Lower Temple, which was built by Wang Yuanlu. Today, this temple serves as an exhibition hall for the Library Cave under the Dunhuang Academy. After his death in 1931, Wang was buried on the eastern bank of the Daquan River in front of the Mogao Caves. His disciple Zhao Yuming and others constructed a stupa over his grave, known as the "Taoist Stupa", which features inscriptions commemorating his life.

## 斯坦因

斯坦因（Marc Aural Stein，1862—1943），英籍匈牙利人，他是第一个骗购敦煌藏经洞文物的外国人，在英国和英属印度政府的支持下，先后完成了三次中亚探险。

1907 年，斯坦因在进行第二次中亚探险时到达敦煌。斯坦因一行不仅在敦煌附近长城沿线掘得大量汉简，更到访莫高窟拍摄了大量洞窟照片，并利用王道士的无知，廉价骗购藏经洞出土敦煌文献 24 箱、绢画和丝织品等 5 箱。斯坦因后来出版的旅行记《沙漠契丹废址记》（1912）和正式的考古报告《西域考

## Marc Aurel Stein

Marc Aurel Stein (1862-1943) was a Hungarian-born British explorer and archaeologist. He was the first foreigner to convince Wang Yuanlu to sell him artifacts from the Library Cave in Dunhuang. With the support of the British and Indian governments, Stein undertook three major expeditions to Central Asia.

Stein arrived in Dunhuang in 1907 during his second expedition to Central Asia. His team not only unearthed a large number of Han-dynasty bamboo slips along the Great Wall near Dunhuang but also visited the Mogao Caves, taking numerous photos of the caves. By exploiting Wang's credulousness, Stein defrauded him into parting with 24 boxes of Dunhuang manuscripts and five boxes of silk paintings and textiles from the Library Cave at a low price. Stein later published travel accounts detailing his findings in *Sand-buried Ruins of Khotan* (1912) and an official archaeological report titled *Serindia: Detailed Report of*

古记》(1921)对敦煌藏经洞均有详细记录。1914年，斯坦因第三次中亚探险时再次来到敦煌，又从王道士手中骗购570余件敦煌文献，这次经历在他的正式考古报告《亚洲腹地考古报告》(1928)中有记录。除了上述的旅行记和考古报告外，斯坦因还编著有《千佛洞：中国西部边境敦煌石窟寺所获之古代佛教绘画》(1921)一书。

这些从敦煌得到的出土文物和文献，主要入藏英国国家博物馆、英国国家图书馆和印度事务部图书馆，以及印度国家博物馆。

*Explorations in Central Asia and Westernmost China* (1921), both of which provide comprehensive records of the Library Cave. In 1914, during his third expedition to Central Asia, he returned to Dunhuang and again defrauded Wang into selling him over 570 pieces of Dunhuang manuscripts. This experience is documented in his *Innermost Asia: Detailed Report of Explorations in Central Asia, Kan-su and Eastern Iran* (1928). In addition to these travel accounts and archaeological reports, Stein also authored *The Thousand Buddhas: Ancient Buddhist Paintings from the Cave-Temples of Tun-huang on the Western Frontier of China* (1921), which focused on the ancient Buddhist paintings found in the Dunhuang Caves.

The artifacts and manuscripts removed from Dunhuang mainly flowed to collections of the British Museum, the British Library, the Library of the Ministry of External Affairs, Government of India, and the National Museum, New Delhi.

# 伯希和

伯希和（Paul Pelliot，1878—1945），法国人，他是骗购敦煌藏经洞出土品精华的探险者，曾多次奉命前往中国购买古籍。1905年，被委任为法国中亚探险队队长，与测量师瓦扬（Louis Vaillant）和摄影师努埃特（Charles Nouette）一起，于1906年至1908年间进入丝绸之路北道，发掘巴楚、库车等地的佛教遗址。

1908年，伯希和一行到达敦煌并来到莫高窟，对全部洞窟进行编号、抄录题记、拍摄大量壁画照片。伯希和精通汉语并熟悉中国古典文献，很快取得王道士好感。王道士允许伯希和在藏经洞中翻阅全部文物，伯希和重点选取佛教大藏经未收的文献、非汉语文献和带有纪年题记的文献。他廉价骗购走大量

## Paul Pelliot

Paul Pelliot (1878-1945) was a French sinologist and explorer known for acquisition of the finest artifacts from the Library Cave in Dunhuang through deceptive purchases. He was commissioned multiple times to travel to China to purchase ancient books. In 1905, he was appointed leader of the French Central Asian Expedition. From 1906 to 1908, he took Louis Vaillant, a surveyor and Charles Nouette, a photographer on a journey across the northern route of the Silk Road to excavate Buddhist sites in regions such as Bachu and Kucha.

In 1908, Pelliot arrived in Dunhuang and visited the Mogao Caves, where he systematically numbered all the caves, transcribed inscriptions, and took numerous photographs of the murals. Fluent in Chinese and well-versed in classical Chinese literature, he quickly won the favor of Wang Yuanlu and access to all the artifacts in the Library Cave. Pelliot specifically sought texts excluded from Chinese Buddhist Canon, non-Chinese literature, and documents with dated inscriptions. He defrauded Wang and removed many high-quality artifacts from the Library Cave including silk paintings and textiles that Stein had missed. In 1909, Pelliot provided Chinese scholars access to some Dunhuang manuscripts at his residence, leading to growing interest in the Library Cave.

藏经洞文献中的精品及斯坦因遗漏的绢画丝织品。1909 年，中国学者在北京伯希和住处看到了他携带的敦煌文献，敦煌藏经洞才引起关注。

这些收集品运回巴黎，文献入藏法国国家图书馆，绢画丝织品等入藏吉美亚洲艺术博物馆。伯希和把在敦煌的发现写成书信，后编为《甘肃发现的一个中世纪文库》一文，汉译文名为《敦煌石室访书记》。回法国后，他将所摄敦煌壁画照片编为《敦煌石窟图录》全六册（1920—1924）；他与各科专家研究带回来的敦煌文献，形成《伯希和中亚探险队丛刊》；他去世后，由法国学者整理出版了《伯希和敦煌石窟笔记》。

The collected items were transported to Paris, and the manuscripts are now housed in the National Library of France, while the silk paintings and textiles are held in Guimet Museum. Pelliot documented his discoveries in Dunhuang in letters which were later compiled into the work titled *Une bibliothèque médiévale retrouvée au Kan-su*. After returning to France, Pelliot compiled the photographs of the Dunhuang murals he had taken into a six-volume catalog titled *Les grottes de Touen-Houang* (1920-1924). Collaborating with various experts, he researched the Dunhuang manuscripts he brought back, which resulted in *Mission Paul Pelliot* (*Documents conservés au Musée Guimet et à la Bibliothèque Nationale*). Following his death, French scholars edited and published his notes under the title *Grottes de Touen-houang: carnet de notes de Paul Pelliot*.

# 三

# 敦煌文物

本章选取记录丝路交通线的汉简《驿置道里簿》、生态环保墙书《四时月令五十条》、反映中原王朝与西域交往的《案验康居王使者献驼册》、描绘书信传递者的《驿使图》，敦煌藏经洞出土代表唐代文化的《新修本草》《全天星图》和雕版《金刚经》，反映唐代文学水平的《秦妇吟》《叶净能诗》《降魔变文》，及反映中外交流的《五印度用甘蔗造砂糖法》《归义军衙府酒破历》和《行脚僧图》进行介绍，这些文物串起了敦煌 2000 多年的文明史，我们能够通过这些文物看到丝绸之路上曾经真实存在过的社会交往与文化交流图景。

# RELICS OF DUNHUANG

This chapter focuses on several artifacts that document the history and culture of Dunhuang including *Yizhi daoli bu* (*The Book of Relay Stations and Distances*), the Han-dynasty bamboo slips which record the transportation routes along the Silk Road; *Sishi yueling wushi tiao* (*Fifty Articles of Seasonal and Monthly Ordinances*), a wall text reflecting principles of environmental conservation; *Anyan kangjuwang shizhe xiantuoce* (*The Official Document Regarding the Investigation of the Camels Presented by the Kangju Envoy*), which illustrates interactions between the Central Plains dynasties and the Western Regions; *The Courier*, depicting a messenger who delivered letters; artifacts from the Library Cave representing Tang-dynasty culture such as *Xinxiu bencao* (*The Newly-Compiled Materia Medica*), *Dunhuang Star Chart*, and the woodblock print *Diamond Sutra*; works that showcase the literary achievements of the Tang Dynasty such as *Qinfu yin* (*Lament of the Lady of Qin*), the *Stories of Ye Jingneng*, and *Transformation Text of Subjugation of Demons*; and texts reflecting Sino-foreign exchanges such as the text on Indian sugar making techniques, *Guiyijun yafu jiupoli* (*The Account Book for the Official Use of Liquor by the Guiyijun Regime*), and *The Traveling Monk*. These artifacts shine light on over 2,000 years of civilization in Dunhuang, providing a glimpse at the social interactions and cultural exchanges that once thrived along the Silk Road.

## 敦煌汉简

敦煌汉简，主要指在汉代敦煌郡境内发现的简牍文书。其发现始于斯坦因1906—1908年的第二次中亚探险，止于2019年阿克塞县双墩子北烽隧遗址发掘。其中，除简牍文书之外，也有少量帛书与纸文书；在时间上，最早始于西汉中期，个别晚至晋代；在地域上，敦煌之外兼有少量属于酒泉郡的文书。

敦煌汉简总数约4万枚，主要包括：1906—1908年斯坦因第二次中亚探险所获3100枚（包括未刊布部分），1913—1916年第三次中亚探险所获200枚；1979年马圈湾遗址发掘1217枚，1990—1992年悬泉置遗址发掘3.5万枚，1998年小方盘城遗址发掘380枚。

这些出土于汉代边塞烽隧和驿站遗址的简牍文书，属于边塞屯戍和驿站日常运作及其管理文书的档案部分，涉及汉代边塞和邮驿系统组织形式、人员结构和具体的防御措施等，对于研究汉代边塞和邮驿的日常管理与社会生活具有非常重要的参考价值。作为汉代第一手的档案资料，敦煌汉简被誉为中国“四大汉简”之一，留下了丝绸之路上“汉匈”“汉羌”“汉胡”等民族交往、交融、交流的重要记录。

## Dunhuang Han-Dynasty Bamboo Slips

Dunhuang Han-dynasty bamboo slips primarily refer to the bamboo-slip documents discovered within the territory of Dunhuang Prefecture during the Han Dynasty. Their discovery began with Stein's second Central Asian expedition from 1906 to 1908 and continued until the excavation of the Shuangdunzi Northern Beacon Tunnel site in Aksay County in 2019. In addition to bamboo slips, a few silk and paper documents were also found. Chronologically, the earliest slips date back to the mid-Western Han Dynasty, with a few extending as late as the Jin Dynasty. Geographically, while most documents are from Dunhuang, a few belong to Jiuquan Prefecture.

The total number of the Han-dynasty bamboo slips in Dunhuang is approximately 40,000 pieces, including 3,100 pieces (including unpublished portions) obtained during Stein's second Central Asian expedition from 1906 to 1908, 200 pieces acquired during his third Central Asian expedition from 1913 to 1916, 1,217 pieces excavated from the Maquanwan Site in 1979, 35,000 pieces unearthed at the Xuanquan Posthouse Site from 1990 to 1992, and 380 pieces discovered at the Xiaofangpan Fort site in 1998.

The bamboo slips excavated from the ruins of the frontier beacon towers and post stations are part of the archival documents related to the daily operations and management of the garrison troops and post stations. They address various aspects such as the organizational structure of the postal relay system, personnel composition, and specific defensive measures of the frontiers at that time. These documents hold significant reference value for studying the daily management and social life at the Han-dynasty frontier. As primary archival materials from the Han Dynasty, the Dunhuang bamboo slips are regarded as one of China's "Four Great Han-dynasty Bamboo Slips", providing important evidence of interactions, integration, and exchanges along the Silk Road among various ethnic groups including the Han, Xiongnu, Qiang, and Hu.

## 悬泉置汉简

1990—1992 年，甘肃省文物考古研究所对悬泉置遗址进行考古发掘，出土各类遗物 7 万件，其中简牍 3.5 万枚。悬泉置汉简是悬泉置日常运作形成的档案文书得以保留下来并被发掘的部分，目前编号整理 1.8 万枚。悬泉置汉简详细记录了作为丝绸之路上汉代邮驿路线的组织机构与运作状况，作为汉与西域交往必经重要驿站的档案文书，其中所见西域地名达 30 多个，涉及大月氏、康居、罽宾、乌弋山离与条支等古国，为探讨汉代中原王朝与西域的交往提供了丰富的资料。

1990 年，悬泉置遗址出土的《驿置道里簿》（简牍编号Ⅱ 90DXT0214 ① :130），记录汉代邮驿交通路线站点及其间距。起于东端的武威郡苍松，经武威、张掖、酒泉，止于敦煌郡最东渊泉置。此简记录的路线与居延汉简 EPT59:582 路线衔接，构成长安经平凉、武威至敦煌郡的完整交通路线。据此可知，当时从长安到敦煌全程有近 60 个驿站，真实展现出丝绸之路长安至敦煌段的历史面貌。

## Han-Dynasty Bamboo Slips, Xuanquan Posthouse Site

From 1990 to 1992, Gansu Institute of Cultural Relics and Archaeology conducted archaeological excavations at the Xuanquan Posthouse Site, bringing to light a total of 70,000 artifacts including 35,000 bamboo slips. These bamboo slips represent a preserved portion of the archival documents generated from the daily operations at the Xuanquan Posthouse Site, with 18,000 pieces currently cataloged and organized. These slips provide detailed records of the organizational structure and operational status of the postal routes along the Silk Road during the Han Dynasty. As essential archival documents from a significant waystation serving interactions between the Han and the Western Regions, they contain over 30 geographical names from the Western Regions, referencing ancient kingdoms such as Yuezhi, Kangju, Jibin, Wuyishanli, and Tiaozhi. This rich information offers valuable insights into the exchanges between the Central Plains and the Western Regions during the Han Dynasty.

In 1990, slips containing *The Book of Relay Stations and Distances* (Slip No. II90DXT0214①:130) were unearthed at the Xuanquan Posthouse Site. The book records the postal traffic routes and stations of the Han Dynasty, along with their distances. The route begins at the eastern end in Cangsong of Wuwei Prefecture, passes through Wuwei, Zhangye, and Jiuquan, and terminates at the easternmost point of Dunhuang Prefecture, Yuanquan Posthouse. This slip documents a route that connects to the route recorded on Juyan Han-dynasty Bamboo Slip EPT59:582, forming a complete transportation route from Chang'an through Pingliang and Wuwei to Dunhuang Prefecture. It indicates the existence of nearly 60 waystations along the journey between Chang'an and Dunhuang, providing an authentic depiction of the historical landscape of the Silk Road segment between the two places.

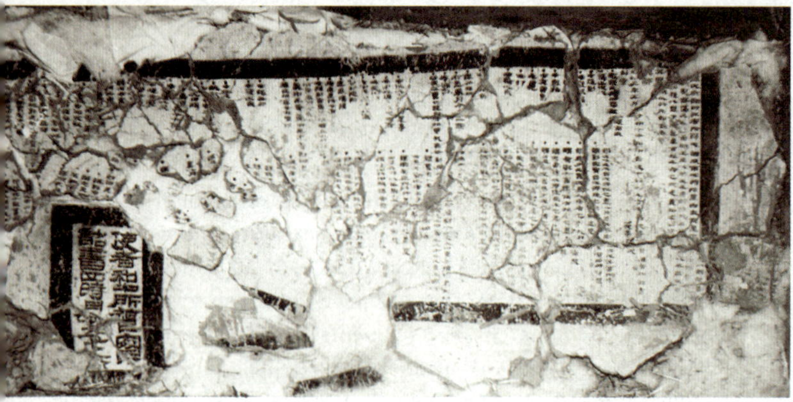

## 西汉生态环保墙书

西汉生态环保墙书指墙壁题记《使者和中所督察诏书四时月令五十条》，1992 年出土于悬泉置遗址。发掘时，文字一面反扣地面，破损严重。复原后长 222 厘米、宽 48 厘米，全文 101 行。此墙书内容为西汉元始五年（公元 5 年）以太皇太后名义颁布的诏书，左下角书写诏书名称，左侧是具体颁布过程，可知其由长安经敦煌郡、效谷县被悬泉置抄写公布在墙上。

墙书中间为诏书正文，详细列出四时及孟仲季 12 个月的具体条文。每条令文首起有“·”标注，上端是正文，下部是具体解释。诏书中说，因为太皇太后有感于西汉末年“阴阳不调、风雨不时”，专门按照《月令》“春生、夏长、秋收、冬藏”之义而制定的条令，如春天不能捣鸟窝，孟夏时不能砍伐大树等。这些观念与现在倡导的环境保护观念相吻合，被称为 2000 年前的“环境保护法”，是迄今为止我国发现最早的一部关于环境保护的法规。其本身既是研究汉代诏书起草、内容、传布形式和过程的典型标本资料，也是研究西汉末年社会政治生活的绝佳素材。

## Eco-Themed Wall Text of the Western Han Dynasty

The eco-themed wall text of the Western Han Dynasty is the inscription of *Fifty Articles of Seasonal and Monthly Ordinances from the Imperial Edict Supervised by the Imperial Envoy and the Zhonghe Office*, which was unearthed in 1992 at the Xuanquan Posthouse Site. During the excavation, one side of the text was found facing the ground and severely damaged. After restoration, it measures 222 centimeters in length and 48 centimeters in width, consisting of 101 lines of text. This wall text is a decree issued in the name of the then empress dowager in 5 AD, in the Western Han Dynasty. The name of the decree is written in the lower left corner, and the left side details the specific process of its issuance. Clearly, the text was copied and publicly displayed on the wall at Xuanquan Posthouse after being transmitted from Chang'an through Dunhuang Prefecture and Xiaogu County.

The center of the wall text contains the main body of the decree, which details specific provisions for each month of the four seasons. Each provision begins with a bullet point ("·") for emphasis, with the main text at the top and specific explanations below. The decree states that the empress dowager, feeling concerned about the "imbalance of *yin* and *yang*, and irregular wind and rain" during the late Western Han Dynasty, specially formulated these regulations based on the principles outlined in *The Book of Rites: Monthly Ordinances*, which underlines "spring growth, summer flourishing, autumn harvest, and winter storage". For instance, it prohibits disturbing bird nests in spring and cutting down large trees in early summer. These concepts align with contemporary environmental protection ideas, earning the text a reputation as "2,000-year-old environmental protection law". It is also regarded as the earliest known legislation concerning environmental protection discovered in China to date. As such, it serves as a valuable reference for the study of the drafting, content, dissemination, and processes of Han-dynasty decrees as well as an excellent resource for the examination of the socio-political life of the late Western Han period.

## 《案验康居王使者献驼册》

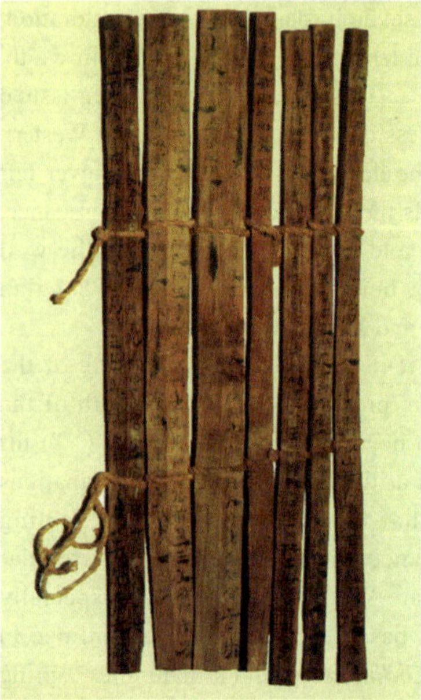

1990年，敦煌悬泉置遗址发掘出土的《案验康居王使者献驼册》（简牍编号Ⅱ90DXT0216②:877—883），出土时编绳完整，全文由7简组成，前4简是康居王使者杨伯刀等人的申诉文书，后3简是各级调查文书。

文书记录了西汉元帝永光五年（前39），康居王使者送给汉朝皇帝的骆驼由白色变黄色、由肥变瘦的申诉。这一外事纠纷事件，由汉朝中央主管“使主客谏大夫汉、侍郎当”联合下文给敦煌郡进行调查。全文借由

## *The Official Document Regarding the Investigation of the Camels Presented by the Kangju Envoy*

In 1990, the document, *The Official Document Regarding the Investigation of the Camels Presented by the Kangju Envoy* (Slip No. II90DXT0216 ② :877-883), was unearthed at the Xuanquan Posthouse Site. It was found with its binding intact and consists of seven slips. The first four slips contain appeal letters from Yang Bodao and other envoys of the king of the State of Kangju, while the last three slips are investigation documents from various levels.

The records detail an incident in 39 BC during the Western Han Dynasty, in which the envoy from the State of Kangju reported that camels presented to the Han emperor had changed from white to yellow and from fat to thin. This diplomatic dispute caused the Han-dynasty officials to jointly issue a directive mandating an investigation in Dunhuang Prefecture. Through this diplomatic dispute, the document reveals the process and manner of interactions between the Han Dynasty and the State of Kangju in the Western Regions, serving as a typical example of ethnic communication and exchanges.

外事纠纷，反映出汉与西域康居国的交往过程和交往方式，是中西交通、民族交往的典型范例。

在丝绸之路开通之后，西域与中原的交往频繁。从悬泉汉简的记录中，可以看到西域各国国王、贵人和使者前往中原的记录。汉宣帝时悬泉置曾在一个月内分两批接待了西域 9 个国家的质子、贵人和使者，汉朝的邮驿为西域的客人们提供饮食车马接待，并派人迎送他们到长安。西域诸国的来客同时出现在悬泉置，也足以说明当时丝绸之路上的西域各国和睦相处。而贡献的物品除了汉王朝重视的良马外，还有折垣王派使者贡献的狮子，康居王派人贡献的骆驼，从而使这一时期西域的大量物产经过敦煌传入中原。

After the trailblazing of the Silk Road, interactions between the Western Regions and the Central Plains became frequent. Records from the Han-dynasty bamboo slips of the Xuanquan Posthouse Site indicate that kings, nobles, and envoys from various Western Regions states traveled to the Central Plains. During the reign of Emperor Xuandi, Xuanquan Posthouse hosted envoys, hostages, and nobles from nine Western Regions states in two waves within a single month. The Han-dynasty's postal system provided food, transportation, and accommodation for these guests, ensuring their safe passage to Chang'an. The simultaneous arrival of visitors from various Western Regions states at Xuanquan Posthouse suggests a harmonious coexistence among the Western Regions along the Silk Road during this period. In addition to the prized horses highly valued by the Han Dynasty, contributes included lions sent by the envoy of the King of Zheyuan and camels by the King of Kangju. This exchange facilitated the introduction of a wide variety of goods from the Western Regions into the Central Plains through Dunhuang during this time.

## 《驿使图》

嘉峪关市魏晋 5 号墓出土的《驿使图》画像砖，长 35 厘米，宽 17 厘米。《驿使图》绘于公元 3—4 世纪前后，画中绘一位驿使，头戴黑帻，身穿白袍，左手执棨。棨是古代的一种木制符信，作为通过关卡、驿站的凭证。驿使座下的马身上有朱红色的斑块，马的四蹄腾空，显示出正在快速奔跑。驿使则稳坐马背，反衬出驿马速度的快捷与信使业务的熟练。《驿使图》生动再现了当时中国西北地区驿使驰送文书的情景，是中国古代邮驿使的珍贵形象资料。这幅图画也被认为是中国最早的邮递员画像。

邮驿是中国传统通信组织形式，现代邮政的前身之一。20 世纪 80 年代初，中国重返万国邮政联盟时，就以《驿使图》作为中国邮政标志物参加了世界万国邮政博览会。如今，《驿使图》悄然成为中国邮政的“形象大使”，经常出现在中国邮政的品牌设计中。

## *The Courier*

*The Courier* is a pictorial brick unearthed from Tomb No. 5 in Jiayuguan City, dating back to the Wei and Jin dynasties (220-420). Measuring 35 centimeters long and 17 centimeters wide, the artwork was created around the 3rd-4th centuries AD. It depicts a courier wearing a black scarf and a white robe, holding a wooden staff in his left hand. This staff, known as *qi*, served as a token to pass through checkpoints and relay stations in ancient times. The horse is marked with bright red spots and leaps with all four hooves in the air, indicating it can move fast. The courier sits firmly on horseback, highlighting the speed of the mount and the courier's expertise at his duties. The picture vividly represents a scene of couriers delivering documents in northwestern China during the period and is considered a precious depiction of ancient Chinese postal couriers. This image is also regarded as one of the earliest representations of postal workers in China.

The postal relay system was a traditional communication organization in China and a precursor to modern postal services. In the early 1980s, *The Courier* was used as a symbol for Chinese postal services at the World Postal Exhibition when China rejoined the Universal Postal Union. Today, it has quietly become the "mascot" of China Post, frequently appearing in logos for the country's postal service.

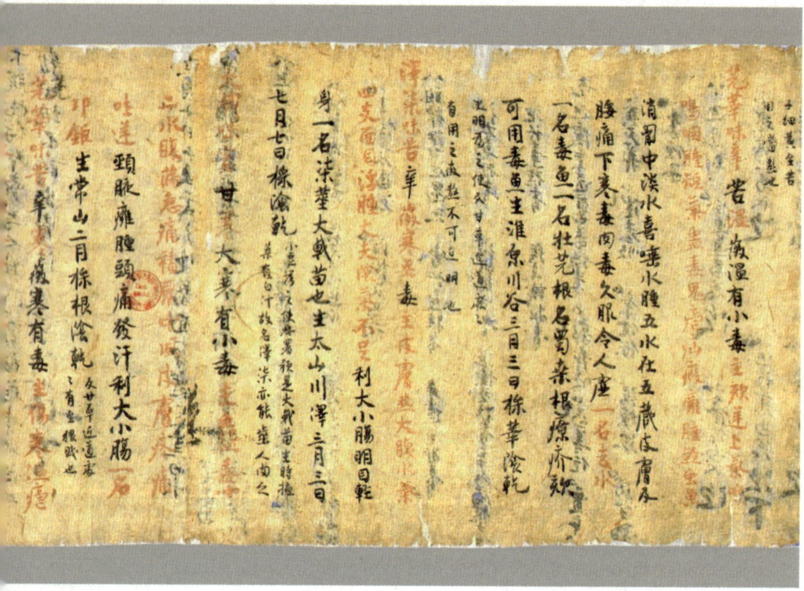

## 《新修本草》

《新修本草》成书于唐显庆四年（659），是唐高宗时由政府组织苏敬等20余人编写的一部医药学大典，也被称为《唐本草》。全书共54卷，收载了844种药物，分为本草、图经、药解三部分，系统总结了唐以前中药学的成就。本草部分记载了药物的性味特点、产地、采集要点、治疗功效等，图经根据药物的实际形态描绘出图样，药解则是对药物的文字说明。书中包括一部分外来药品，如安息香、龙脑香、胡椒等；甚至还记载了用白锡、银箔调配成补牙用的填充剂——这也是世界医学史上最早关于补牙的文献记载。

## *The Newly-Compiled Materia Medica*

*The Newly-Compiled Materia Medica* was completed in 659, Tang Dynasty. It is a significant medical compendium compiled by over 20 scholars including Su Jing, a prominent physician and pharmacologist, and organized by the government. Also known as *Tang Materia Medica*, the work consists of 54 volumes and catalogs 844 types of medicinal substances, divided into three sections: materia medica, illustrations, and medicinal explanations. It systematically summarizes the achievements of traditional Chinese medicine prior to the Tang Dynasty. The materia medica section records the properties, origins, harvesting notes, and therapeutic effects of various medicinal herbs. The illustrations provide depictions based on the actual appearance of the herbs, while the medicinal explanations offer written descriptions of their uses. The text includes some foreign medicinal products such as benzoin, borneol, and pepper, among others. It even documents the use of white tin and silver foil as dental filling material, marking the earliest records of dental filling in the history of world medicine.

敦煌藏经洞出土的《新修本草》共6件，分别藏于中国国家图书馆、日本杏雨书屋、法国国家图书馆及英国国家图书馆等。《新修本草》内容丰富，一经问世立刻四散传播。唐代来中国求法的日本僧人把它带回日本，对日本医学界影响很大，当时的日本“凡医生皆读苏敬《新修本草》”。该书图文并茂，是此前1000多年中国药学知识的集大成之作。作为官方组织编写并颁布的药典，它比欧洲最早的药典——1498年出版的《佛罗伦萨处方集》早了800多年，它是全世界最早的国家药典，显示了当时中国在医学领域的领先水平。

A total of six copies of *The Newly-Compiled Materia Medica* were discovered in the Library Cave, and they are currently housed in various institutions including the National Library of China, Akinoya Bookstore in Japan, the National Library of France in Paris, and the British Library. Rich in content, the work spread rapidly upon its release. Japanese monks who came to China to study during the Tang Dynasty brought it back to Japan, influencing Japanese medicine at the time to such a great extent that there was a saying that "all doctors in Japan read Su Jing's *Newly-Compiled Materia Medica*". This book is richly illustrated and represents a comprehensive compilation of Chinese pharmacological knowledge accumulated across more than 1,000 years. As an official pharmacopeia compiled and published by the government, it predates Europe's earliest pharmacopeia, the *Florentine Codex*, published in 1498, by over 800 years. It is recognized as the world's earliest national pharmacopeia, showcasing China's leadership in the field of medicine at that time.

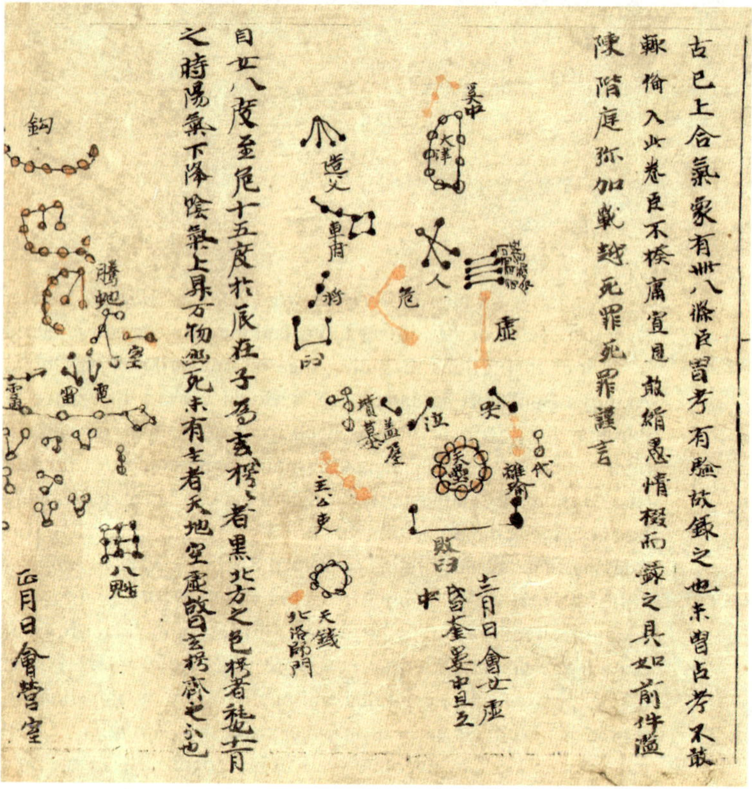

## 敦煌星图

敦煌文献 S.3326《全天星图》和敦博 076《紫微垣星图》，又分别被称为敦煌星图甲本、乙本。其中《全天星图》总长 330 厘米，卷首不存，现存前半部为《云气占》，后半部为《全天星图》，尾部绘一电神并有题记。《全天星图》的原作者被认为是唐初著名的天文星占家李淳风。

《全天星图》绘制于 1300 多年前，它包括 13 幅图和相应的说明文字，描绘了唐朝皇家观星台中肉眼所能见到的 1348 颗

## Dunhuang Star Maps

*Dunhuang Star Chart* (S.3326) and *The Purple Forbidden Enclosure* (Dunbo 076) are referred to as Dunhuang Star Maps, with the former known as Version A and the latter Version B. *Dunhuang Star Chart* measures a total length of 330 centimeters, but the beginning is missing. The preserved front half contains *Meteorological Divination*, while the latter half presents *Dunhuang Star Chart*, with a depiction of a lightning deity and an inscription at the end. The original author of *Dunhuang Star Chart* is believed to be Li Chunfeng, a renowned astrologer from the early Tang Dynasty.

*Dunhuang Star Chart*, created over 1,300 years ago, consists of 13 illustrations accompanied by explanatory texts depicting 1,348 stars visible to the naked eye from the Tang-dynasty royal observatory. It holds the distinction of being the oldest, most comprehensive star chart in existence, recording the highest number of stars. The chart portrays the entire night sky in a

星星。它是世界上现存记录星数最多，也是最古老的一幅星图。它用一种相当“现代”的方式描绘了整个星空，前 12 幅用圆柱形投影法绘制十二时角图，最后一幅又用方位投影法绘制环北极星图。

敦煌星图在世界天文学史上占有十分重要的地位。英国著名的中国科技史学家李约瑟博士甚至说：“欧洲在文艺复兴以前可以和中国天图制图传统相提并论的东西，可以说很少，甚至簡直就没有。”

remarkably "modern" manner, with the first 12 illustrations using cylindrical projection to create 12-celestial-hour-angle diagrams, while the final illustration employs azimuthal projection for a polar star diagram.

Dunhuang Star Maps occupy a significant position in the history of world astronomy. Dr. Joseph Needham, a renowned British historian of Chinese science and technology, stated that there were very few, if any, comparable traditions in Europe before the Renaissance that could be likened to China's tradition of astronomical cartography.

## 《金刚经》

《金刚经》全称为《金刚般若波罗蜜经》，现藏于英国国家图书馆，它是世界上现存最早的、有明确刊印日期的雕版印刷品。这件《金刚经》为鸠摩罗什译本，全卷首尾完整，由 7 纸相连成卷，总长近 500 厘米，每纸高约 27 厘米，宽约 75 厘米。每纸刻印佛经 48—52 行不等，每行 18—21 字不等，有上下书栏。卷首第 1 纸为版画，其余 6 纸为佛经，经卷的尾部书写题记。从这些文字可知它印刷于唐咸通九年（868）农历四月十五，因为有准确的刊印时间，它成为中国印刷史上的一件标

## *The Diamond Sutra*

*Vajracchedikā Prajñāpāramitā Sūtra*, or *The Diamond Sutra*, housed in the British Library, is recognized as the oldest known printed book in the world with a specific publication date. This edition is a translation by Kumārajīva, and it remains complete with both the front and back pages intact. It consists of seven connected sheets totaling nearly 500 centimeters in length, with each sheet measuring 27 centimeters in height, 75 centimeters in width. Each sheet features 48 to 52 lines of text, with each line containing 18 to 21 characters, along with margins at the top and bottom. The first sheet of the scroll includes a woodblock print, while the remaining six sheets contain the sutra text. The colophon at the end of the scroll indicates that it was printed on the 15th day of the fourth month in 868. Due to this precise printing date, *The Diamond Sutra* has become a significant artifact in the history of Chinese printing, with the British Library referring to it as "the earliest printed book in the world".

志物，并被英国国家图书馆称为“世界上最早的印本书籍”。

这件《金刚经》的卷首版画，表现《金刚经》的序品部分，描绘佛祖释迦牟尼乞食回到给孤独园坐定，长老须菩提向他提问，于是佛祖开始讲说《金刚经》。整部佛经上的文字端正大方，有颜柳楷书风骨。版画和文字都显示出雕版的刀法娴熟，印刷墨色匀称、清晰，属上乘的印刷作品。1914 年，这部《金刚经》第一次在英国国家博物馆展出，1973 年被转交给了英国国家图书馆。

The frontispiece of *The Diamond Sutra* features a woodblock print illustrating the preface section of the sutra. It depicts Sakyamuni returning to the Jeta Grove after begging for alms, where Subhūti poses a question to him, prompting the Buddha to begin his discourse on *The Diamond Sutra*. The text throughout the sutra is elegantly formatted, showcasing the style of the regular script by Yan Zhenqing (709-784) and Liu Gongquan (778-865), both renowned calligraphers of the Tang Dynasty for their regular script. Both the print and text demonstrate the skillful carving techniques of woodblock printing, with the ink color being uniform and clear, marking it as a superior example of printing craftsmanship of the time. In 1914, this edition was exhibited for the first time at the British Museum, and in 1973, it was transferred to the British Library.

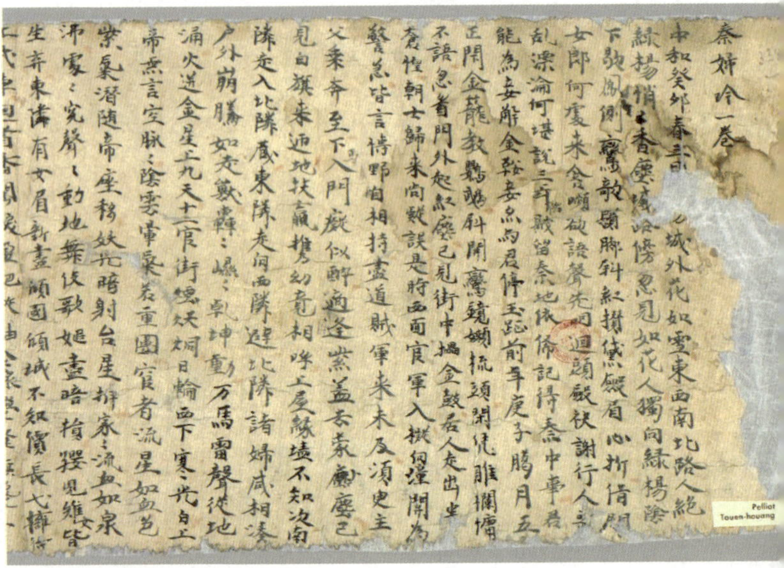


## 《秦妇吟》

《秦妇吟》全诗七言 238 句、1666 字，被誉为“唐朝第一长诗”。作者韦庄在广明元年（880）因黄巢起义被困长安，他在中和三年（883）将自己目睹的战乱情形，借诗中主人公“秦妇”之口讲述出来，写成了极具现实主义色彩的长篇叙事诗。这首纪实长诗的时间跨度达三年之久，空间范围涉及长安、洛阳两京，

## *Lament of the Lady of Qin*

*Lament of the Lady of Qin* by Wei Zhuang, an outstanding poet and lyricist of the Tang Dynasty, is a lengthy poem consisting of 238 lines and 1,666 Chinese characters, earning it the title of "the longest poem of the Tang". Wei was trapped in Chang'an in 880, during the turmoil of the Huang Chao Rebellion (875-884). Three years later, he narrated the war-torn conditions he witnessed through the voice of the poem's protagonist, the "Lady of Qin", crafting a long narrative poem rich in realism. Spanning three years, the poem covers significant geographical areas including the capitals of Chang'an and Luoyang, and vividly depicts the historical upheaval and the suffering of the common people. A monumental piece of documentary poetry, it offers a detailed, vivid portrayal of the social landscape during the late Tang Dynasty compared to official historical records.

所描绘的是历史的沧桑巨变和百姓的苦难遭遇。作为纪实性的史诗巨作，该诗比正史更加形象细致地描绘了唐末的社会景象。

《秦妇吟》自诞生之时就在民间广为流传，当时的人甚至称韦庄为“《秦妇吟》秀才”。历史上这首诗曾一度失传，世人只知其名不得其文。敦煌文献发现的《秦妇吟》写卷共计 10 件，其中 6 件带有题记，分别记载它们曾经属于寺学学子、私学学子以及普通百姓的情况。正是因为敦煌藏经洞的意外开启，世人在今天才能一睹韦庄名作《秦妇吟》的真容。

Since it was written, *Lament of the Lady of Qin* had been widely circulated among the populace, with contemporaries even referring to Wei Zhuang as the "lyricist of *Lament of the Lady of Qin*". Historically, the poem faced a period of obscurity, wherein many knew its title but no verses. The Dunhuang cache included a total of 10 copies of *Lament of the Lady of Qin*, six of which contained inscriptions indicating previous ownership by students from monasteries, private academies, and ordinary people. Thanks to the discovery of the Library Cave, the modern world can appreciate the original form of Wei Zhuang's masterpiece—*Lament of the Lady of Qin*.

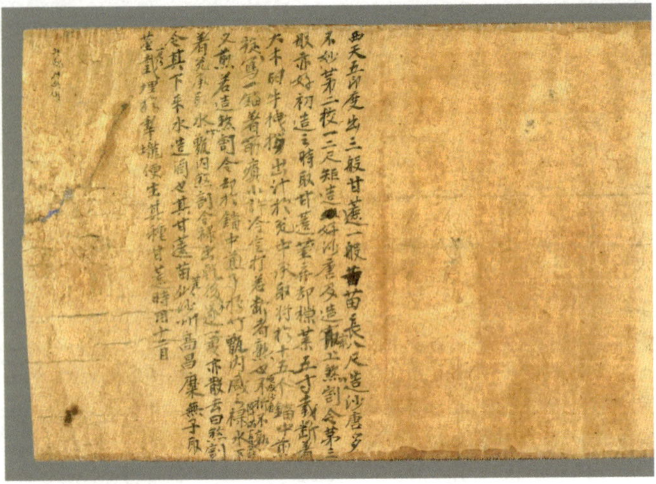

## 印度制糖法文献

虽然中国人很早就种植甘蔗，但在印度制糖法传入之前，却只能熬煮浓缩甘蔗汁制造粗糖。唐太宗贞观二十一年（647）专门派出使者到印度学习制糖技术，唐高宗龙朔元年（661）又从印度将制糖专家请到中国。经过唐初的技术和人才的引进，中国终于生产出口感超过印度的石蜜和砂糖，这时的糖已经跟现在的糖非常接近了。

敦煌文献 P.3303V《五印度用甘蔗造砂糖法》是一件记录印度制糖法的文献。它写在一张佛经的背后，短短的几百字涉及了甘蔗的种类、制砂糖法、糖的种类、甘蔗酿酒等一系列问题。这件文献先讲如何选择适合制糖的甘蔗，之后讲具体的制糖方法。文献中也提到了石蜜的制作方法，熬完石蜜的水还可以造甘蔗酒。

季羡林先生曾说，糖本是一件小东西，然而在它身上却驮着长达 1000 多年的中印两国文化交流的历史。

## Literature on Indian Sugar Production Methods

Although the Chinese had been cultivating sugarcane for a long time, they could only boil and concentrate sugarcane juice to produce raw sugar before Indian sugar production methods were introduced. In 647, Emperor Taizong of the Tang Dynasty specifically dispatched envoys to India to learn sugar production techniques. In 661, sugar production experts from India were invited to China. With the introduction of these technologies and talent during the early Tang Dynasty, China eventually began to make sugar products such as rock candy and granulated sugar, which surpassed India's offerings in flavor. This technology made sugar very similar to what we have today.

The Dunhuang manuscript P.3303V, titled *Methods of Producing Sugar from Sugarcane in the Five Indian Regions*, is a document recounting Indian sugar production techniques. Written on the back of a Buddhist scripture, this brief text of a few hundred words addresses various topics including types of sugarcane, methods of producing granulated sugar, types of sugar, and distilling alcohol from sugarcane. The manuscript begins by discussing how to select suitable sugarcane for sugar production, followed by detailed methods. It also mentions a method for making rock candy, noting that leftover water from rock candy making can be used to brew sugarcane wine.

Renowned Chinese scholar Ji Xianlin once commented that despite being such a small item, sugar carries a history of cultural exchanges between China and India that spans over a thousand years.

## 北宋敦煌官府的酒账

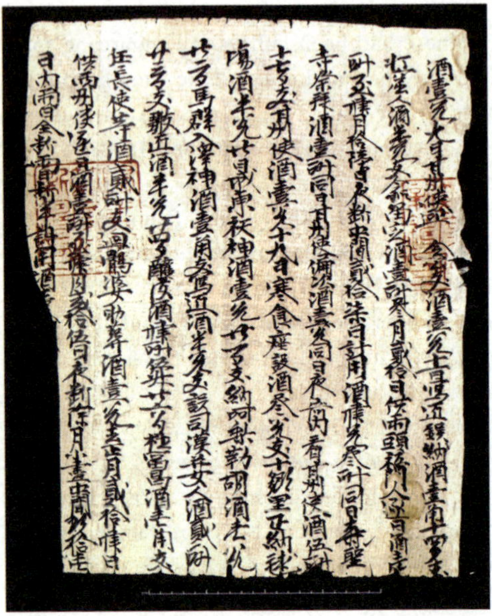

敦煌文献《归义军衙府酒破历》常常被简称为《酒账》，里面记录了北宋时期敦煌当地官府200多笔用酒支出。《酒账》上盖有曹元忠执政时期归义军的官印。曹元忠是归义军节度使中统治时间最长的一位，他积极发展与周边民族的关系，并与中原的后晋、后汉、后周和北宋保持联系，使敦煌地区得以稳定发展。

这件《酒账》所有项目都是归义军政府的公费支出，立账严格、条目清楚，并形成了一整套制度。这件《酒账》里有多条接待甘州、西州、伊州、于阗等地使者的记载，说明这时候的敦煌地区仍是西北各地的纽带，连接着东西的广大地区。为了

## *Wine Accounts of the Dunhuang Government During the Northern Song Dynasty*

The Dunhuang manuscript, *Wine Accounts of the Dunhuang Government During the Northern Song Dynasty* is often referred to simply as the *Liquor Ledger*. It records over 200 instances of wine expenditures by the local government in Dunhuang during the Northern Song Dynasty (960-1127). The manuscript features the official seal of the Guiyijun Regime from the period of Cao Yuanzhong's administration. Cao was the longest-serving commander of the Guiyijun Regime and actively worked to develop relationships with surrounding ethnic groups. He maintained contact with the Later Jin, Later Han, Later Zhou, and Northern Song dynasties, which contributed to the stable development of the Dunhuang region.

All the text in the *Liquor Ledger* documents public expenditures by the Guiyijun Regime. It is characterized by strict record-keeping and clear entries, forming a complete set of regulations. The manuscript includes multiple records of receptions for envoys from places such as Ganzhou, Xizhou, Yizhou, and Yutian, indicating that during this time, the Dunhuang region served as a vital link among various areas in the northwest, connecting vast regions of the East and West. To facilitate communication, the Guiyijun Regime also employed many interpreters, demonstrating that Dunhuang was a hub of frequent interactions with surrounding ethnic groups and regions, a gathering place for diverse cultures.

交流方便，归义军衙府还有很多翻译官，这说明敦煌当时与周边民族和地区交往频繁，是多种文化的汇集之地。

《酒账》在流传的过程中曾经被分为三段：第一段一直保存在敦煌研究院；第二段流落到日本，1997 年由日本友人青山庆示捐赠敦煌研究院；第三段收藏于法国。现在利用数字化技术，我们能够重新看到《归义军衙府酒破历》的原貌。

The *Liquor Ledger* was divided into three sections over time during its spread. The first section has been preserved at the Dunhuang Academy. The second section was once lost to Japan but donated to the Dunhuang Academy by Japanese friend Keiji Aoyama in 1997. The third section is housed in France. Modern digital technology has made it possible to reproduce the document as it originally looked.

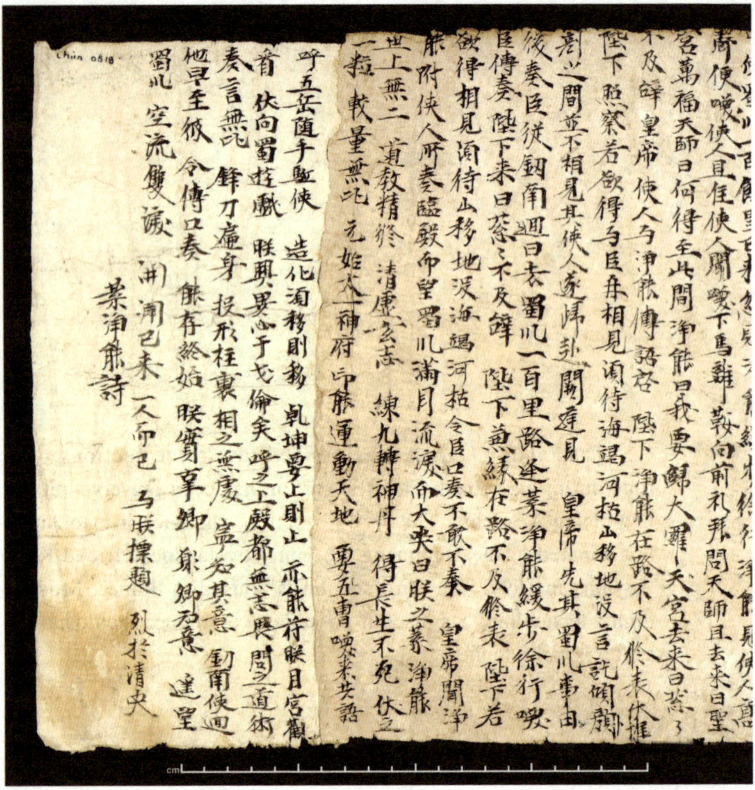

## 《叶净能诗》

话本是说唱故事的底本，隋唐时把讲故事称为“说话”，“说话”的底稿或记录都可以称为话本。原来一般认为话本小说开始于宋代，直到藏经洞中出土了唐代话本，大家才认识到唐代不仅孕育着话本小说的雏形，甚至远在西北的敦煌都已经广泛传抄。敦煌文献 S.6836《叶净能诗》出自于藏经洞，这件文献虽然卷末题名为“叶净能诗”，但其实并不是诗作，而是一部像小说一样的话本。

## *The Stories of Ye Jingneng*

The term "*huaben*" refers to scripts used for storytelling, which were known as "*shuohua*" during the Sui and Tang dynasties. Therefore, the manuscripts, or records of *shuohua*, can also be called *huaben*. Previously, most believed that *huaben* novels began in the Song Dynasty. However, the discovery of Tang-dynasty *huaben* in the Library Cave made it clear that the Tang Dynasty nurtured the embryonic form of *huaben* novels, but such works were already widely copied in far-off Dunhuang in the northwest. The Dunhuang manuscript S.6836, titled *The Stories of Ye Jingneng*, was also founded in the Mogao Caves. Although this document is titled *The Stories of Ye Jingneng* at the end, it is not a collection of poems but rather a *huaben* resembling a novel.

《叶净能诗》充满了奇幻色彩。叶净能是唐高宗、武则天时有名的方士。在这件话本中，叶净能在会稽山修道有成，赴长安途中降妖除害；后来被唐玄宗召见，斩龙祈雨，还带着玄宗神游剑南观灯，并在中秋游月宫。《叶净能诗》里的各种怪谈，在唐人多部笔记小说中已有记载，这件话本是把已有的奇幻故事编排到叶净能的身上。特别是其中“唐明皇游月宫”的情节，这个充满想象力的人类登月故事，在唐代就有多种版本并逐渐成为一个广为流传的题材，后来还以此创作出杂剧、小说、绘画等。

*The Stories of Ye Jingneng* is filled with elements of fantasy. Ye Jingneng was a renowned sorcerer during the reigns of Emperor Gaozong and Empress Wu Zetian of the Tang Dynasty. In this *huaben*, Ye attains enlightenment while practicing Taoism in Kuaiji Mountain and encounters various demons and hazards on his way to Chang'an. Later, he is summoned by Emperor Xuanzong of Tang to slay a dragon and pray for rain. He also takes Xuanzong on a magical journey to Jian'nan to observe lanterns and even visits the Moon Palace during the Mid-Autumn Festival. The various strange tales in *The Stories of Ye Jingneng* have been documented in many Tang-dynasty notes and novels. This *huaben* compiles existing fantastical stories and attributes them to Ye Jingneng. Notably, the episode in which *Emperor Xuanzong of Tang Visits the Moon Palace* features an imaginative narrative about human lunar exploration which had multiple versions during the Tang Dynasty and gradually became a widely-circulated theme. This story later inspired various forms of art including dramas, novels, and paintings.

## 《降魔变文》

敦煌文献《降魔变文》主要讲述建造祇园精舍的曲折故事，重点讲以智慧第一著称的佛弟子舍利弗与六师外道的代表劳度叉多次神变斗法的故事。敦煌藏经洞出土了多件《降魔变文》，其中敦煌文献 P.4524 讲唱手卷最有价值。本件文献正面绘有 5 组图像，从右到左依次绘出金刚击山、狮子啖牛、象踏宝池、金翅鸟战毒龙、毗沙门天王降夜叉。横卷的背面存有 5 段文字，内容与正面画面情节一一对应。9 至 10 世纪敦煌地区讲唱文艺流行，"于是张翠幕，列画图，扣洪钟，奏清梵"。通常只需要一位或两位故事讲述人，边吟唱韵文或者讲解故事，边展示画

## *The Transformation Text of Subjugation of Demons*

Dunhuang manuscript, *The Transformation Text of Subjugation of Demons*, primarily tells the intriguing story of the construction of Jetavana Monastery. It focuses on the tale of Shariputra, a foremost disciple of Buddha known for his wisdom, engaging in a series of miraculous battles with Raudrākṣa, a representative figure of the Six Heretics. Several copies of the *Transformation Text of Subjugation of Demons* were discovered in the Library Cave, among which the handscroll manuscript P.4524 is the most valuable. The front of this manuscript is adorned with five groups of images. From right to left, they depict the Vajra striking the mountain, a lion devouring a bull, an elephant trampling a pool of treasures, a garuda fighting a venomous dragon, and the deity Vaisravana subduing the Yaksha. On the back of the horizontal scroll are five sections of text, each corresponding to the scenes on the front. During the 9th and 10th centuries, storytelling performances were popular in the Dunhuang region, where "curtains were raised, paintings were displayed, bells were struck, and chants were performed". Typically, only one or two storytellers were needed. They would recite rhymed verses or explain the story while displaying the scroll illustrations. This particular manuscript is currently the only known scroll of *Transformation Text of Subjugation of Demons* that has been used for storytelling performances, providing tangible evidence of the practice of illustrating and narrating tales in this form of literature.

卷。这件文献是目前找到的唯一作讲唱用途的《降魔变文》手卷，它以实物形式证实了讲唱文学中观图听讲这一事实。

敦煌壁画也绘有这个斗法的故事，这一题材的经变画叫《劳度叉斗圣变》。敦煌壁画共绘有 19 铺《劳度叉斗圣变》，莫高窟、榆林窟、西千佛洞和五个庙石窟均有绘制。这个题材的经变和变文对中国古典神魔小说产生了巨大的影响，如《西游记》中孙悟空与二郎神、孙悟空与羊力大仙的神变斗法，就和舍利弗与劳度叉斗法的情节十分相似。

The story of the miraculous battle is also depicted in Dunhuang murals, where this theme is referred to as *Raudrākṣa's Contest with Śāriputra*. A total of 19 murals depicting the theme can be found in Dunhuang, including the Mogao Caves, Yulin Caves, Western Thousand-Buddha Caves, and the Five-Temple Caves. This theme of scriptural transformation and narrative exerted a significant influence on Chinese classical supernatural fiction. For example, the divine battles in *Journey to the West*, such as those between Sun Wukong (the Monkey King) and Erlang Shen, or between Sun Wukong and the Goat-Strength Immortal, bear a striking resemblance to the battle between Shariputra and Raudraksa.

## 《行脚僧图》

敦煌的《行脚僧图》一共有 20 幅，画面多数为僧人携虎而行。敦煌壁画中有 8 幅，敦煌藏经洞出土有 12 幅纸画和绢画，分别收藏于法国吉美博物馆、法国国家图书馆、韩国国立中央博物馆和俄罗斯艾尔米塔什博物馆。

敦煌绢画 EO.1138 是其中最精美的一幅。这件创作于 9 世纪的唐代绢画，现存法国吉美博物馆。僧人身着交领的法衣，领口露出白色的内衣。他左手执木杖、右手提数珠，腰间挂锥子、小刀、熏炉等物，裸足穿凉鞋。他背着一个满载经卷、像背篓一样的巨大竹笈，前方悬着一个金色香囊，竹笈的后方有一根木头挂着拂尘、幡和净瓶等物。僧人上方的云端，有一尊坐在莲台上的小佛像，此即宝胜如来。僧人

## *The Traveling Monk*

A total of 20 traveling-monk paintings have been found in Dunhuang. The scenes often depict monks walking accompanied by tigers. The scenes often depict monks walking accompanied by tigers. Eight of them are murals and 12 paper and silk paintings, which were brought to light from the Library Cave. These works are now held in various collections including Guimet Museum in France, the National Library of France, the National Museum of Korea, and Hermitage Museum in Russia.

The Dunhuang silk painting, *The Traveling Monk with a Tiger*, is considered the most exquisite of its kind. The Tang-dynasty silk painting, created in the 9th Century, is currently housed in Guimet Museum in France. The monk in the painting is dressed in a robe with a crossed collar, revealing a white undergarment at the neckline. He holds a wooden staff in his left hand and a string of prayer beads in his right hand. Various items such as an awl, a knife, and an incense burner hang from his waist, and he wears sandals over bare feet. Strapped to his back is a large bamboo basket packed with scriptures and resembling a carrying frame. A golden incense pouch hangs from the front of the basket, while a stick at the back carries a fly-whisk, banners, and a purification bottle. Above the monk, a small Buddha, seated on a lotus throne and identified as Ratna-sambhava, hovers on the cloud. Following closely behind the monk is a calm, obedient tiger, and nearby, birds

的身后，有一只乖顺的老虎随行，路边的小鸟也驻足观看。

这幅绢画设色淡雅、精细入微，僧衣及竹笈上以金泥彩描。画家出色地塑造出一位求法之路上的僧人形象，他身负重物，却眼神坚定，一人一虎执着前行。历史上，有很多僧人曾往来于丝绸之路，他们对佛教的传播是东西方文化交流的重要内容，《行脚僧图》形象地记录了这些古代文化传播者的形象。

pause along the road to watch.

The painting is delicately colored, with an elegant, subtle palette. Fine gold paint highlights the monk's robe and bamboo basket. The artist masterfully portrays the monk's steadfast determination as he carries his heavy load on his quest for wisdom. Despite the burden, his gaze remains resolute, and together with the tiger, he continues his journey. Historically, many monks traveled the Silk Road, playing a key role in the spread of Buddhism and the exchanges between ancient Chinese civilization and various other cultures along the Silk Road. This painting vividly captures the image of these ancient cultural ambassadors.

# 四

# 敦煌石窟

敦煌石窟群包括 800 多个洞窟、5 万多平方米壁画和 2000 多身彩塑。古人将无限的智慧投入到石窟的营建当中，为我们保留了全世界规模最大、内容最丰富的佛教艺术长廊。那些远远望去状如蜂房的一处处石窟，在没有摄影摄像设备的时代，以绘画的方式形象记录着从公元 5 至 14 世纪 1000 多年间丝绸之路上的世事变迁。本章重点介绍敦煌石窟的标志性建筑、经典洞窟、壁画与彩塑，讲述那些反映丝路交流交往历史的壁画形象。一窟一世界，在这里，每一个洞窟、每一身彩塑、每一处壁画都是一个时代的投射、一段中华文明史和中外交流史的缩影。

# THE DUNHUANG CAVES

The Dunhuang Caves complex consists of 800-plus caves, 50,000-plus square meters of murals, and 2,000-plus painted sculptures. The ancient builders poured immense wisdom into the construction of these caves, leaving behind the world's largest, most comprehensive Buddhist art gallery. These caves, resembling beehives from a distance, serve as visual records of the changing events along the Silk Road from the 5th to the 14th centuries—long before the advent of photography or video. This chapter focuses on the iconic structures that compose the Dunhuang Caves, the evolution of the grottoes, and the murals and sculptures found within. It takes a close look at the mural images that reflect the history of cultural exchanges along the Silk Road. Each cave is a world unto itself in which every sculpture and mural is a reflection of its era, offering a snapshot of the history of Chinese civilization at one time through its exchanges with other cultures.

## 敦煌石窟群

敦煌石窟是对中国古代敦煌郡和晋昌郡就岩镌凿之佛教石窟的总称，位于今甘肃省敦煌市、瓜州县、肃北蒙古族自治县和玉门市境内，范围包括今敦煌莫高窟、西千佛洞，瓜州榆林窟、东千佛洞、水峡口下洞子石窟，肃北五个庙石窟、一个庙石窟和玉门昌马石窟。因其最大的石窟莫高窟位于古敦煌郡，各石窟的艺术风格又同属一脉，且古敦煌郡为两郡之政治、经济、文化中心，故以敦煌石窟作为统称。

## The Dunhuang Caves Complex

"The Dunhuang Caves" is the collective term for the Buddhist caves carved into the cliffs of ancient Dunhuang and Jinchang prefectures. These caves are located in present-day Dunhuang City, Guazhou County, Subei Mongolian Autonomous County, and Yumen City in Gansu Province. The complex includes several key sites: the famous Mogao Caves, the Western Thousand-Buddha Caves, the Yulin Caves in Guazhou, the Eastern Thousand-Buddha Caves, the Shuixiakou Lower Caves, the Five-Temple Caves and the One-Temple Cave in Subei, and the Changma Caves in Yumen. The Mogao Caves is the largest and most famous of these sites, located in ancient Dunhuang Prefecture, which served as the political, economic, and cultural center of the region. Despite their geographic spread, all the caves share a common artistic lineage, which is why they are collectively referred to as the Dunhuang Caves.

敦煌石窟中现存规模最大的是莫高窟，并因此成为敦煌石窟的代表而名闻天下。实际上，这里的每一座石窟都曾有过自己的辉煌，并保存着独具特色的艺术成就。其中，西千佛洞位于敦煌古城与阳关之间，根据文字记载，其开凿时间早于莫高窟；榆林窟所在地瓜州位于河西走廊的西端，与敦煌同为古代丝绸之路上的重镇，集中体现敦煌晚期艺术的精华；东千佛洞位于榆林窟以东，是一个以藏传密教内容为主的佛教石窟群，反映出 11 世纪以后中印佛教文化交流的情况；下洞子石窟、五个庙石窟、一个庙石窟和昌马石窟，这四处石窟洞窟虽数量不多，现存壁画均为五代之后的作品，但也是古代敦煌艺术地域范围的实物见证。如果说莫高窟是一部完整的中国中古艺术史，那敦煌石窟群中的其他石窟则各有各的绮丽，为这部艺术史锦上添花，散发出神秘迷人的光彩。

The largest in the Dunhuang Caves Complex is the Mogao Caves, which has gained worldwide recognition as a representative site of the Dunhuang Caves. In fact, each cave once enjoyed a specific reputation and preserves unique artistic achievements. Among them, the Western Thousand-Buddha Caves is located between the ancient cities of Dunhuang and Yangguan. Historical records show that these caves were carved before the Mogao Caves. The Yulin Caves, situated at the western end of the Hexi Corridor in Guazhou—an important hub along the ancient Silk Road, exemplifies the essence of late Dunhuang art. The Eastern Thousand-Buddha Caves, located east of the Yulin Caves, primarily features content related to Tibetan Tantric Buddhism, reflecting the influence of Indian Buddhism after the 11th Century. The Lower Caves, Five-Temple Caves, One-Temple Cave, and Changma Caves may be fewer in number in terms of caves, but their existing murals date from after the Five Dynasties (907-960) and serve as tangible evidence of the ancient artistic landscape of Dunhuang. If the Mogao Caves represents a comprehensive history of Chinese medieval art, each of the other caves in the Dunhuang Caves Complex contributes distinctly unique beauty, enriching the area's artistic history with an enchanting, mysterious allure.

## 敦煌莫高窟

敦煌莫高窟，俗称千佛洞，位于甘肃省敦煌市区东南 25 千米的鸣沙山东麓断崖上。莫高窟现存洞窟 735 个、壁画 4.5 万多平方米、彩塑 2000 余身，是由石窟建筑、壁画和彩塑三者结合的立体艺术。它是敦煌石窟群中规模最大、延续时间最长、保存最完好的一处石窟，被誉为“全世界最大的画廊”“东方卢浮宫”。整个窟区分南北两区，其中南区为礼佛区，有壁画和彩

## The Mogao Caves at Dunhuang

The Mogao Caves, commonly known as the Thousand-Buddha Caves, is located on the eastern slope of the Sounding Sand Hill, approximately 25 kilometers southeast of Dunhuang City. The complex consists of 735 existing caves, with over 45,000 square meters of murals and more than 2,000 painted sculptures, creating a multidimensional artistic space that combines cave architecture, murals, and sculptures. As the largest, longest-lasting, and best-preserved site within the Dunhuang Caves Complex, the Mogao Caves has been celebrated as "the largest art gallery in the world" and the "Louvre on the Orient". The entire cave system is divided into two main areas: The southern zone, where caves are adorned

塑的洞窟集中于此，北区多数洞窟都无壁画和彩塑，主要是僧人禅修、生活和瘗埋死者的所在。

据记载，莫高窟第一个洞窟由僧人乐僔于前秦建元二年（366）开凿。其后经北凉、北魏、西魏、北周、隋、唐、五代、北宋、沙州回鹘、西夏、元代共11个时代的相继营建形成今天的规模。莫高窟现存洞窟不仅在艺术上完整地保存了5—14世纪的中国中古美术史，而且作为丝绸之路的重要见证者，以图像方式形象地记录了东西方交流与古人的生活。它既是中华优秀传统文化的杰出作品，也是人类文明的智慧结晶。

with murals and sculptures concentrated, serves as a worship area, while the northern zone caves mostly lack wall paintings or sculptures, and are primarily used by monks for meditation, daily living, and burial of the deceased.

Historical records indicate that the first cave of the Mogao Caves was excavated by Monk Yue Zun in 366 during the Sixteen Kingdoms period. Subsequently, the caves were developed over a span of 11 different periods, including the Northern Liang, Northern Wei, Western Wei, Northern Zhou, Sui, Tang, Five Dynasties, Northern Song, Shazhou Uighur, Western Xia, and Yuan dynasties, shaping the complex into its present scale. The existing Mogao caves not only provide a complete artistic record of Chinese medieval art from the 5th to the 14th centuries but also serve as a significant witness to the Silk Road, vividly capturing the exchanges between China and various countries along the route, as well as aspects of ancient life. It survives not only as an outstanding legacy of China's rich traditional culture but also a testament to the wisdom of human civilization.

## 敦煌藏经洞

1900 年，一个名叫王圆箓的道士，意外发现了莫高窟第 16 窟甬道北壁隐藏的密室，即莫高窟第 17 窟——藏经洞。藏经洞内保存了 7 万余件古代文献，这些文献内容广泛，官私文书是其中最具史料价值的部分，还有大量古藏文、回鹘文、于阗文、粟特文、梵文等各种文字写成的文献材料，极大地丰富了少数民族生活和中外交流的历史记录。同时，藏经洞出土的绢画、麻布画、纸画、丝织品、刺绣等难以留存的艺术品，在敦煌这样干燥密闭的环境下非常完好地保存下来，有着无法估量的价值。

## The Library Cave

In 1900, a Daoist priest named Wang Yuanlu accidentally discovered a hidden chamber in the northern wall of the passageway in Cave 16 of the Mogao Caves, known as the Library Cave (Cave 17). This cave preserved over 70,000 pieces of ancient literature, encompassing a wide range of content, with government and private documents and letters being most historically significant. The cave contains a wealth of manuscripts in various languages, including ancient Tibetan, Uighur, Khotanese, Sogdian, and Sanskrit, greatly enriching the historical records of ethnic minority's life as well as Sino-foreign exchanges between the central Chinese regime and the Western Regions, and beyond. Additionally, the Library Cave preserved delicate art such as silk paintings, linen paintings, paper artworks, textiles, and embroidery—items that seldom survive. These artifacts were lucky enough to have been exceptionally well preserved in the dry, enclosed environment here, and they hold

藏经洞内的发现无论从时间、内容、数量、价值等各方面均堪称独一无二。但由于被发现时中国正值国力衰落，这批文献文物经多次流散，现在分藏于世界各地，并引发了一门世界性的显学——敦煌学。中国学者从 1909 年开始关注藏经洞的出土资料，在学术研究上奋起直追，使中国的敦煌学从“学术伤心史”转变成“学术自强史”。

immeasurable value.

The discoveries in the Library Cave are unparalleled in terms of time, content, quantity, and value. However, due to China's decline at the time of their discovery, these cultural relics and documents were scattered multiple times and are now stored in various parts of the world, leading to the emergence of a global academic discipline known as Dunhuang Studies. Chinese scholars began to focus on the excavated materials from the cave in 1909, making significant academic progress and transforming China's Dunhuang Studies from a "history of academic sorrow" into a narrative of academic self-improvement.

## 敦煌壁画

敦煌壁画是敦煌石窟艺术的主要组成部分之一。因敦煌石窟崖体不适合雕刻，所以古代先民在开凿洞窟之后，在窟顶和墙面抹泥涂白粉，令壁面平整再在上面作画。与石刻相比，绘画费工少，易于描绘细节，人物场景的一点一滴都可以精细入画，表现出的佛经内容及社会风情都比石刻更广泛、丰富和详尽。

敦煌壁画总面积5万多平方米，按绘制的题材，可以归纳为尊像画、佛传故事画、本生故事画、因缘故事画、汉族神话题材图画、佛教史迹画、经变画、供养人像（含出行图）、装饰图案画共九大类。其中，本生故事画是描绘释迦牟尼前生累世

## Dunhuang Murals

Dunhuang murals are one of the central components of Dunhuang cave art. Because the cliffs of the Dunhuang caves are not suitable for carving, the ancient people plastered the ceilings and walls with mud and chalk after excavating the caves, creating a smooth surface for painting. Compared to stone carvings, painting requires less labor, making it easier to depict details. Every little aspect of the figures and scenes can be rendered with precision, allowing for a broader, richer, and more detailed interpretation of Buddhist texts and social customs than stone carvings.

The total area of Dunhuang murals exceeds 50,000 square meters. Based on the themes depicted, they can be categorized into nine major types: portraits, stories of Buddha's life, Jātaka tales, stories of causes and conditions, Han Chinese mythological illustrations, paintings of Buddhist historical sites, sutra transformation paintings, donor portraits (including pilgrimage scenes), and decorative patterns. Among them, Jātaka tales depict the various good deeds of Siddhartha Gautama in his previous lives,

的各种善行，佛传故事画描绘释迦牟尼从出生到涅槃的一生事迹；经变画是敦煌最具代表性的绘画形式，通常专指将一部佛经的主要内容组织成有始有终、主次分明的大幅画。莫高窟现存经变画 33 种，内容丰富，形式多样，是珍贵的文化遗产。

敦煌壁画绘制的内容以佛教题材为主，兼有中国古代的神话题材和社会生活的场景，既是一部延续千年的美术史，同时又是中国古代社会、政治、经济、军事、文化、民族关系、中外交流等历史形象的资料宝库。

while the stories of Buddha's life portray his journey from birth to nirvana. Sutra transformation paintings are the most representative form of Dunhuang art, usually focusing on organizing the main content of Buddhist scriptures into large paintings with a clear beginning, end, and hierarchy. The 33 types of sutra transformation paintings currently within the Mogao Caves are rich in content and diverse in form, representing invaluable cultural heritage.

The themes of Dunhuang murals primarily revolve around Buddhism, but they also include ancient Chinese mythological themes and scenes of social life. They represent a continuous history of art spanning thousands of years and serve as a treasure trove of historical data reflecting ancient Chinese society, politics, economics, military affairs, culture, ethnic relations, and exchanges between Chinese and other cultures.

## 音乐窟

莫高窟第220窟位于莫高窟九层楼南，又名“翟家窟”，建于公元642年。甬道南壁龛外墨书翟氏“检家谱”，即翟氏一家较为简明扼要的家谱。敦煌翟氏家族不仅开凿了这一洞窟，其后300年间还对此窟进行了维护。本窟是莫高窟初唐洞窟的代表，壁画线描、色彩、晕染均属中原一脉，其场面恢宏、色彩瑰丽、人物形象真实，反映出大唐开国的博大胸怀和繁华富丽的景象。

此窟南北壁绘通壁大幅经变画。在北壁和南壁的东、西方净土变中，中央绘佛和菩萨等主要人物，下方平台上是乐舞场面，舞伎们正在表演西域传来的舞蹈，乐伎们在两旁伴奏，整个画面洋溢着佛国的欢乐气氛。壁画反映了当时宫廷舞乐盛况，共绘乐器50多件，其中埙的图像，莫高窟仅此一例，花边阮仅见两例，故此窟又被称为“音乐窟”。

## The Music Cave

Cave 220 of the Mogao Caves, located south of the Nine-Story Building, is also known as the "Zhai Family Cave" and was built in 642. The ink inscription on the southern wall of the corridor describes Zhai's genealogy with a concise record of the family lineage. The Dunhuang Zhai family not only excavated the cave but also maintained it for the following 300 years. This cave is a representative example of early Tang-dynasty caves in the Mogao Caves, characterized by its line drawings, colors, and shading that reflect the artistic traditions of the Central Plains. The grand scenes, vibrant colors, and realistic depictions of figures reflect the broad vision and opulent splendor of the founding of the early Tang Dynasty.

This cave features full-wall sutra transformation paintings on its northern and southern walls. The central compositions portray the Buddha and Bodhisattvas as the primary figures within the Eastern and Western Pure Land transformations depicted on these walls, while the lower platform displays scenes of music and dance. Dancers perform in Western Regions styles, presumably, accompanied by musicians on either side. The entire scene radiates a joyful atmosphere of the Buddhist realm. The murals reflect the grandeur of court music and dance during that time, depicting over 50 musical instruments. Notably, the depiction of the *xun* (a type of ancient Chinese vessel flute) is unique to this cave, and the image of the flower-bordered *ruan* (a plucked string instrument) appears only twice in the whole Mogao Caves, hence the name "Music Cave".

## 室内第一大佛

莫高窟最大一尊佛像营造于初唐，即第96窟的弥勒大佛，俗称北大像。这尊大佛为石胎泥塑，即先在崖面上凿出佛像石胎，后以草泥垒塑，再用麻泥细塑，然后敷色彩绘。佛像高35.5米，依壁倚坐，两腿自然下垂，慈目下视，右手上扬，左手平伸。因其塑于窟内，且高度居全世界之首，故被称为“室内第一大佛”。

武则天称帝前曾制造社会舆论，授意薛怀义、法明等人编造《大云经疏》，暗示她是弥勒降世。第96窟及弥勒大佛最早由禅师灵隐及居士阴祖等造于公元695年，正是武则天称帝后的五年，说明敦煌人当时也顺应形势，迎合武氏称帝思想。此窟后经多次重修，大佛现存外表只有两只胖乎乎的大脚是初唐原作，未经改动，由此也可看出唐代以丰肥为美的特点。1928年敦煌当地人刘骥德、易昌恕等重修时，彩绘中衣及土红袈裟，并在袈裟垂裾边沿绘清式云龙纹，1987年由敦煌研究院主持重塑了大佛的双手。

## Largest Indoor Buddha

The largest Buddhist statue in the Mogao Caves, known as the Maitreya Buddha in Cave 96, was created in the early Tang Dynasty and is commonly referred to as the "Northern Great Buddha". The statue was first carved out of the rock face, then shaped with a mixture of clay and straw, followed by detailed modeling with fine clay, and finally painted with colors. It stands 35.5 meters tall, seated against the wall with its legs naturally hanging down, eyes looking downward with compassion, right hand raised, and left hand extended horizontally. It has been dubbed the "Largest Indoor Buddha" because it is sculpted inside the cave and is the tallest of its kind in the world.

Before declaring herself emperor, Wu Zetian sought to influence public opinion by ordering monks including Xue Huaiyi and Fa Ming to compile the *Commentary to the Mahāmegha Sūtra* in a way that implied that she was Maitreya Buddha's incarnation. The Maitreya Buddha statue in Cave 96 was originally created in 695 by Chan master Ling Yin and lay Buddhist Yin Zu five years after Wu Zetian's ascension to the throne. The people of Dunhuang were apparently aligning with the prevailing circumstances and supporting Wu's imperial aspirations. This cave has undergone multiple renovations, and the only remaining original features of the large statue from the early Tang time are its two plump feet, which have not been altered, reflecting Tang-dynasty's aesthetic preference for fullness. In 1928, Liu Jide, Yi Changshu, and other local residents restored the statue, adding painted clothing and a reddish-brown kasaya with Qing-style cloud and dragon patterns on the hem. In 1987, the Dunhuang Research Academy oversaw the reconstruction of the Buddha's hands.

## 九层楼

九层楼，即莫高窟第96窟的木构窟檐，是现在莫高窟的标志性建筑。其主体为木结构建筑，依崖而建，俯临窟体，视野开阔，与岩体巧妙地融为一体，是防止风沙雨雪侵蚀洞窟的主要保护措施。

莫高窟第96窟始建于初唐时期，初为四层，其后几经重修，多次增建，直至1935年建成如今九层楼建筑。九层楼攒尖高耸，檐牙错落，铁马叮咚，其历经千年，已成为莫高窟、敦煌乃至甘肃的重要标志性建筑。

## Nine-Story Building

The Nine-Story Building, located at Cave 96 of the Mogao Caves, is a wooden structure with the iconic architectural feature of the Mogao Caves. This main building is constructed of wood and built against the cliff, overlooking the caves and providing a broad view, cleverly blending into the rock formation. It serves as a primary protective measure against wind, sand, rain, and snow that could erode the caves.

Cave 96 of the Mogao Caves was first established during the early Tang Dynasty, initially comprising four stories. It underwent several renovations and expansions over the years, eventually culminating in the completion of the current nine-story structure in 1935. The Nine-Story Building rises sharply with staggered eaves, creating a distinctive silhouette. Withstanding the test of time and numerous renovations, it has become a significant landmark for the Mogao Caves, Dunhuang, and Gansu Province.

## 唐代彩塑群像

莫高窟彩塑全面系统地反映了中国彩塑艺术的发展演变过程，是一部真实系统的彩塑史，第 45 窟更是莫高窟彩塑艺术的代表之作。莫高窟第 45 窟现存一佛二弟子二菩萨二天王共七尊像，是敦煌石窟中保存最完整、人物形象最生动写实的一组彩塑像。

主佛结跏趺坐在束腰式金刚座上，他面相丰满圆润，双目修长，口端鼻正，内着僧祇支，外穿通肩式袈裟，衣纹流畅自如，色彩浑厚深沉。身后的头光和身光，及一道道凸起的泥条

## Tang-Dynasty Painted Statues Group

The painted statues in the Mogao Caves comprehensively reflect the development and evolution of Chinese painted sculpture art, composing a genuine, systematic history of the form. Cave 45 is particularly noted as a representative work of the painted sculpture art in the Mogao Caves. Currently, Cave 45 houses a group of seven statues: one Buddha, two disciples, two Bodhisattvas, and two Heavenly Kings. This group is the most complete, vividly realistic collection of the painted sculptures preserved in the Dunhuang Caves.

The main Buddha is seated in a lotus position on a waist-bound Diamond Throne. With a full and round face, elongated eyes, straight nose, and a well-defined mouth, the Buddha wears a monastic robe underneath and an outer shoulder drape with flowing garment patterns and rich, deep colors. The halo behind his head and body set against raised clay strips adorned with golden decorations creates a striking interplay that enhances the three-dimensionality and opulence of the figures. On either side stand Kasyapa and Ananda, one old, one young; the former is composed and dignified, while the latter youthful and carefree, creating a sharp contrast between aged wit and innocence.

金饰，绘塑互映，更显得层次分明，富丽堂皇。分立在两旁的迦叶和阿难，一老一少，一个老成持重，一个年轻洒脱，一个睿智达练，一个童心外溢，形成鲜明的对比。

两身菩萨，面带微笑，温婉慈祥，袒露上身，肌肤洁白如玉，斜披的飘带以及华美的长裙，与婀娜多姿一波三折的S形躯体，巧妙结合在一起，既超凡脱俗，又雍容华贵。南北两侧的天王，上穿金甲，下着战裙，瞪目张口，一手掐腰，一手挥拳，威武凶猛，与温柔的菩萨和虔诚的弟子，一武一文，形成强烈的对比。整铺造像显得有动有静，动静结合，内心世界明显，性格各异，实为中国彩塑艺术的精华。

The two Bodhisattvas wear gentle smiles, exuding warmth and kindness. Their upper bodies are bare, with skin as white as pure nephrite. The draped ribbons and luxurious long skirts elegantly complement their graceful, curvaceous S-shaped figures, creating a harmonious blend of the ethereal and the opulent. The Heavenly Kings on the northern and southern sides are clad in golden armor and war skirts, with fierce expressions and wide-open mouths. One hand rests on their hips while the other is raised in a threatening fist, presenting a fearful, imposing demeanor. This creates a stark contrast with the graceful Bodhisattvas and devoted disciples, showcasing both gentleness and powerfulness. The overall composition of the sculptures conveys a dynamic interplay between movement and stillness, clearly reflecting the distinct inner worlds and diverse personalities of each figure. This truly represents the essence of Chinese painted sculpture art.

## 飞天

飞天，是敦煌壁画中的经典艺术形象。在佛教中，飞天一般指八部护法中的乾闼婆和紧那罗，被视为佛国世界的香音、歌舞之神。飞天，早在印度阿旃陀等石窟中已出现，传入中国后，成为一种极富民族特色的艺术形象，遍布所有石窟。仅敦煌莫高窟内，现共保存从十六国时期到元代历代所绘飞天 6000 余身，呈现出各个时期的不同风格和特点。

## Apsaras

Apsara (flying celestial nymph) is a classic artistic figure found in the murals of Dunhuang. In Buddhism, it generally refers to Gandharva and Kiṁnara, who are regarded as the deities of music and dance in the Buddhist paradise. The image of apsaras appeared as early as the rock caves of Ajanta in India, and after being introduced to China, it evolved into an art form rich in national characteristics, becoming prevalent across all rock caves. In the Mogao Caves of Dunhuang alone, over 6,000 apsaras have been preserved, spanning the period from the Sixteen Kingdoms to the Yuan Dynasty (1271-1368), showcasing the various styles and characteristics of different historical periods.

敦煌石窟飞天表现形式多样，姿态各异。以初唐莫高窟第321窟中的“双飞天”最为著名，故又称此窟为“飞天洞”。这些飞天或绘于经变画中，或绘于龛楣中。他们两个一组，一前一后或一左一右，结伴飘行。向下的飞天迎风而降，裙带飞舞；向上的飞天姿态优雅，缓缓而上。他们前后呼应，构成统一和谐的整体，具有很强的艺术感染力。此外，西千佛洞第9窟主室西壁南端还存有以白描手法绘制的飞天多身，其造型简练，线条流畅，比例协调，轻盈飘逸，分别手持长笛、芦笙、琵琶、箜篌等乐器，是西千佛洞壁画的代表作品。

飞天已成为深入人心的经典形象，1983年中国国家广播电视总局举办第三届全国优秀电视剧评奖活动时，将该奖正式命名为“中国电视剧飞天奖”。“飞天奖”是中国电视剧唯一的政府奖，也是中国国内创办时间最早、历史最悠久的电视剧奖项。

The apsaras in the Dunhuang Caves display a diverse range of forms and postures, among which the Double Apsaras in Cave 321 of the Mogao Caves is the most famous. This cave is also known as the Apsara Cave. These apsaras can be found painted within the transformation murals or within the niches. They appear in pairs, either one in front and the other behind or one to the left and the other to the right, gracefully floating together. The descending apsara was depicted as going down against the wind, her skirt flowing, while the ascending one has an elegant posture, rising slowly. Their mutual correspondence creates a unified, harmonious whole, exuding a strong artistic appeal. Still, more apsaras were drawn with a fine line style at the southern end of the western wall of the main hall in Cave 9 of the Western Thousand-Buddha Caves. These figures are characterized by their simple yet fluid shapes and well proportioned but light, ethereal quality, each holding musical instruments such as the flute, *lusheng* (a type of reed instrument), *pipa*, or *konghou* (a type of harp). This work is representative of the murals in the Western Thousand-Buddha Caves.

The apsara has become a deeply ingrained classic image in Chinese culture. In 1983, during the 3rd National Excellent TV Drama Awards organized by the National Radio and Television Administration of China, the award was officially named the "Feitian (Apsara) Award for Chinese TV Dramas". It is the only official award for Chinese TV dramas as well as the earliest, longest-running TV drama award in China.

## 九色鹿

九色鹿见于莫高窟第257窟西壁壁画《鹿王本生》，全图生动描绘了古印度恒河边九色鹿王搭救溺水人，溺水人见利忘义最终恶有恶报的故事。画面整体布局紧凑、主旨突出，并以富有动感的山峦分割情节，绘制了8组场景。

画面采用横卷连环画的表现形式，按两头开始、中间结束的特殊顺序绘制。左一为九色鹿救起溺水之人，画中一人骑在鹿背上，紧抱鹿颈，鹿王从水中将其驮出。左二落水人跪在九色鹿面前，向鹿王许诺保守秘密。右一为王后向国王撒娇要九色鹿皮做坐褥、用鹿角做拂柄，图中国王与王后坐在宫殿之中，王后以右臂揽国王肩膀，扭头朝向国王，一只脚丫翘起外露，撒娇之态跃然画上。门外，溺水之人正背信弃义向国王告密。

## Nine-Colored Deer

The Nine-Colored Deer appears in the mural Deer King Jātaka on the western wall of Cave 257 in the Mogao Caves. The mural vividly depicts the story of the Nine-Colored Deer King who saves a drowning man by the banks of the Ganges River in ancient India. The man, however, being ungrateful and treacherous, ultimately faces dire consequences for his selfishness. The overall layout of the mural is compact, with a clear theme, and the dynamic mountains divide the narrative, illustrating eight distinct scenes.

The mural employs a horizontal scroll format, depicting the narrative in a unique order that begins at both ends and concludes in the middle. On the far left, the Nine-Colored Deer rescues a drowning man, who is shown riding on the deer's back, tightly clutching its neck, as the Deer King carries him out of the water. To the right, the drowning man kneels before the Nine-Colored Deer, promising to keep the secret. On the far right, the queen coyly begged the king for the Nine-Colored Deer's hide to make a saddle blanket and its antlers for a fly-whisk handle. The scene illustrates the king and queen sitting in a palace, with the queen hugging the king's shoulder with her right arm, turning her head toward him while one of her feet is playfully raised, vividly portraying her flirtatious demeanor. Outside the door, the drowning man, having betrayed the deer, is maliciously informing the king. On the second

右二为一人驾马车，是国王和王后在溺水人的带领下同乘一辆马车前往围猎九色鹿。画面中部是国王等人惊醒了沉睡中的九色鹿，九色鹿毫不畏惧，向国王痛诉溺水者的忘恩负义。在国王及侍从之后，是手指九色鹿居处的溺水人，这个告密者满身白点，代表恶有恶报，全身生疮。

这组壁画在 1981 年由上海美术电影制片厂制作成动画片，成为中国本土动画片的经典之作。

right, a man is driving a carriage, taking the king and queen to hunt the Nine-Colored Deer, led by the perfidious drowning man. In the center of the mural, the king and others awaken the sleeping Nine-Colored Deer, who, unafraid, passionately recounts the ungratefulness of the drowning man to the king. Behind the king and his attendants is the drowning man, pointing to where the Nine-Colored Deer resides. This informant is covered in white spots, symbolizing the notion of karma, as he is afflicted with sores all over his body as a consequence of his betrayal.

This set of murals was adapted into an animated film by the Shanghai Animation Film Studio in 1981, becoming a classic in China's domestic animation.

## 反弹琵琶

反弹琵琶，是敦煌石窟乐舞壁画的代表形象。佛教壁画中为了表现净土世界的美好、讲经说法的精彩，往往在经变画最前方的平台上绘制乐舞表演的场景。唐代之后，这类画面中居

## *Playing the* Pipa *from the Back*

*Playing the* Pipa *from the Back* is a representative image of the music and dance murals in the Dunhuang Caves. In Buddhist murals, scenes of music and dance performances are often painted on the platforms at the forefront of the sutra transformation

正中的舞者经常为反弹琵琶，其中又以莫高窟第112窟的这一形象最为经典。

画中舞者两侧各有三人组成的乐队，分别演奏琵琶、阮咸、箜篌、鼗鼓、横笛、拍板，伎乐天伴随着仙乐翩翩起舞，举足旋身，使出“反弹琵琶”的绝技。画师妙笔传神，人物造型丰腴饱满，线条流畅，一气呵成，将伎乐天神态悠闲雍容、落落大方之态跃然壁上。其丝帛绕身，璎珞庄严，天衣裙裾如游龙惊凤，摇曳生姿，上身微曲，双手将琵琶置于项背，屈身向右，吸右腿，边弹边舞。画师将伎乐天刹那间动势定格在壁画中，同时也描绘出净土世界的庄严、极乐、热烈与辉煌。反弹琵琶这种极具难度的乐舞表演，在中国人对敦煌舞的不断探索中，已于今天的舞台上得以再现。

paintings to depict the beauty of the Pure Land and the brilliance of sermons. After the Tang Dynasty, the dancer in the center of such scenes is often depicted as "playing the *pipa* from the back", with the image from Cave 112 of the Mogao Caves being the most classic.

The painting depicts an ensemble of three musicians on each side of the dancer playing instruments such as the *pipa*, *ruan*, *konghou*, *tao* drum, flute, and clapper. The musicians accompany the celestial dancer, who gracefully performs the technique of playing the *pipa* from the back, moving with elegance and poise. The artist's skillful brushwork captures the figures in a full, rich manner, smooth in lines that flow seamlessly, vividly portraying the dancer's leisurely and dignified demeanor. Draped in silk and adorned with elaborate jewelry, the dancer's garments flow like swimming dragons and soaring phoenixes, swaying gracefully. With a slight bend, she holds the *pipa* against her neck and back, leaning to the right while drawing in her right leg, playing and dancing simultaneously. The artist freezes this moment of dynamic movement in the mural while depicting the solemnity, bliss, warmth, and brilliance of the Pure Land. This challenging dance posture of playing the *pipa* from the back, through the ongoing exploration of Dunhuang dance by the Chinese, has been brought back to life on today's stage.

## 胡旋舞

莫高窟第220窟南壁绘出一个巨大的露天舞场，两侧方形大地毯上坐着两组乐队，共16人，手持琵琶、古琴、箜篌、横笛、排箫、长鼓、铜钹等乐器。这些乐工头梳高髻，戴宝冠，上身半裸，斜披罗巾，项饰璎珞，佩戴手镯、臂钏等饰物。中央两块圆形小花毯上有一对舞伎，身穿长裙，手舞彩带，脚踩花毯，旋转相顾，翩翩起舞。这对舞伎表演的以快速旋转为特点的舞蹈，符合史籍对“胡旋舞”的记载，表现的应该就是由

## Sogdian Whirl Dance

The southern wall of Cave 220 in the Mogao Caves depicts a vast outdoor dance floor with two groups of musicians seated on large square carpets on either side, totaling 16 people. They hold various instruments such as the *pipa*, *guqin*, *konghou*, transverse flute, panpipe, long drum, and cymbals. These musicians sport high topknots and wear jeweled crowns, with their upper bodies partially bare, draped in thin silk shawls, and adorned with necklaces, bracelets and armlets. In the center, two small circular flower carpets feature a pair of dancers dressed in long skirts, waving colorful ribbons as they dance gracefully, their feet on the carpets, spinning and gazing at each other. The dance performed by this pair, characterized by rapid spins, aligns with historical records of the Sogdian Whirl Dance, which is believed to have originated from the Western Regions. This grand musical and dance scene occupies a third of the lower part of the entire wall, beautifully rendered and well preserved, making it one of the most representative images for understanding and studying the Sogdian Whirl Dance.

西域传来的胡旋舞。这组宏大的乐舞场景占据了整个壁面下部的三分之一，绘制精美，保存较佳，是我们了解和研究胡旋舞最具代表性的图像。

唐代是中原和西域乐舞艺术大交流、大融合的兴盛时期。唐代歌舞一方面继承和发展了民族舞乐的传统，另一方面也大量吸收了西北各族和中亚各国舞乐的特长，创造了新的民族舞乐。在宫廷和民间广泛流传从西域传来的胡腾舞、胡旋舞、柘枝舞等，节奏欢快，一经传入，就深受人们喜爱，得到广泛传播，风行一时。

The Tang Dynasty was a flourishing period of extensive exchanges and integration of musical and dance arts between the Central Plains and the Western Regions. Tang-dynasty dance and music inherited and developed the traditions of many different ethnic dance and music forms, absorbing the flavors of various ethnic groups in the northwest and countries in Central Asia, creating new forms of national dance and music. The dances of Hu Teng, Sogdian Whirl Dance, and Zhe Zhi, which originated in the Western Regions, became widely popular both in the royal court and among the common people. With their lively rhythms, these dances quickly gained favor and spread widely, becoming fashionable at the time.

## 美人菩萨

莫高窟初唐第57窟洞窟规模虽小，但整窟壁画绘制极其精湛，南壁所绘观音菩萨更是众多的唐代菩萨画像中的上乘佳作。观音菩萨是西方净土的主要人物，以“闻声救度”而获得信众的欢迎。此尊菩萨体态婀娜，容颜秀丽，长目细眉，唇红鼻直，无髭须，头微侧，目俯视，身躯略作S形，尽显文静典雅的女子柔美之姿。菩萨额上、鬓边、眼睑、两颊、下颏均以淡朱晕染，突显肌肤光洁细腻之感。衣饰各种花纹均勾白线，显出丝绸织物之绮丽。

人物冠饰、璎珞、臂钏皆以沥粉堆金制成，尽显华贵之感。沥粉堆

## *Beauty Bodhisattva*

Cave 57 of the Mogao Caves, dating from the early Tang Dynasty, is relatively small in scale, but the murals within are exquisitely crafted. The depiction of Avalokiteshvara (Guanyin) on the southern wall stands out as a premier example among the many Bodhisattva images from the Tang Dynasty. Guanyin is a central figure in the Western Pure Land, revered for her ability to "hear the cries of the world and offer salvation", which has won her the devotion of many believers. This Bodhisattva is portrayed in a graceful figure and a beautiful face, featuring elongated eyes and slender brows, red lips, a straight nose, and no facial hair. Her head is slightly tilted, with her gaze directed downwards, and her body is subtly curved in a gentle "S bend", showcasing the quiet elegance and feminine beauty of a refined woman. Her forehead, hairline, eyelids, cheeks, and chin are adorned with a light rosy hue, highlighting the smooth, delicate quality of her skin. The clothing is detailed with various patterns outlined in white, enhancing the splendor of the silk fabric.

The adornments on the figure including the crown, jewelry, and armlets are made with the technique of "sprinkling powder to pile up gold", showcasing a sense of opulence. "Sprinkling powder

金是传统彩画工艺之一，即用尖端有孔的管子，其后装有胶和土粉混合成的膏状物，按彩画图案先挤出隆起的花纹，上面再贴以金箔。这一工艺的特殊之处在于纹样高出物面，并在它的上面贴金、银箔及上色等，呈现出图案的立体感。这种古老的民间制作工艺，早在盛唐时期已被广泛采用。从这尊菩萨像上，可窥知唐人生活的富足和初唐艺术的富丽。敦煌壁画虽然绘有大量的菩萨形象，但被誉为“美人菩萨”的只此一尊，莫高窟第 57 窟也因其得名为“美人窟”。

to pile up gold" is one of the traditional painting techniques, which employs a piping bag fitted with a narrow nozzle to apply an adhesive-clay composite paste, forming embossed motifs based on the underlying painted design. Gold leaf is subsequently gilded onto the raised surfaces. The uniqueness of this technique lies in its raised motif, which allows for the application of gold and silver leaf, or color, presenting a three-dimensional quality to the patterns. This ancient folk crafting method was widely adopted as early as the High Tang period. From this Bodhisattva image, one can glimpse the affluence of Tang lifestyles and the richness of early Tang art. Although Dunhuang murals depict a vast number of Bodhisattva images, only this one is renowned as the *Beauty Bodhisattva*, leading Cave 57 to be nicknamed the "Cave of Beauty".

## 睒子本生

“睒子本生”是在印度和中国都深受欢迎的故事题材，在印度、犍陀罗地区及中国石窟、造像碑中均有出现，通常以壁画或浮雕的形式表现。故事来源于《佛说睒子经》，古印度迦夷国中有人名睒子，随盲父母居于山中，采果汲溪水供养父母。一日，国王射猎时进山误伤身披鹿皮的睒子，睒子将其一家修行之事告知国王。国王深悔，到睒子家通知其父母，父母来到河边，见睒子尸，抚尸恸哭。睒子孝感动天，天神使其复活，并使其父母复明。

## Śyāmaka Jātaka

The Śyāmaka Jātaka tale is a popular narrative theme in both India and China, appearing in various forms in Indian and Gandhara art, as well as in Chinese caves and stele, typically represented in murals or reliefs. The story originates from *Śyāmaka Jātaka*, which tells of a boy named Śyāmaka who lives in the mountains with his blind parents, gathering fruits and fetching water to support them. One day, while hunting, the king mistakenly shoots Śyāmaka, who is dressed in a deer skin. The dying Śyāmaka informs the king about his family's ascetic practices. The king, filled with remorse, goes to Śyāmaka's home to notify his parents. Upon arriving at the riverbank, they receive their boy's body and weep in sorrow. Moved by Śyāmaka's filial piety, the heavenly deities revive him and restore his parents' sight.

敦煌石窟从北周至隋代绘有多幅睒子本生故事画，莫高窟第 299 窟为这一题材的代表作品。全图共包括 6 个情节。整幅画面的叙事从两头开始，画面中心既是故事的高潮也是故事的结尾。

中国传统二十四孝故事中的“鹿乳奉亲”，讲的是郯子为父母入山取鹿奶差点被误杀的经历，主人公的原型是中国春秋时期郯国的国君郯子和佛经记载的睒子相结合而成。孝顺父母是中国人的传统美德，睒子故事的流行，充分体现了外来佛教为适应中国本土文化特点，从原来倡导出世离家到更注重孝道的转变。

The Dunhuang Caves feature numerous paintings of the Śyāmaka Jātaka tale from the Northern Zhou to the Sui dynasties, with Cave 299 being a representative work of this theme. The painting comprises six scenes in total, with the narrative starting from both ends and culminating at the center, which serves as both the climax and conclusion of the story.

Another traditional Chinese tale of filial piety, *Offering Deer Milk to Parents*, tells the story of Tanzi's experience of nearly being killed in the mountains while fetching deer milk for his parents. It combines the protagonist's archetype of the king of the state of Tan from the Spring and Autumn Period (770-476 BC) with the figure of Śyāmaka as recorded in Buddhist scriptures. As a traditional virtue, filial piety is a recurring theme in China, and the popularity of the Śyāmaka tale reflects how Buddhism, as a foreign religion, adapted to Chinese cultural values.

## 《张骞出使西域图》

公元前 138 年和前 119 年，汉武帝两次派张骞出使西域，使中原与西域第一次有了直接交往。历史上把张骞通西域的壮举称为“凿空”，从此仿佛打开了一扇中国通向西方世界的大门，东西方世界被这条后来称为“丝绸之路”的交通线连接起来。莫高窟初唐第 323 窟北壁绘制了著名的《张骞出使西域图》，以唐代佛教徒的视角将这一重大历史事件以图像方式记录下来。

## *Zhang Qian's Diplomatic Missions to the Western Regions*

In 138 BC and 119 BC, Emperor Wudi of the Han Dynasty sent Zhang Qian (164-114 BC), a prominent diplomat and explorer, on two missions to the Western Regions, marking the first direct exchange between the Central Plains and the Western Regions. Historically, Zhang Qian's accomplishments connecting with the Western Regions have been referred to as "cutting through the solid", as if opening a door for China to go west. This connection ultimately established the transportation route later known as the "Silk Road", linking East and West. The northern wall of Cave 323 of the Mogao Caves from the early Tang Dynasty features the famous mural *Zhang Qian's Diplomatic Missions to the Western Regions*, capturing this significant historic event from the perspective of Tang Buddhist practitioners.

此幅作品整体呈“U”字形叙事结构，融于青绿山水环境中，以山峦来引导、分割故事情节，在敦煌壁画中首次采用透视原理中的近大远小手法绘制而成。整个故事由三个画面组成：一是左上角汉武帝得到匈奴祭天金人，并将两尊金人安置在甘泉宫，武帝常亲自前来礼拜。二是底部汉中宗不知金人名号，于是派博望侯张骞出使西域问其神名。画中是张骞辞别汉中宗，骑在高头大马上的是汉中宗，在马前跪拜的是张骞。三是右上角张骞所遣副使经过万水千山最终抵达大夏国，问得金人原来就是佛像。

历史上，派张骞出使西域的是汉武帝而非汉中宗，两次出使的目的分别是联合大月氏、乌孙夹击匈奴和通好西域，打通丝绸之路并保证其畅通。这里，唐代佛教徒对“张骞出使西域”进行了改编，使其成为一个讲述佛教如何传入中国的故事，也赋予了张骞出使西域在文化交流上的新意义。

The overall composition of this work is a U-shaped narrative structure integrated into a landscape of green mountains and blue water. The mountains guide and divide the storyline, employing the technique of perspective—where objects appear larger in the foreground and smaller in the background—used for the first time in Dunhuang murals. The entire story is composed of three scenes:

1. In the upper left corner, Emperor Wudi receives some golden statues for worship from the Huns and places two such statues in Ganquan (Sweet Spring) Palace, where he often comes to pay his respects personally.

2. At the bottom, curious about the name of the golden statues, Emperor Zhongzong of the Han sends Zhang Qian to the Western Regions to inquire about their divine names. The painting depicts Zhang bidding farewell to the emperor, who is mounted on a tall horse, while Zhang kneels in front of him.

3. In the upper right corner, Zhang Qian's deputy, having traversed many rivers and mountains, finally arrives in Daxia and learns that the golden statue is, in fact, a Buddhist statue.

Historically, it was Emperor Wudi of Han who sent Zhang Qian on a mission to the Western Regions, not Emperor Zhongzong. The purposes of these two missions were to unite the Yuezhi and Wusun in attacking the Huns, establish friendly relations with the Western Regions, and keep the route operating. In this context, Tang Buddhist practitioners adapted the story of *Zhang Qian's Diplomatic Missions to the Western Regions*, transforming it into a narrative about how Buddhism was introduced to China, thereby imbuing Zhang's missions with new significance in terms of cultural exchanges.

## 丝路各民族群像

贞观初年，因周边地区前来向唐朝朝贡，唐太宗命画家阎立本绘制了各国使者的形象，并以文字叙述所绘人物的国家，这个图文并茂的图卷就是《职贡图》。同样，敦煌壁画从初唐贞观十六年（642）营建的莫高窟第220窟开始，《维摩诘经变》中前来听法的人物就有身穿不同服饰的各国国王、王子和使者的形象，呈现出丝路各民族的群像。

## Portrait of Ethnic Groups Along the Silk Road

In the early years of the reign of Emperor Taizong of the Tang Dynasty, many tribute missions arrived from regions surrounding the Tang, so the emperor ordered painter Yan Liben to depict the images of envoys along with texts describing the countries represented by these figures. This illustrated scroll is known as *The Envoy with Tribute Bearers*. Similarly, the Dunhuang murals, starting from Cave 220, which was built in 642, feature characters attending sermons in the *Vimalakīrti Nirdeśa Sūtra Illustration*. These characters include kings, princes, and envoys from various countries dressed in different attire, showcasing the diverse ethnic groups along the Silk Road.

第 220 窟的《维摩诘经变》的这一画面，原本是表现维摩诘居士居家称病，各国国王、王子、大臣、长者前往问疾的场景。画中维摩诘居士帐下，前来听法的各国国王、王子和使者，面貌各异，肤色和服饰尽显民族特色。站在队伍最前方的皮肤黝黑者来自南海诸国，其身后穿锦边袍服者来自西域、戴鸟羽冠者来自朝鲜半岛。画面中的人物，实为唐代以前敦煌壁画所未见的各族人物群像，应是敦煌画师根据长安传来的粉本加工而成，是初唐时期往来于丝绸之路上的各族人物的真实写照。既反映出唐朝与周边政权之间的交往，也展现出广义丝绸之路上的各民族往来。

In this scene from the *Vimalakīrti Nirdeśa Sūtra Illustration* of Cave 220, the original depiction showcases a situation with Vimalakīrti, a revered lay Buddhist, feigning illness at home, with the true intention of taking the opportunity to give preaching while kings, princes, ministers and elders from various countries visit to inquire about his health. In the painting, under Vimalakīrti's canopy, the kings, princes, and envoys attending the sermon exhibit diverse appearances, with varying skin tones and attire reflecting their ethnic characteristics. The person at the front of the line, with dark skin, hails from the South Sea, while those behind him in brocade robes come from the Western Regions, and those wearing feathered crowns are from the Korean Peninsula. The figures depicted in this work represent a diverse array of ethnic groups previously unseen in Dunhuang murals prior to the Tang Dynasty. Experts observe that Dunhuang artists crafted the figures based on the models brought from Chang'an to create an authentic portrayal of the various ethnic groups traveling along the Silk Road during the early Tang period, not only reflecting interactions between the Tang Dynasty and its surrounding cultures but also showcasing the exchanges among the various peoples along the broader Silk Road.

## 胡商

中国古代将域外和西北少数民族商人称为“胡商”，来往于丝路进行贸易的胡商以中亚的粟特人居多。唐代敦煌县从化乡就是居住在敦煌的粟特人建立起来的，沙州城东还有袄神庙。在唐、五代、宋初的敦煌商业经济活动中，粟特人非常活跃，他们经营酒店、贩卖胡粉，往往获利颇丰。

莫高窟北周第296窟《福田经变》中，在描绘利益众生的公益事业之一的“安设桥梁”时，绘制了胡汉商队过桥相遇的画面。画中桥梁平坦，两侧有栏杆，桥上有两头毛驴驮货前行，后面跟随正要上桥的骑马的汉人商队。桥的另一侧，一胡商牵着骆驼等待过桥，后有一商人赶着两头毛驴。这幅画面，应是当时丝绸之路上商队的真实写照。

## Hu Merchants

In ancient China, foreign merchants and Northwest ethnic minority traders were referred to as "Hu merchants". Among those who traded along the Silk Road, the Sogdian people from Central Asia made up a significant group. In the Tang Dynasty, the village of Conghua in Dunhuang County was established by these Sogdian people, and to the east of Shazhou City, a temple was dedicated to a Zoroastrian deity. From the Tang and Five Dynasties through the early Song Dynasty, or approximately from the 7th to the 10th centuries, the Sogdians were highly active in Dunhuang, running hotels and selling goods such as "Hu powder" (primarily lead carbonate, used in cosmetics or as a pigment), often reaping substantial profits.

A mural found in Cave 296 of the Northern Zhou period at the Mogao Caves themed at bridges there is a scene depicting a meeting between Hu and Han merchant caravans on a bridge, an illustration of a Buddhist text about public welfare projects such as building bridges, aimed at benefiting sentient beings. The bridge in the painting is flat and features railings on both sides. Two donkeys loaded with goods are crossing the bridge, followed by a Han merchant caravan on horseback, preparing to ascend. On the other side of the bridge, a Hu merchant is leading a camel, while another merchant drives two donkeys behind him. This scene is likely a true representation of the merchant caravans that traveled along the Silk Road at that time.

莫高窟盛唐第45窟《观音经变》中还绘有胡商遇盗图。画中商人显现出高鼻深目、络腮满面的面部特征，是典型的西域胡商形象。这队胡商在山谷行进过程中，遭遇了三个强盗。强盗们手持长刀，欲行劫盗。六位商人背后跟着驮负货物的毛驴，地上放着一捆白色丝绸和一个红色包袱。此时胡商均双手合十，口诵观音名号求救。这幅图像既描绘了丝绸之路上可能遇到的危险，又反映出丝绸是当时丝路贸易的主要商品，也说明了毛驴曾是丝绸之路上进行运输的主要畜力。

Murals depicting the merits of Avalokiteshvara Bodhisattva in Cave 45 of the Mogao Caves from the High Tang period also features a scene of Hu merchants encountering bandits. The merchants portrayed in the painting exhibit prominent facial features typical of Sogdian, characterized by high noses, deep-set eyes, and full beards. While traveling through a valley, they are confronted by three robbers. The bandits are armed with long knives, ready to attack. Behind the six merchants are donkeys laden with goods, with a bundle of white silk and a red package placed on the ground. The Hu merchants are clasping their hands together and reciting the name of Avalokiteshvara to pray for help. This image not only depicts the dangers that could be encountered along the Silk Road but also indicates that silk was a primary commodity in Silk Road trade at the time, and that donkeys were a significant mode of transport along this route.

## 《五台山图》

五台山，属太行山脉的一支，位于今山西省境内。从唐代开始，被认定成文殊菩萨的道场，并产生了专门描绘五台山面貌的《五台山图》。中唐时期，该图传入敦煌，其中最为著名的即莫高窟五代第 61 窟西壁的巨幅《五台山图》。

## *Map of Mount Wutai*

Wutai Mountain, part of the Taihang Mountain range, is located in present-day Shanxi Province. Since the Tang Dynasty, it has been recognized as the sacred site of Manjushri Bodhisattva, leading to the creation of specific depictions known as Mount Wutai maps. During the mid-Tang period, these maps arrived in Dunhuang, the most famous example being a large *Map of Mount Wutai* found on the western wall of Cave 61 in the Mogao Caves.

这幅《五台山图》长 13 米、高 3.6 米，面积达 46.8 平方米。全图可分为三部分，上部主要绘菩萨赴会和各种“灵异”“化现”内容，中部主要表现五台及山中寺院、佛塔等圣迹，下部重点描绘出入五台山的两条交通要道。图中共有榜题 195 条。其中，还可以看到北印度罽宾国僧人佛陀波利巡礼五台山，以及山中的新罗送供使队伍，反映出当时五台山信仰在整个东亚地区的影响力。这幅巨作不仅是一幅佛教史迹画，也是一幅山水人物画，更是一幅翔实细致的历史地理地图，为佛教史、社会史、交通史、地理史和古代建筑史的研究都提供了图像资料。

The map is 13 meters long and 3.6 meters high, covering an area of 46.8 square meters. The entire painting can be divided into three sections. The upper section primarily depicts Bodhisattvas attending a gathering and various "supernatural" and "transformation" scenes. The middle section focuses on the sacred sites of the mountain including temples and pagodas. The lower section highlights two main routes leading into and out of the mountain. The map contains a total of 195 labels. The painting also depicts Jibin monk Buddha-bhadra making a pilgrimage to Wutai Mountain, along with a procession from Silla (Korea) offering tribute, illustrating the influence of the mountain as a center of Buddhist faith at that time. The grand work is not only a depiction of Buddhist historical sites but also a landscape featuring figures, as well as a detailed, accurate historical geographic map. It serves as an important visual resource for the study of Buddhist history, social history, transportation history, geography, and ancient architecture.

# 《唐僧取经图》

中国古典四大名著之一《西游记》讲述了唐僧师徒四人历经磨难去西天取经的故事。故事中“唐僧”的原型，是撰写了《大唐西域记》、实现中印文化交流的翻译家——高僧玄奘。《西游记》成书于明代，而早在西夏时期，唐僧取经的故事就被画入了敦煌壁画。敦煌石窟现存 6 幅《唐僧取经图》，出现在榆林窟和东千佛洞的西夏壁画中。这 6 幅《唐僧取经图》的内容和表现手法基本一致，大都不是独立画面，而是绘制在《水月观音变》或《普贤变》的一角。

## *Xuanzang Going on a Pilgrimage for Buddhist Scriptures*

One of China's Four Great Classics, *Journey to the West*, tells the story of the Tang Monk and his three disciples enduring hardships to travel to the Western Heaven in quest of Buddhist scriptures. The character called "Tang Monk" in the story is based on the historical figure Xuanzang, an eminent monk and translator who authored *Records of the Western Regions of the Great Tang* and facilitated cultural exchanges between China and India. The story of his journey had already been depicted in Dunhuang murals during the Western Xia period (1038-1227), although *Journey to the West* was written during the Ming Dynasty (1368-1644). Six confirmed depictions of *Xuanzang Going on a Pilgrimage for Buddhist Scriptures* have been found so far in the Dunhuang Caves—the Western Xia murals in the Yulin Caves and the Eastern Thousand-Buddha Caves. These six illustrations share similar content and artistic styles, most of which are not standalone paintings but part of larger murals, often appearing in the corners of Water-Moon Guanyin or Samantabhadra transformation scenes.

榆林窟第2窟西壁门北的水月观音，斜倚岩壁坐于透明的圆光之中。观音对面的岩岸上，唐僧身穿袈裟，双手高举合十，面朝观音遥拜，其后猴行者穿窄袖衫、束腿裤，一手牵马，一手搭凉棚，仰望观音。榆林窟第3窟南侧的《普贤变》，普贤菩萨手持梵夹坐于六牙白象背上的莲座上，周围梵天、天王、菩萨、罗汉等护从。画面左边的崖岸上，唐僧立于岸边，身体微躬，双手合十而拜，猴行者与白马并排站立，紧随其后。猴行者毛发浓密，面露凶相，双目圆睁，张口露齿，亦双手合十礼拜。白马背驮包袱，包袱放出光芒，可见装有真经，据此可知这一画面是取经后返回东土的情节。这些西夏时期的《唐僧取经图》说明，早在《西游记》成书之前300多年，民间已流传唐僧取经的传奇故事。

In Yulin Cave 2, on the western wall north of the door, *Water-Moon Guanyin* is depicted reclining against a rock, seated within a transparent halo. Opposite Guanyin, the Tang Monk, wearing a kasaya, stands with his hands raised in prayer, facing Guanyin with reverence. Behind him, the itinerant monk is dressed in narrow-sleeved clothing and pants tied at the legs. He leads a horse with one hand while shading his eyes with the other, gazing up at Guanyin. In Cave 3 of Yulin, on the southern side, the *Samantabhadra Transformation* scene shows Samantabhadra Bodhisattva holding a palm-leaf manuscript while seated on a lotus throne atop a six-tusked white elephant. Surrounding the Bodhisattva are Brahma, heavenly kings, bodhisattvas, and arhats. To the left of the painting, the Tang Monk is depicted standing by the riverbank, slightly bowing with his hands clasped in prayer. The itinerant monk and the white horse stand side by side behind him, following closely. The itinerant monk is shown with thick hair, a fierce expression, bulging eyes, and bared teeth, yet he is also shown with hands clasped in prayer. The white horse carries a bundle that emits light, indicating it contains the true scriptures and revealing that this scene depicts the return journey after obtaining the scriptures from India. These scenes centered around the theme of *Xuanzang Going on a Pilgrimage for Buddhist Scriptures* from the Western Xia period suggest that the legendary tale of the monk's journey had already been circulating in folk culture over 300 years before *Journey to the West* was published.

五

# 守望敦煌

敦煌的文化遗产是全世界独一无二的千年文明瑰宝。1944 年，国立敦煌艺术研究所成立，结束了敦煌石窟 400 年无人管理、任人损毁、屡遭破坏偷盗的历史。从此，越来越多的有识之士凭着对敦煌的热爱、对历史使命与行动价值的清醒认识，把青春年华和全部精力都奉献给了这里。正是在他们的努力之下，才有了今天敦煌文化事业蒸蒸日上的面貌。本章主要介绍保护、研究和弘扬敦煌文化遗产的中国专业机构、团队和外籍专家，并重点介绍百年敦煌学出版的重要学术成果和以敦煌为主题创作的文艺作品，以及当下敦煌文化的创造性转化和创新性发展成果。

# GUARDING DUNHUANG

Dunhuang's cultural heritage is a unique treasure of civilization that developed over a thousand years. In 1944, the National Dunhuang Art Research Institute was established, ending 400 years of neglect, destruction of caves, damage, and theft. Since then, more and more individuals, driven by love of Dunhuang and a clear understanding of the historical mission and value of action, have dedicated their lives and energy to this cause. Dunhuang's cultural undertakings have flourished thanks to such dedicated efforts. This chapter discusses the professional institutions, teams, and foreign experts dedicated to the preservation, research, and promotion of Dunhuang's cultural heritage. It also highlights significant academic achievements in Dunhuang studies over the past century and the artistic works inspired by Dunhuang, as well as the current innovative transformation and development of Dunhuang culture.

## 敦煌研究院

敦煌研究院的前身是1944年成立的国立敦煌艺术研究所，1950年改名为敦煌文物研究所，1984年扩建为敦煌研究院。敦煌研究院负责管理世界文化遗产敦煌莫高窟、天水麦积山石窟、永靖炳灵寺石窟、中国重点文物保护单位瓜州榆林窟、敦煌西千佛洞、庆阳北石窟寺共6座石窟。

敦煌研究院本部位于中国甘肃省敦煌市莫高窟，并设有兰州分院。敦煌研究院坚持“保护、研究、弘扬”的工作方针，现已成为在世界具有相当影响力的遗址博物馆、敦煌学研究实体、中国古代壁画与土遗址保护科研基地。2010年在巴西召开的世界遗产委员会第34届会议上，莫高窟被誉为“有效保护与可持续旅游管理方法的典范”。现在，敦煌研究院正努力建设成为世界文化遗产保护的典范和敦煌学研究的高地。

## Dunhuang Academy

The Dunhuang Academy traces its origins to the National Dunhuang Art Research Institute, established in 1944. In 1950, it was renamed Dunhuang Cultural Relics Research Institute, and in 1984, it was expanded and upgraded to the Dunhuang Academy. The Academy oversees management of six cave complexes: the world cultural heritage sites of the Mogao Caves in Dunhuang, the Maiji Mountain Grottoes in Tianshui, the Bingling Caves in Yongjing, and other key protected cultural relics sites in China including the Yulin Caves in Guazhou, the Western Thousand-Buddha Caves in Dunhuang, and the North Cave-Temple in Qingyang.

The headquarters of the Academy is located in the city of Dunhuang, Gansu Province, China. The Dunhuang Academy also operates a branch office in Lanzhou. Guided by the policy of "protection, research, and promotion", the Academy has become a site museum with considerable influence worldwide, a research entity for Dunhuang studies, and a scientific research base for the protection of ancient Chinese murals and earthen sites. At the 34th session of the World Heritage Committee held in Brazil in 2010, the Mogao Caves was praised as "a model" for effective protection and sustainable tourism management. Today, the Academy is striving to become a model for the protection of world cultural heritage and a pedestal for the research of Dunhuang studies.

## 敦煌研究院文物保护利用群体

2020 年 1 月，中共中央宣传部向全社会发布敦煌研究院文物保护利用群体的先进事迹，授予其“时代楷模”称号。

80 年来，敦煌研究院文物保护利用群体几代人薪火相传，择一事终一生，扎根大漠，舍小家顾大家，以强烈的使命担当、无私的奉献精神，精心保护和修复莫高窟珍贵文物，潜心研究和弘扬敦煌文化艺术，合理探索推进文化旅游合理开发，取得了令世人瞩目的巨大成就。充分彰显了为国为民奉献的家国情怀、为事业无怨无悔坚守的敬业品格、为文化传承发展拼搏奋斗的执着追求，以实际行动诠释了莫高精神。

## Dunhuang Academy's Relics Protection and Utilization Team

In January 2020, the Publicity Department of the Central Committee of the Communist Party of China recognized the advanced achievements of the Academy's relics protection and utilization team, awarding it the title of "Model of the Times".

For 80 years, generations of the Academy's relics protection and utilization team have passed down their expertise to successors after committing their lives to the single cause. They have thrown down roots in the desert, prioritizing the greater good over personal interests. With a strong sense of mission and selfless dedication, they have meticulously protected and restored the precious relics in the Mogao Caves, deeply studied and promoted Dunhuang culture and art, and explored the sustainable development of cultural tourism. Their remarkable achievements have attracted global attention, radiated a patriotic spirit of serving the country and the people, and demonstrated professional integrity and unwavering commitment to the work. Their painstaking efforts to inherit, disseminate, and develop Chinese culture flavor the Mogao Spirit continuously.

## 敦煌研究院文物保护团队

2024 年 1 月“国家工程师奖”表彰大会上，敦煌研究院文物保护团队荣获“国家卓越工程师团队”称号。

从 1944 年国立敦煌艺术研究所成立保护研究组，开展敦煌石窟积沙清理、壁画修复、崖体加固等工作，再到 2014 年设立敦煌石窟监测中心，敦煌研究院在保护实践中逐渐形成了一支集产、学、研、用一体化的近 200 名技术人员的高质量保护技术团队。

## Academy's Team for Relics Protection and Utilization

The relics protection team from the Dunhuang Academy was granted the title of "National Outstanding Engineering Team" at the commendation ceremony of the National Engineer Award in January 2024.

The Dunhuang Academy has gradually assembled a high-quality protection technology team of nearly 200 technical personnel. They integrate production, learning, research, and application. In 1944, the National Dunhuang Art Research Institute established a protection and research team for clearing sand, restoring murals, and reinforcing cliff bodies in the Dunhuang caves. In 2014, the team opened the Dunhuang Caves Monitoring Center to enhance its protection efforts.

这支团队几代人不忘初心，接续奋斗，在大漠深处、摩崖之间显身手，攻克古代壁画保护、土遗址与石窟寺保护、丝路遗产监测预警与预防性保护、文物出土现场保护、岩土质文物保护等方面的多项技术难题。他们让文化遗产华光永续，是技术的革新突破，也是与自然的较量、与时间的对抗。敦煌研究院文物保护团队不断突破的技术理念被推广至全国，并沿着“一带一路”惠及更多国家的文化遗产保护工作。

This team, spanning several generations, remains true to its original mission and continues to strive in the depths of the desert and between the cliffs. They tackle various technical challenges hindering the protection of ancient murals and the safeguarding of earthen sites and cave temples by monitoring and implementing preventive protection of Silk Road heritage, relics at excavation sites, and rock and soil artifacts. While ensuring the everlasting brilliance of cultural heritage, they work extremely hard to make breakthroughs in technological innovation and fight against nature as well as time. The technological concepts continuously developed by the team have been promoted nationwide and benefited the cultural heritage protection efforts of other countries along the Belt and Road Initiative (BRI) route.

## 兰州大学敦煌学研究所

兰州大学敦煌学研究所是由兰州大学和敦煌研究院联合建立的中国教育部人文社会科学重点研究基地。其前身是1979年兰州大学成立的敦煌学研究小组，是中国最早开展敦煌学研究的高校机构之一。1980年创办了全国首份敦煌学专业期刊《敦煌学辑刊》。1985年建立中国敦煌吐鲁番学会兰州大学资料中心。1998年获得历史文献学（含敦煌学、古文字学）博士学位授予权，成为中国

## Institute of Dunhuang Studies, Lanzhou University

The Institute of Dunhuang Studies (IDS), Lanzhou University is a key research base for humanities and social sciences jointly established by Lanzhou University and the Dunhuang Academy. It is accredited by the Ministry of Education of China. Its predecessor was Dunhuang Studies Research Group established at Lanzhou University in 1979, making Lanzhou one of the earliest higher education institutions in the country to conduct research on Dunhuang studies. In 1980, the IDS launched the first national professional journal on Dunhuang studies, *Journal of Dunhuang Studies*. In 1985, it established Lanzhou University Documentation Center for the Institute of Dunhuang and Turfan Studies of China (LUDCIDTSC). In 1998, it was awarded the authority to confer doctoral degrees in historical literature (including Dunhuang studies and ancient script studies), becoming the first doctoral program in Dunhuang studies in China. In 1999, it was selected as one of the first key research bases for humanities and social sciences by the Ministry of Education.

第一个敦煌学博士点。1999 年入选为首批教育部人文社会科学重点研究基地。

该所下设敦煌文献研究室、敦煌石窟艺术研究室、宗教学研究室、国际佛教艺术与文化研究中心、藏传佛教艺术中心、中国敦煌吐鲁番学会兰州大学资料中心、《敦煌学辑刊》编辑部等机构，主要研究方向为敦煌文献研究、敦煌石窟艺术研究、敦煌学史研究、敦煌与西北历史研究。作为高校研究机构，该所建立起包括硕士、博士和博士后在内的学位授权点及科研流动站，拥有一套完整的人才培养体系，并持续加强与国内外学术界的交流联系。经过 40 多年的建设，兰州大学敦煌学研究所已成为国际知名的敦煌学研究、人才培养、学术交流的重要平台。

The IDS includes various departments and centers such as Dunhuang Literature Research Office, Dunhuang Cave Art Research Office, Religious Studies Research Office, International Buddhist Art and Culture Research Center, Tibetan Buddhist Art Center, LUDCIDTSC, and the editorial office of *Journal of Dunhuang Studies*. It specializes in Dunhuang literature, Dunhuang cave art, the history of Dunhuang studies, and the study of Dunhuang and Northwest history. As a higher education research institution, the IDS has established degree-granting programs covering master's, doctoral, and postdoctoral levels, along with research mobility stations, forming a comprehensive talent cultivation system, while continuously strengthening its communication and collaboration with academic circles both domestically and internationally. After more than 40 years of development, it has become an internationally renowned platform for Dunhuang studies, talent development, and academic exchanges.

## 《敦煌劫余录》

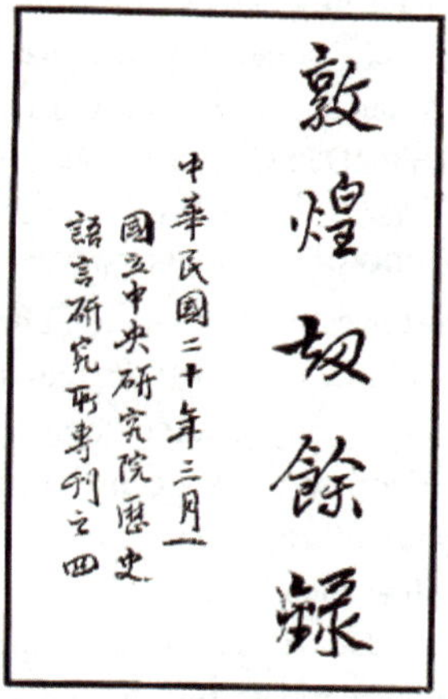


《敦煌劫余录》是由中国学者陈垣编撰的当时北平图书馆（今中国国家图书馆）共计 8679 件敦煌文献的总目录，1931 年由中国中央研究院历史语言研究所刊行，是全世界最早的敦煌汉文文献分类目录。该书以“劫余”为书名，表明了中国学者认为敦煌藏经洞文物被西方探险家骗购盗劫、流失海外的立场。

该书先在总目内依佛经种类和次序汇编全部写经、排成目次，并在每部经名下记录该经收藏的总数；在正录内依佛经目

## *An Analytical List of the Tun-Huang Manuscripts in the National Library of Peiping*

*An Analytical List of the Tun-Huang Manuscripts in the National Library of Peiping* is a comprehensive directory compiled by Chen Yuan (1880-1971), a prominent Chinese scholar, historian, and librarian, listing a total of 8,679 Dunhuang documents held by Peking Library (now the National Library of China) at the time. Published in 1931 by the Institute of History and Philology of the Academia Sinica, it is the earliest classification catalog of Dunhuang Chinese literature in the world. The title "劫余 (jieyu)" ("remnant") reflects the stance of Chinese scholars that the Dunhuang Caves manuscripts and artifacts were fraudulently acquired, robbed, and smuggled abroad by Western explorers.

The book first is a compilation of all the scriptures according to the types and order of Buddhist texts in the general catalog, arranging them into a table of contents, and recording the total number of each scripture under its title. The main catalog lists each document according to the Buddhist text catalog, noting the document's start and end, number of pages, number of lines, and quality. In the supplementary notes, it transcribes the colophons and any missing details of the manuscripts. This work has become a significant model in both organization of Dunhuang literature and cataloging methods.

次，记录每件文献的起讫、纸数、行数及品次，并在附记内抄录题记及写本残缺情况。本书无论在敦煌文献的整理工作抑或是编目方法上，都成为相当重要的范例。

由陈寅恪为该书撰写的序言中，评价此书为“诚治敦煌学者，不可缺之工具”。同时，也提出了“敦煌学”一词，并针对当时中国流行“敦煌学者，吾国学术之伤心史也”的说法提出自己的观点。他认为，敦煌藏经洞出土的新材料，带动了当时全世界敦煌学研究的新潮流，并举例说明留存在中国的敦煌文献也有很多有价值的精品，意在鼓励中国学者奋起直追，使中国学者能够屹立于国际敦煌学之林。

In the preface written by Chen Yinke, the book is described as "an essential tool for scholars of Dunhuang studies". Chen also introduced the term "Dunhuang studies" and addressed the prevailing sentiment in China at the time that "Dunhuang studies represent the lamentable history of our country's scholarship". He argued that the new materials unearthed from the Dunhuang Caves had sparked a global trend in Dunhuang studies. He provided examples to illustrate that many valuable pieces of Dunhuang literature remain in China, aiming to encourage Chinese scholars to march forward so as to stand tall in the international field of Dunhuang studies.

## 敦煌遗书与《敦煌文献全集》

敦煌遗书，现在多称为“敦煌文献”，是指1900年在中国敦煌莫高窟藏经洞发现的公元4—11世纪的写卷、写本、印本和拓片等文献资料。据敦煌研究院敦煌文献研究所最新统计，现存敦煌文献总计7万余件，分藏于中、英、法、俄、日等国的近百家公私收藏机构和个人手中。

2023年，全彩印《敦煌文献全集》出版工作启动。本次高清彩印，兼重文献价值和文物价值，不仅吸纳百余年间在定名、缀合等方面的学术成果，而且在编排上最大限度还原敦煌文献的原始形态。截至2025年4月，《法国国家图书馆藏敦煌文献》（第1—110册）、《甘肃藏敦煌文献》（第1—30册）、《重庆藏敦煌文献》（第1—3册）、《中国国家图书馆藏敦煌文献》（第1—80册）已正式出版，其他各卷出版工作也在陆续推进中。《敦煌文献全集》作为对敦煌文献的全面汇编，必将推动世界性显学敦煌学向前发展。

## Dunhuang Documents and *Complete Collection of Dunhuang Manuscripts*

Dunhuang documents, now commonly known as "Dunhuang literature", refer to written scrolls, manuscripts, printed materials, and rubbings discovered in the Library Cave at the Mogao Caves in Dunhuang in 1900, dating from the 4th to the 11th centuries. According to the latest statistics from the Dunhuang Literature Research Institute under the Dunhuang Academy, over 70,000 pieces of Dunhuang literature are currently held in nearly 100 public and private collections across countries such as China, the UK, France, Russia, and Japan.

The year 2023 saw the official commencement of the publication of the full-color *Complete Collection of Dunhuang Literature*. This high-quality edition emphasizes both the literary value of the documents and their value as historical relics, incorporating academic achievements over the past century regarding naming, collation, and more. The compilation aims to restore the original form of Dunhuang literature to the greatest extent possible. As of April 2025, *Dunhuang Manuscripts in the Bibliothèque Nationale de France* (Vol. 1-110), *Dunhuang Manuscripts Preserved in Gansu* (Vol. 1-30), *Dunhuang Manuscripts Preserved in Chongqing* (Vol. 1-3), and *Dunhuang Manuscripts Preserved in the National Library of China* (Vol. 1-80) have been officially published, while the publication of other volumes is also progressing. As a comprehensive compilation of Dunhuang literature, the *Complete Collection of Dunhuang Literature* is sure to promote the advancement of Dunhuang studies as a significant academic field worldwide.

# 《敦煌石窟全集：莫高窟考古报告》

《敦煌石窟全集：莫高窟考古报告》将最先进的测绘技术运用到考古工作中，实现了石窟考古测绘的重大突破。这一考古报告打破了过去仅限于文字、绘图和摄影结合的方法手段，融汇了考古、历史、美术史、佛教、测量、计算机、摄影、化学、物理学、信息资料等多学科方法。

该报告得到了国内外学术界的高度肯定，也为其他石窟寺遗址考古报告的撰写提供了范例。法兰西学院金石美文学院将“第二届汪德迈中国学奖”授予了该丛书的负责人樊锦诗先生，不仅是对樊锦诗主持的莫高窟考古报告学术成就的褒奖，也

## *The General Collection of the Dunhuang Caves: Archaeological Report of the Mogao Caves*

*The General Collection of the Dunhuang Caves: Archaeological Report of the Mogao Caves* applied the most advanced surveying technologies to archaeological work to achieve significant breakthroughs in cave archaeological mapping. This archaeological report transcends traditional methods limited to text, drawings, and photography by integrating interdisciplinary approaches from archaeology, history, art history, Buddhism, surveying, computer science, photography, chemistry, physics, and information studies.

The report was acclaimed by the academic community both domestically and internationally and became a model for writing archaeological reports on other cave temple sites. École des Hautes Études en Sciences Sociales awarded the 2nd Léon Vandermeersch Prize of Chinese Studies to Fan Jinshi, the chief editor of the series. The award not only recognizes the academic achievements of the Mogao Caves' archaeological report under Fan's leadership, but also signifies the international academic community's keen interest in and acknowledgment of the archaeological and world heritage preservation achievements at the Mogao Caves.

意味着国际学术界对敦煌莫高窟的考古与世界遗产保护成就的高度关注与认同。

考古报告的出版，有利于永久保存、保护敦煌莫高窟及其他敦煌石窟的科学档案资料，推动敦煌石窟文化遗产的深入研究、满足国内外学者和学术机构对敦煌石窟资料的需求，在石窟随时间逐渐劣化的威胁下，为全面复原提供可靠的依据。

The publication of this archaeological report is beneficial for the permanent preservation and protection of the scientific archival materials related to the Mogao Caves and other Dunhuang caves. It promotes in-depth research into the cultural heritage of the Dunhuang Caves and meets the demands of domestic and international scholars and academic institutions for information about the caves. This report provides foundational evidence for the comprehensive restoration under the threat of progressive deterioration in the cave temples.

## 《敦煌学大辞典》

《敦煌学大辞典》是至今为止最全面、最权威的敦煌学专业大型工具书。本书第一版由中国敦煌吐鲁番学会、敦煌研究院与上海辞书出版社联合发起，由中国著名学者、北京大学季羡林教授担任主编，全国老中青三代专家学者100余人参与，历经13年编纂而成。

2024年12月，《敦煌学大辞典》第二版正式问世。第二版图书由郝春文主编，敦煌学界近160位学者历时6年共同编纂而成，词条数量和图片数量均增添一倍。不仅增加了20世纪以来重要的敦煌学考古成果和20世纪末以来重要的敦煌文献刊布与整理研究成果，还系统增加了现代科技在敦煌学研究与保护应用方面的词条和现当代重要的国内外敦煌学人物类词条，与敦煌古代历史相关的人、事、物类词条，以及第一版未收录的其他重要门类如碑铭赞、尊像画等。

该辞典是迄今为止海内外唯一一部以工具书形式，全方位展示20世纪至21世纪初敦煌学研究成果的大型辞典，首次系统、全面地对敦煌学进行总结，集中反映了中国敦煌学整体研究水平。

## *Dictionary of Dunhuang Studies*

The *Dictionary of Dunhuang Studies* (*Dunhuangxue Dacidian*) is the most comprehensive, authoritative large reference work in the field of Dunhuang studies to date. Publication of the first edition was jointly undertaken by the Institute of Dunhuang and Turfan Studies of China, the Dunhuang Academy, and Shanghai Lexicographical Publishing House. It was edited by renowned Chinese scholar Prof. Ji Xianlin from Peking University and features participation from over 100 experts and scholars across the country. It took 13 years to complete the compilation of the book.

In December 2024, the *Dictionary of Dunhuang Studies* (2nd Edition) was officially published. Edited by Hao Chunwen and collaboratively compiled over six years by nearly 160 scholars in the field, this edition doubles the number of entries and illustrations compared to its predecessor. The new edition not only incorporates major archaeological discoveries in Dunhuang studies since the 20th Century and critical publications and researches on Dunhuang manuscripts since the late 20th Century, but also systematically expands entries on modern technologies applied in Dunhuang research and conservation as well as content on prominent international and contemporary Dunhuang scholars, historical figures, events, and artifacts related to ancient Dunhuang. Stelae eulogies and sacred deity paintings are among previously excluded but important categories.

As the only comprehensive reference work worldwide to present Dunhuang scholarship from the 20th to the early 21st centuries, this dictionary marks the first systematic and comprehensive summation of Dunhuang studies, reflecting China's leading research capabilities in the field.

## 《敦煌艺术大辞典》

《敦煌艺术大辞典》是敦煌研究院组织编写的敦煌艺术工具书，2019 年 12 月出版。该书由樊锦诗、赵声良领衔，集结敦煌学界 70 余位学者共同完成。

该书是以敦煌石窟、遗迹遗物、塑像、壁画、人物、题记、藏经洞艺术品、石窟保护等为主题的石窟考古与艺术研究领域学术词汇和专业知识的集释。正文按照类别进行编排，共 28 个类别，收录词条近 3000 条、1000 余幅图片，约 140 万字。

## *Dictionary of Dunhuang Art*

The *Dictionary* of *Dunhuang Art* (*Dunhuang Yishu Dacidian*) is a reference book on Dunhuang art organized and compiled by the Dunhuang Academy. Published in December 2019, it is a joint effort by over 70 scholars from the field of Dunhuang studies led by Fan Jinshi and Zhao Shengliang, who are known for their expertise in the study of Dunhuang art as well as Chinese art history in general.

This book serves as a comprehensive compilation of academic vocabulary and specialized knowledge in the field of cave archaeology and art research, focusing on themes such as the Dunhuang Caves, relics, sculptures, murals, figures, inscriptions, artworks from the Library Cave, and cave protection. The main text is organized into 28 categories including nearly 3,000 entries and over 1,000 images, totaling around 1.4 million words. It provides a thorough overview of Dunhuang cave art and the latest achievements in academic research, featuring a large number of high-resolution color images and line drawings that vividly showcase the rich, profound Dunhuang art.

全面展示了敦煌石窟艺术的整体面貌和学术研究的最新成果，书中配置了大量高清彩色图片及线描图，图文并茂，形象地展示了博大精深的敦煌艺术。

这是第一部全面介绍和诠释敦煌石窟考古与艺术的大型工具书，是敦煌艺术的百科全书。该书凝结了敦煌艺术研究领域几代专家、学者长期以来的集体智慧，反映了敦煌艺术领域的最新成果和研究动向，具有学术性、准确性、权威性；推动了敦煌石窟艺术研究的发展和敦煌文化的普及，对传承弘扬中华优秀传统文化具有重要价值。

This is the first comprehensive reference book to introduce and interpret the archaeology and the art of the Dunhuang Caves, an encyclopedia of Dunhuang art. The book captured the collective wisdom of several generations of experts and scholars in the field of Dunhuang art research, reflecting the latest achievements and research trends in this area. Characterized by its academic rigor, accuracy, and authority, the book has promoted the development of Dunhuang cave art research and the popularization of Dunhuang culture, holding significant value for the inheritance and promotion of outstanding traditional Chinese culture.

## 《中国石窟：敦煌莫高窟》

《中国石窟：敦煌莫高窟》，俗称“五卷本”，由敦煌文物研究所（第二版更名为“敦煌研究院”）编著、文物出版社与日本平凡社合作出版。季羡林为其撰写序言《中日友谊，万古长青》，回顾了中日两国人民长达几千年的友好交往，肯定了这套丛书是中日友谊的结晶。该书于 1991 年获中国“首届全国美术图书特别金奖”，1994 年获中国“首届国家图书奖”。

本丛书第一卷至第五卷收录了敦煌莫高窟不同时期的彩塑和壁画，并附有几位中日学者的代表性论文。这是 20 世纪 80 年代对敦煌石窟研究成果的一次高度总结，具有划时代的意义。

## *Chinese Grottoes: The Mogao Caves in Dunhuang*

The *Chinese Grottoes: The Mogao Caves in Dunhuang*, commonly referred to as the *Five-Volume Edition*, was compiled by the Dunhuang Cultural Relics Research Institute (renamed "Dunhuang Academy" in the second edition) and published in collaboration with the Cultural Relics Publishing House and Japan's HEIBON-SHA. Prof. Ji Xianlin wrote a preface titled *Everlasting Sino-Japanese Friendship*, reflecting on the long-standing friendly exchanges between the people of China and Japan over thousands of years, affirming that this series is a product of Sino-Japanese friendship. The book won the First National Special Golden Award for Art Books in 1991 and the First National Book Award in 1994, both in China.

The first five volumes of this series include colored sculptures and murals of the Mogao Caves from different periods, with accompanying representative articles by noted Chinese and Japanese researchers. This work serves as a significant summary of the research achievements related to the Dunhuang Caves in the 1980s, which marked a groundbreaking period in the field.

## 《敦煌石窟全集》

敦煌研究院主编《敦煌石窟全集》(26卷)于2000—2005年由香港商务印书馆出版。本丛书是对敦煌石窟资料的专题研究成果的系统刊布。

这套丛书收录了敦煌石窟的建筑、雕塑、壁画及藏经洞出土品等文物图片约6000幅，总计160万字的说明文字。《敦煌石窟全集》是20多位中国敦煌学专家多年通力合作的研究成果，全面总结并展示了敦煌研究院多年来在敦煌石窟考古、石窟艺术及藏经洞出土品研究方面的成果，全面系统地揭示了敦煌石窟的丰富内涵和珍贵价值。

## *Complete Collection of the Dunhuang Caves*

The *Complete Collection of the Dunhuang Caves* (26 volumes), edited by the Dunhuang Academy, was published by the Hong Kong Commercial Press from 2000 to 2005. This series systematically presents specialized research findings related to the Dunhuang Caves.

It includes approximately 6,000 images of artifacts such as architecture, sculptures, murals, and items excavated from the Mogao Caves alongside 1.6 million words of explanatory text. The book is the result of years of collaborative research by over 20 Chinese Dunhuang scholars. It comprehensively summarizes and showcases the achievements of the Dunhuang Academy in the fields of Dunhuang cave archaeology, cave art, and the study of items excavated from the Mogao Caves, and systematically addresses the rich connotations and precious value of the Dunhuang Caves.

## 井上靖《敦煌》

日本文坛巨匠、芥川龙之介奖得主井上靖于1959年在讲谈社首次出版长篇小说《敦煌》。井上靖（1907—1991）一生27次访问中国，曾到新疆、甘肃等地实地考察，著有以西域为题材创作的《楼兰》《敦煌》《丝绸之路诗集》等作品，其中《楼兰》《敦煌》在1960年获得日本“每日艺术大奖”，并有多个中译本。

《敦煌》讲述了宋仁宗天圣年间，书生赵行德进京赶考，却因瞌睡错过了考试，前往刀兵四起、黄沙漫天的敦煌，命运由此发生了剧烈的转折。一块写有西夏文的神秘布片，牵引出北

## Inoue Yasushi's *Dunhuang*

Japanese literary master Inoue Yasushi (1907-1991), a recipient of the Akutagawa Prize, authored the novel *Dunhuang* in 1959, which was published by Kodansha. Yasushi visited China 27 times throughout his life, conducting field research in regions such as Xinjiang and Gansu. He is known for works inspired by the Western Regions including *Ro-ran (Lou-Lan)*, *Tonkō (Tun-huang)*, and *Silk Road Poetry Collection*. Both *Ro-ran* and *Tonkō* won Japan's Mainichi Art Award in 1960 and have several Chinese translations.

*Dunhuang* recounts the story of Zhao Xingde, a scholar during the reign of Emperor Renzong of the Song Dynasty. On his way to the capital for the imperial examination, Zhao accidentally sleeps in and misses the exam. His journey leads him to the war-torn and sandy lands of Dunhuang, where his fate takes a dramatic turn. A mysterious piece of cloth inscribed with Tangut script leads him through a series of misadventures. The novel is set against the historical backdrop of the Tangut occupation of Dunhuang and connects the protagonist's story to the mystery surrounding the closure of the Dunhuang Caves, which were said to have been sealed to escape the threats posed by the Tangut.

宋书生赵行德一路踉跄的人生。小说以西夏占领敦煌前后为历史背景，采用了敦煌藏经洞封闭为“避西夏之难”的说法，将主人公与敦煌藏经洞封闭之谜联系到一起。

无数读者从这部小说开始关注中国西部并踏上前往敦煌的漫长旅程。井上靖对中国文化的感情至为深厚，他通过《敦煌》对人生和历史寄予了独特思考，对中国史传文学的叙事模式亦有秉承和借鉴。1988 年，为纪念中日邦交正常化十周年，由佐藤纯弥担任导演，改编自这部小说的中日合拍同名电影《敦煌》上映，该片当年即荣获第 12 届日本电影金像奖最佳影片、最佳导演和最佳男主角奖，成为中日友好交往的重要见证。

Countless readers began to focus on western China and embark on the long journey to Dunhuang through this novel. Inoue Yasushi had a deep affection for Chinese culture, and through *Tonkō (Tun-huang)*, he expressed unique reflections on life and history while inheriting and referencing the narrative patterns of Chinese historical literature. In 1988, to commemorate the 10th anniversary of the normalization of diplomatic relations between China and Japan, a Sino-Japanese co-production film titled *Tonkō (Tun-huang)*, directed by Junya Sato and adapted from this novel, found its way to the big screen. The film won the Best Film, Best Director, and Best Actor awards at the 12th Japan Academy Prize, becoming an important testament to the Sino-Japanese friendship.

## 《敦煌岁时节令》

2018年，敦煌研究院微信公众号推出“敦煌岁时节令”系列推文。这一系列以“传承、人文、诗意、生活”为核心理念，多学科协同深入挖掘敦煌文化的多元价值，对敦煌的珍贵壁画，彩塑和文献进行重新整理，创新性地结合了中国传统文化——岁时节令，将中国古代民俗、礼俗、岁时、节令和日常生活引入当代人的视野，让中国传统岁时节令别具人文内涵，重现敦煌

## *Time and Seasons of Dunhuang*

In 2018, Dunhuang Academy's public WeChat account launched a series of articles titled *Time and Seasons of Dunhuang*. The series, centered on the core concepts of "inheritance, humanity, poetry, and life", employs a multidisciplinary approach to explore the diverse values of Dunhuang culture. It reorganizes the precious murals, sculptures, and documents of Dunhuang and creatively integrates traditional Chinese culture—especially seasonal festivals—into the contemporary context. This initiative brings ancient Chinese customs, rituals, seasonal events, and daily life into the modern view, endowing traditional seasonal festivals with unique cultural significance and recreating ancient scenes of Dunhuang. Building on this foundation, a series of short videos titled *Time and Seasons of Dunhuang* was launched in 2022, making it an important digital brand for promoting Dunhuang culture and excellent traditional culture of China.

古代生活图景。以此为基础，2022 年推出《敦煌岁时节令》系列短视频，使《敦煌岁时节令》成为宣传敦煌文化和中华优秀传统文化的重要数字品牌。

2022 年，由敦煌研究院编著的人文读物《敦煌岁时节令》中文版、日文版正式出版。全书以中国二十四节气和重要民俗节日为线索，生动展示了中国传统节令之美，以及中国古代农业科技、天文历法、传统民俗中的智慧与哲理。该书集学术性与文化审美价值于一身，自出版以来深受好评。

In 2022, the Dunhuang Academy published Chinese and Japanese versions of the cultural reading material *Time and Seasons of Dunhuang*. The book covers China's 24 solar terms and significant folk festivals, vividly showcasing the beauty of traditional Chinese seasonal festivals as well as the wisdom and philosophy found in ancient agricultural science, astronomy, and traditional customs. This work combines academic rigor with cultural and aesthetic value and has received widespread acclaim since its publication.

## 敦煌仙子莫伽瑶

敦煌仙子莫伽瑶，是敦煌研究院官方推出的首位虚拟代言人，其原型出自敦煌莫高窟壁画中声音婉转如歌的妙音鸟“迦陵频伽”。以青少年形象出现的莫伽瑶，在服装配饰上，为凸显敦煌艺术的美感，加入了大量莫高窟经典壁画元素及供养人服饰造型；在形象设计上，着重体现古典气韵与娇俏少女的灵动感。

莫伽瑶作为敦煌研究院的“形象代言人”，已参加过内容丰富的各类创意传播项目。未来，莫伽瑶将作为首位数字敦煌文化大使和“云游敦煌”小程序首位数字讲解员，继续以展览虚拟直播、丝路文化科普、IP 创新跨界合作等方式与大众见面，带来更丰富的文化内容互动，带领更多人领略敦煌文化的魅力。

## Dunhuang Fairy Mo Jiayao

Mo Jiayao, a Dunhuang fairy, was the first virtual spokesperson officially launched by the Dunhuang Academy. Her character is inspired by the melodious "kalavinka", a songbird depicted in the murals of the Mogao Caves. Represented as a youthful figure, Mo Jiayao's clothing and accessories incorporate numerous classic mural elements and donor attire from the Mogao Caves to highlight the beauty of Dunhuang art. The design emphasizes a blend of classical elegance and the lively spirit of a charming young girl.

As the "image ambassador" of the Dunhuang Academy, Mo Jiayao has participated in various creative communication projects. In the future, she will serve as the first digital ambassador for Dunhuang culture and the inaugural digital guide for the "Cloud Tour Dunhuang" mini-program. She will continue to engage with the public through virtual live exhibitions, Silk Road cultural outreach, and innovative cross-border IP collaborations and endeavor to enrich cultural content interactions and guide more people to appreciate the charm of Dunhuang culture.

## 敦煌画派

中国敦煌研究院第一任院长常书鸿毕生致力于弘扬敦煌石窟艺术，他在 20 世纪 80 年代提出对新美术流派“敦煌画派”形成的期待。“敦煌画派”是一个跨越时间、超越地域、逾越画种的画派，其形成主要有两个重要因素：一是古代工匠创造的辉煌成果，二是当代艺术家传承的探索成就。敦煌画派主要由赴敦煌考察、临摹并开展保护工作，以敦煌石窟壁画、彩塑、装饰纹样等特征鲜明、传承有序的艺术体系为基础，以敦煌为精神象征的地域性艺术家团体构成。

从老一辈艺术家董希文《哈萨克牧羊女》，敦煌文物研究所集体创作的《姑娘追》《猎归》等作品中可以看出，他们的作品一方面继承了敦煌壁画的绘画传统，一方面探寻出敦煌艺术的创新之路。敦煌画派实际上是以敦煌为中心的当代美术创新，是中国艺术发展的重要现象和敦煌文化在当代的不断延伸。

## Dunhuang School of Painting

The first president of the Dunhuang Academy, Chang Shuhong (1904-1994), was a renowned Chinese painter and art educator who devoted his life to promoting the art of the Dunhuang Caves. In the 1980s, he expressed hope for the formation of a new art movement known as the "Dunhuang School of Painting". Aiming to break the limits of time, geography, and art forms, this school is primarily influenced by two significant factors: the brilliant achievements of ancient craftsmen and the exploratory accomplishments of contemporary artists. The Dunhuang School of Painting mainly consists of artists who have visited Dunhuang for research, replication, and conservation work. It is based on a distinct, orderly artistic system characterized by the murals, colored sculptures, and decorative patterns of the Dunhuang Caves. This group of regional artists are united by Dunhuang as a spiritual symbol.

Works by older artists such as *The Kazakh Shepherdess* by Dong Xiwen (1914-1973), as well as collectively-created pieces like *Girl Chasing* and *Returning from Hunt*, by the Dunhuang Cultural Relics Research Institute, all show that such artists not only inherit the painting traditions of Dunhuang murals but also explore innovative pathways for Dunhuang art. The Dunhuang School of Painting represents a contemporary art innovation centered around Dunhuang, reflecting an important phenomenon in the development of Chinese art and the continuous extension of Dunhuang culture in modern times.

六

# 互鉴共进

中国的敦煌，也是人类共同的文化遗产。文明交流互鉴是人类历史的核心，没有任何一个文明可以独自存在。古代的丝绸之路上，使者相望于道、商旅不绝于途。今天的敦煌，仍然在国际交流上不断迈进。敦煌文化遗产的保护与传承，得益于全世界的关注与支持。敦煌学从诞生之日起，就是一门国际性显学，是全世界学者共同关注和开展国际合作的热点。本章主要介绍在敦煌文化遗产保护、研究、弘扬中做出重要贡献的中国敦煌吐鲁番学会和中国以外的学术机构，支持这一事业发展的各基金会、国际合作的成功案例及敦煌文物资源的全球共享平台。

# MUTUAL LEARNING AND COMMON PROGRESS

Although physically located in China, Dunhuang is a shared cultural heritage of humanity. Exchanges and mutual learning among civilizations is the heart of human history; no civilization has ever existed in isolation. Along the ancient Silk Road, envoys shuttled and merchants hustled. Today, Dunhuang continues to make strides in international exchanges. Protection and inheritance of Dunhuang's cultural heritage benefit from the attention and support of the entire world. Since its inception, Dunhuang studies have been an international scholarly field and a hotspot for scholars worldwide to collaborate and engage. This chapter covers the significant contributions of the Institute of Dunhuang and Turfan Studies of China (IDTSC) and academic institutions outside of China towards the protection, research, and promotion of Dunhuang's cultural heritage as well as various foundations that support the development of this cause, international cooperation, and global platforms sharing Dunhuang cultural resources.

## 敦煌文博会

SILK ROAD (DUNHUANG) INTERNATIONAL CULTURAL EXPO

丝绸之路（敦煌）国际文化博览会

开幕式暨高峰会议

致首届丝绸之路（敦煌）国际文化博览会的贺信

值此首届丝绸之路（敦煌）国际文化博览会开幕之际，我谨代表中国政府和中国人民，并以我个人的名义，向文博会的召开致以热烈的祝贺！向出席文博会的各国嘉宾和朋友表示诚挚的欢迎！

2000多年前，贯通亚欧的古丝绸之路架起了一座东西方友好往来、文明交流的重要桥梁。敦煌是历史上东西方文化交汇的重要枢纽，不同文化在这里汇聚和交融，塑造了独具魅力的敦煌文化。历史表明，世界各民族文化互鉴共进是人类文明的基本特征，也是人类文明发展的重要动力。这次文博会以推动文化交流、共谋合作发展为主题，为丝绸之路沿线各国合作交流提供了一个重要平台。要坚持多样共存、互鉴共进、合作共享，加强文化交流，倡导文化平等，保护文化遗产，推动文化创新，加强文化合作，让人类创造的丰富多彩的文化造福更多民众，让世界更加美好。

2016年9月20日

敦煌文博会，全称“丝绸之路（敦煌）国际文化博览会”，是“一带一路”建设的重要载体，是丝绸之路沿线国家人文交流合作的战略平台，承载着重要的国家使命。

敦煌文博会以“推动文化交流、共谋合作发展”为宗旨，以丝绸之路精神为纽带，以文明互鉴与文化交流合作为主题，以实现民心相通为目标，着力打造国际化、高端化、专业化的国家级文化博览会，成为中国与丝绸之路沿线国家开展文化交流合作的重要平台、推动中华文化走出去的重要窗口、丝绸之路经济带建设的重要支撑。

2016年9月，首届敦煌文博会在甘肃省敦煌市举办。截至2024年底，敦煌文博会共举办七届。

## Dunhuang Cultural Expo

Dunhuang Cultural Expo (DCE), officially known as the "Silk Road (Dunhuang) International Cultural Expo", is an important platform for the BRI and serves as a strategic platform for cultural exchanges and cooperation among countries along the Silk Road, carrying significant national missions.

Opening Ceremony & Summit Conference

**Congratulatory Letter for the First Silk Road (Dunhuang) International Cultural Expo**

Xi Jinping

September 20th, 2016

On the occasion of the opening of the First Silk Road (Dunhuang) International Cultural Expo, I hereby, on behalf of the Chinese government and people, and in my own name, would like to extend warm congratulations on the Cultural Expo and express sincere welcome to all the distinguished guests and friends from different countries present at the Cultural Expo.

Over 2,000 years ago, the ancient Silk Road connecting Asia with Europe served as an important bridge for friendly exchanges and civilization communications between the East and West. In the history, Dunhuang was the significant hub of cultural interactions between the East and West. Here different cultures converged and integrated, shaping the unique Dunhuang Culture with great charms. The history proves that mutual learning and common progress of all national cultures around the world are the basic features of human civilization as well as the driving force of its development. With Promoting Cultural Exchange and Development through Cooperation as its theme, the Cultural Expo will provide a significant platform for cooperation and interaction among the countries along the Silk Road. We should insist on diversity and coexistence, mutual learning and common progress, cooperation and mutual benefit, to strengthen cultural exchange, promote cultural equality, protect cultural heritage, enhance cultural innovation and reinforce cultural cooperation, to help more people enjoy the rich and colorful cultures created by the human beings, and to make the world a better place.

DCE aims to promote cultural exchanges and seek cooperative development. It reinvigorates the spirit of the Silk Road as a bond and focuses on mutual learning among civilizations and cultural exchange cooperation, with a goal of achieving connections between hearts. It seeks to create an internationalized, high-end, and specialized national cultural expo, become an important platform for cultural exchanges and cooperation between China and countries along the Silk Road, serve as a big window for promoting Chinese culture abroad, and provide vital support for the construction of the Silk Road economic belt.

The first DCE was held in September 2016 in Dunhuang, Gansu Province. As of the end of 2024, DCE had been held seven times.

## 《敦煌宣言》

2016年9月，在首届敦煌文博会高峰会议上，与会丝路沿线国家就进一步加强文化交流合作达成共识，共同发布了《敦煌宣言》。

《敦煌宣言》本着“推动文化交流、共谋合作发展”的宗旨，回顾了亚欧大陆人民共同开辟丝绸之路这条友谊之路的丰硕成果，赞扬了“和平合作、开放包容、互学互鉴、互利共赢”的丝路精神，肯定了敦煌文化是不同文明交流互鉴的典范，强调了深化人文交流，共建“一带一路”的决心，并就进一步加强文化交流合作达成四点共识，即坚持文化多样性平等性包容性、保护传承各国历史文化遗产、加强各层次文化对话与合作、促进文化贸易与文化产业合作。

《敦煌宣言》公布了以后各方的协同工作计划，包括：丝路沿线国家将举办高级别论坛，开展政府间高层次文化对话，协商制定政府间文化合作框架，制定行动纲领，以制度性安排推动政府间文化对话的持续高效；同时，扩大民间往来和学界、智库的交流，广泛开展文学艺术、新闻出版、广播影视、人文社科等领域合作交流，举办各类主题鲜明、彰显特色的文化活动，共同推进重大合作项目。《敦煌宣言》的践行，必将促进丝路沿线国家的文化交流和文明互鉴。

## *Dunhuang Declaration*

At the summit meeting of the first DCE in September 2016, countries along the Silk Road reached consensus on further strengthening cultural exchanges and cooperation and collectively issued the *Dunhuang Declaration*.

The *Dunhuang Declaration* is based on the principle of "promoting cultural exchanges and seeking cooperative development". It reviewed the fruitful achievements of the peoples of the Eurasian continent since blazing the Silk Road as a path of friendship, praised the Silk Road Spirit of "unity and mutual trust, equality and mutual benefits, inclusiveness and mutual learning, and win-win cooperation", affirmed that Dunhuang culture exemplifies the exchanges and mutual learning among different civilizations, and emphasized determination to deepen cultural exchanges and jointly build the Belt and Road. The Declaration also reached four points of consensus to strengthen cultural exchanges and cooperation: 1. Adhere to cultural diversity, equality, and inclusiveness; 2. Protect and inherit the historical and cultural heritage of all countries; 3. Strengthen cultural dialogue and cooperation at all levels; 4. Promote cultural trade and cooperation in the cultural industry.

After the announcement of the *Dunhuang Declaration*, a collaborative work plan was made that included organization of high-level forums in countries along the Silk Road, scheduling of intergovernmental high-level cultural dialogues, negotiation of an intergovernmental cultural cooperation framework, and formulation of an action plan. Institutional arrangements will be made to promote sustained, efficient intergovernmental cultural dialogue. Moreover, efforts will be made to expand exchanges among civil societies, academia, and think tanks, and carry out cooperation and exchanges in fields such as literature, arts, news, broadcasting, and film as well as humanities and social sciences. Various cultural activities with distinct themes and characteristics will be organized to jointly advance major cooperation projects. The implementation of the *Dunhuang Declaration* will undoubtedly promote cultural exchanges and mutual learning among all the cultures along the Silk Road.

## 敦煌论坛

“敦煌论坛”原为敦煌研究院主办的大型国际学术研讨会品牌。2010 年 7 月，第一次敦煌论坛“2010 敦煌论坛：吐蕃时期敦煌石窟艺术国际研讨会”在莫高窟召开，来自日本、法国、瑞士、新加坡、中国大陆及台湾地区等 30 多家高校和科研机构近 50 位学者出席了会议，集中展示了老中青三代学者在敦煌吐蕃石窟艺术研究方面的丰硕成果。

## Dunhuang Forum

The Dunhuang Forum was originally a large international academic seminar organized by the Dunhuang Academy.

In July 2010, the first Dunhuang Forum, titled "2010 Dunhuang Forum: International Symposium on Dunhuang Cave Art During the Tubo Period", was held at the Mogao Caves. Nearly 50 scholars from more than 30 universities and research institutions in Japan, France, Switzerland, Singapore, Chinese mainland, and China's Taiwan region attended and showcased fruitful results of research on Dunhuang Tubo cave art.

2016 年，首届敦煌文博会将“敦煌论坛”这一学术会议品牌纳入其常设活动，论坛以打造敦煌文化制高点、文旅融合新样板、国际交流新高地为重点，深入挖掘丝路文化精髓，着力打造敦煌学研究高地，为该领域国际的对话与合作搭建良好学术交流平台。

2023 年第六届敦煌文博会，围绕传承弘扬丝路精神、共建“一带一路”等分别举办 12 场“敦煌论坛”，从不同文化背景、不同领域、不同角度深入阐述文明交流互鉴的重要作用、主要特征及实现途径，为落实全球文明倡议、推动共建“一带一路”高质量发展、创造人类文明新形态贡献了真知灼见。

In 2016, the first DCE included the Dunhuang Forum as one of its permanent activities. The forum focuses on establishing a high point for Dunhuang culture, a new model for the integration of culture and tourism, and a new pedestal for international exchanges. It explores the essence of Silk Road culture extensively and aims to elevate Dunhuang studies by providing a platform for academic exchanges, dialogues, and cooperation in this field.

At the sixth DCE in 2023, 12 Dunhuang Forums were organized, themed around inheriting and promoting the Silk Road Spirit and jointly building the BRI. These forums featured in-depth discussions on the important role, main characteristics, and methods of realizing civilizational exchanges and mutual learning from various cultural backgrounds, fields, and perspectives, contributing valuable insights for implementing global civilization initiatives, promoting high-quality development of the BRI, and creating a new form of human civilization.

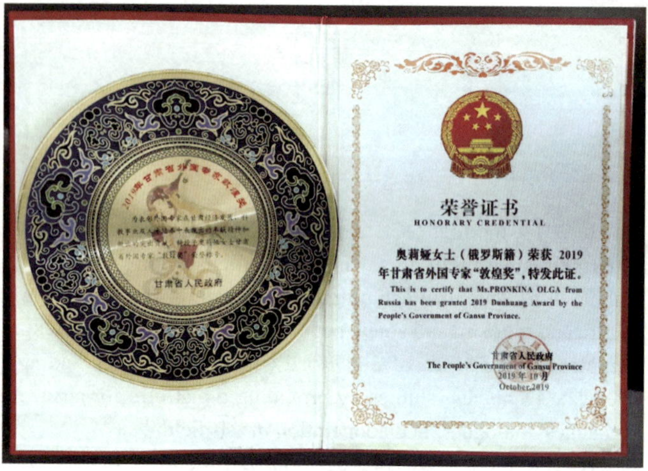


## 敦煌奖

“敦煌奖”是甘肃省人民政府于 1996 年 10 月设立的外国专家荣誉奖项，旨在表彰在甘肃省经济社会发展中做出突出贡献的外国专家。

该奖项每三年评选一次，有多位致力于敦煌文化遗产保护与敦煌文化传播的外国友人获此殊荣，如 2016 年获得者为美国人倪密·盖茨（Mimi Gates），是美国敦煌基金会理事会主席，西雅图艺术博物馆前任馆长。2019 年获得者俄罗斯人普隆金娜·奥莉娅（Pronkina Olga），现任甘肃政法大学教授。2022 年获得者为英国人海瑟·安·威尔斯（Heather Viles），现任牛津大学教授。

## Dunhuang Award

The Dunhuang Award is an honorary award established by the Gansu Provincial People's Government in October 1996 to recognize foreign experts who have made outstanding contributions to the economic and social development of Gansu Province.

This award is granted every three years, and several foreign friends who have become dedicated to the protection and promotion of Dunhuang cultural heritage have received the honor. For instance, the recipient in 2016 was Mimi Gates from the United States, chair of the Dunhuang Foundation and former curator of the Seattle Art Museum. The 2019 recipient was Pronkina Olga from Russia, who is a professor at Gansu University of Political Science and Law. The 2022 recipient was Heather Viles from the UK, who is currently a professor at the University of Oxford.

## 敦煌纪录片

1954年，许珂编导的纪录片《敦煌壁画》在中央新闻纪录电影制片厂出品，这是中国第一部敦煌主题的纪录片。1980年，日本放送协会（NHK）和中国中央电视台（CCTV）联合制作的纪录片《丝绸之路》上映，该片走进古代贯穿欧、亚的丝绸之路，探索其间的壮丽景观、历险故事、文化艺术及沿途人民生活状况，其中第3集重点介绍了敦煌，让全世界注意到了敦煌文化和敦煌艺术。

2008年，日本放送协会推出《敦煌莫高窟：美的全貌》，集中展示了莫高窟30个代表洞窟面貌。2010年，敦煌研究院与中视传媒股份有限公司共同出品了大型人文纪录片《敦煌》，从国外探险家、莫高窟、藏经洞、壁画、彩塑、乐舞、丝绸之路、敦煌守望者等角度，展示了敦煌地区1000多年的历史和生

## Dunhuang Documentaries

In 1954, the documentary *Dunhuang Murals*, directed by Xu Ke, was produced by the Central News Documentary Film Studio, marking the first Dunhuang-themed documentary in China. In 1980, *The Silk Road*, co-produced by the Japan Broadcasting Corporation (NHK) and China Central Television (CCTV), premiered. This film explored the ancient Silk Road that connected Europe and Asia, showcasing its magnificent landscapes, adventurous stories, culture and arts, and the living conditions of those along the route. Its third episode focuses on Dunhuang, drawing global attention to Dunhuang culture and art.

In 2008, NHK released *Dunhuang Mogao Caves: The Complete Beauty*, which presented an overview of 30 representative caves at Mogao. In 2010, the Dunhuang Academy and China Television Media Co., Ltd. jointly produced the large-scale cultural documentary *Dunhuang*, showcasing over 1,000 years of history and life in the Dunhuang region from various perspectives, including foreign explorers, the Mogao Caves, the Library Cave, murals, sculptures, music and dance, the Silk Road, and the guardians of Dunhuang. It premiered on the CCTV News Channel the same year and exerted a significant impact on society. From this documentary, many learned about Dunhuang for the first time and subsequently became advocates and guardians of Dunhuang culture.

活。该纪录片于同年在中国央视新闻频道首播，在社会上引起了极大反响。因为这部纪录片，许多人第一次知道了敦煌，继而成为敦煌文化的传播者和守护者。

此后，随着对敦煌文化的日益关注，中国陆续推出了系列敦煌纪录片，多角度讲述敦煌作为古代丝路重镇、东西方文明交流十字路口所蕴含的丰富的历史、艺术、科技和文化价值。

With the growing attention on Dunhuang culture since, China has successively launched a series of Dunhuang documentaries, which narrate the rich historical, artistic, technological, and cultural values embodied by Dunhuang as an ancient hub on the Silk Road and a crossroads for exchanges between Eastern and Western civilizations from multiple perspectives.

## 《丝路花雨》

《丝路花雨》1979年诞生于中国西北的兰州，由中国甘肃省歌舞团（今甘肃敦煌艺术剧院）创作并首演，是取材于敦煌壁画的中国大型民族舞剧。该剧是以中国唐朝极盛时期为背景的六场历史舞剧，歌颂了老画工神笔张和歌伎英娘父女俩的艺术劳动，描写了他们的悲欢离合，以及他们与波斯商人伊努斯之间的纯洁友谊。高度颂扬了中原和西域人民源远流长的友谊，再现了唐朝内政昌明、对外经济文化交往频繁的盛况。其中，女主角英娘表演的“反弹琵琶”，成为中国舞的经典造型。

《丝路花雨》搬上舞台40多年来，历久弥新，不仅是中国甘肃的一张名片，更享有“中国民族舞剧之最”“中国民族舞剧里程碑”“东方的天鹅湖”等美誉。该剧久演不衰，所到之处盛况空前。该剧被誉为“中国民族舞剧的典范”，并作为20世纪中国舞蹈经典剧目载入中华民族艺术史册。

## *Along the Silk Road*

*Along the Silk Road* was created and premiered in 1979 in Lanzhou, northwestern China, by Gansu Song and Dance Troupe (now Gansu Dunhuang Arts Theatre). It is a large-scale Chinese ethnic dance drama inspired by Dunhuang murals. The play consists of six historical dance dramas set against the backdrop of the Tang Dynasty at its peak, celebrating the artistic labor of the old painter Zhang and his daughter, Ying Niang, a singer. It depicts their joys and sorrows, as well as their pure friendship with a Persian merchant named Yinus. The drama celebrates the long-standing friendship between the people of the Central Plains and the Western Regions, showcasing the flourishing internal governance and frequent economic and cultural exchanges during the Tang time. Notably, the *Playing the* Pipa *from the Back* performed by the female lead has become a classic pose in Chinese dance.

*Along the Silk Road* has been staged for over 40 years and remains as fresh as ever. It is not only a calling card for Gansu, China, but also enjoys reputation as "the best Chinese ethnic dance drama", "a milestone in Chinese ethnic dance drama", and "Swan Lake of the East". The play has been performed extensively, drawing unprecedented crowds wherever it has been shown. Regarded as a "model of Chinese ethnic dance drama", it has been included in the annals of Chinese national art history as a classic work of 20th-century Chinese dance.

## 中国敦煌吐鲁番学会

中国敦煌吐鲁番学会于 1983 年 8 月在兰州成立，以组织与团结国内敦煌吐鲁番学研究者开展相关学术研究与文物保护、推进国际学术文化交流为宗旨。第一任会长为国学大师季羡林，学会秘书处先设立于北京大学，2000 年转至首都师范大学。学会主办学术集刊《敦煌吐鲁番研究》和《敦煌学国际联络委员会通讯》。

## Institute of Dunhuang and Turfan Studies of China

The Institute of Dunhuang and Turfan Studies of China (IDTSC) was established in August 1983 in Lanzhou with an aim to organize and unite domestic researchers in Dunhuang and Turfan studies to conduct relevant academic research and cultural relic protection, as well as promoting international academic and cultural exchanges. The first president was the Chinese scholar Ji Xianlin, and the society's secretariat was placed at Peking University, but moved to Capital Normal University in 2000. It publishes the academic journals *Dunhuang and Turfan Studies* and *Dunhuang Studies International Liaison Committee Newsletter*.

学会与英、美、日、法、俄等敦煌学研究的重要机构合作，先后在日本京都、美国普林斯顿、俄罗斯圣彼得堡、英国剑桥大学等地举办国际性的敦煌学学术会议，有效促进了全世界敦煌学者之间的联系。学会的成立从根本上改变了“敦煌在中国，敦煌学在国外”的状况。近年来，学会集中力量实施“敦煌文献系统性保护整理出版工程”，这项工程不但保持中国敦煌吐鲁番学的可持续发展，同时也为全世界的学者刊布最全面的敦煌吐鲁番学资料。

Over the past few years, the IDTSC has collaborated with major institutions in Dunhuang studies from the UK, the U.S., Japan, France, and Russia, hosting international academic conferences in locations such as Kyoto, Princeton, St. Petersburg, and Cambridge, thus effectively facilitating connections among Dunhuang scholars worldwide. The establishment of the society has fundamentally changed the situation when many sighed, "Dunhuang is in China, but Dunhuang studies are done abroad". In recent years, the IDTSC has focused on implementing the Systematic Protection, Organization, and Publication Project of Dunhuang Literature, which has not only ensured the sustainable development of Dunhuang and Turfan studies in China, but also provided scholars worldwide with the most comprehensive resources on Dunhuang and Turfan studies.

## 东京艺术大学敦煌项目

东京艺术大学是日本唯一的艺术类国立大学，在日本国内被公认为日本最高的艺术家培养学府。

20 世纪 70 年代末，日本著名画家平山郁夫第一次访问敦煌莫高窟。受到敦煌壁画艺术强烈冲击的他，开始为敦煌石窟的保护与研究四处奔走，募集资金。20 世纪 80 年代，平山郁夫先生积极促成东京艺术大学携手敦煌研究院，在敦煌学、石窟考古、文物保护等领域开展合作，双方有计划地互相派遣学者进行专业研修培训和学术考察。

## The Dunhuang Project by Tokyo University of the Arts

Tokyo University of the Arts (TUA) is Japan's only national university for the arts and the highest institution for training artists in Japan.

In the late 1970s, famous Japanese painter Ikuo Hirayama (1930-2009) visited the Mogao Caves in Dunhuang for the first time. Deeply impressed by the art of Dunhuang's murals, he began to advocate for the protection and research of the Dunhuang caves and raise funds for the cause. In the 1980s, Hirayama actively facilitated collaboration between TUA and the Dunhuang Academy in fields such as Dunhuang studies, cave archaeology, and cultural relic preservation. Both parties planned to send scholars for professional training and academic investigations.

自1983年开始，敦煌研究院陆续派遣了50余位研究人员到东京艺术大学进行研修学习，在敦煌文物事业发展和敦煌学各专业领域发挥了重要作用。东京艺术大学也已派遣近百名美术、修复等专业的学生到敦煌研究院研修，定期或不定期合作轮流举办学术交流报告会，合作成果交流共享。1988年8月，时任日本首相的竹下登到访中国，访问了敦煌莫高窟，随后援助建成敦煌石窟保护研究陈列中心。

Since 1983, the Dunhuang Academy has successively sent over 50 researchers to TUA for training and study, hence playing an important part in the development of Dunhuang relics and various specialized fields of Dunhuang studies. TUA has also sent nearly 100 students majoring in fine arts, restoration, and other fields to the Academy for training. The two institutions have frequently arranged academic exchange seminars to share the results of their collaboration. In August 1988, Noboru Takeshita (1924-2000), then prime minister of Japan, visited China and toured the Mogao Caves in Dunhuang, after which Japan provided assistance on establishing the Dunhuang Cave Protection & Research Exhibition Center.

## 美国盖蒂保护研究所敦煌保护项目

美国盖蒂保护研究所是盖蒂基金会的组成部分，成立于1985年。中国敦煌研究院自1989年与美国盖蒂保护研究所开始合作，至今已有30多年，双方长期展开研究项目合作，尤其是在莫高窟第85窟壁画保护项目长达7年的合作时间里，从壁画的价值评估到修复材料的准备，再到成功修复，解决了以往壁画修复中存在的诸多难题。作为该机构敦煌项目的文物保护专家，内维尔·阿格纽（Neville Agnew）获得了中国政府友谊奖和国际科学技术合作奖。

盖蒂保护研究所在文物保护领域多方面都拥有先进的理念和丰富的经验，中美双方在项目合作中找到更多的共鸣，并从中改善壁画修复技术、修复程序及管理理念，通过项目合作、创新方法和模式保护策略，总结出一整套既符合国际惯例又适合中国国情的先进壁画保护理念和遗址管理方法。

## Getty Conservation Institute: Dunhuang Preservation Project

The Getty Conservation Institute (GCI) is part of the Getty Foundation, established in 1985. The Dunhuang Academy has collaborated with the Getty Conservation Institute for nearly 30 years since 1989. The two parties have engaged in long-term research project cooperation, particularly in the preservation of the murals in Cave 85 of the Mogao Caves, which lasted seven years. This collaboration addressed many challenges previously encountered in mural restoration, ranging from value assessment of the murals to the preparation of restoration materials and successful restoration efforts. Neville Agnew, a conservation expert on the Dunhuang project, received the Chinese government's Friendship Award and the International Scientific and Technological Cooperation Award for his contributions.

The GCI boasts advanced concepts and extensive experience in the field of cultural heritage conservation. Through project collaboration, China and the United States found great resonance in improving mural restoration techniques, restoration processes, and management philosophies. Working together on projects and employing innovative methods and model protection strategies, participants have summarized a comprehensive set of advanced mural protection concepts and site management methods that align with international practices while being suitable for China's specific conditions.

## 法国远东学院与敦煌学

法国远东学院（简称 EFEO）前身为 1898 年成立的法国印度支那考古学调查会，1900 年改为现名。该机构的主要任务是研究亚洲的古典文明，已在亚洲的多个国家和地区共设立了 18 个联络中心。

20 世纪初，伯希和作为 1899—1911 年的法国远东学院成员，从敦煌带来数量巨大的古代文献，现被收藏于法国国家图书馆和吉美亚洲艺术博物馆。这些敦煌收集品，为中世纪中国历史、汉传佛教、佛教中国化以及中古佛

## École Française d'Extrême-Orient

École Française d'Extrême-Orient (EFEO), formerly known as the French Indochina Archaeological Survey Committee, was established in 1898 and renamed in 1900. Specializing in the study of the classical civilizations of Asia, EFEO has established 18 liaison centers in various countries and regions across Asia.

In the early 20th Century, Paul Pelliot, a member of EFEO from 1899 to 1911, brought back vast quantities of ancient texts from Dunhuang, which are housed in the National Library of France and Guimet Museum. These Dunhuang collections provide new materials for the study of medieval Chinese history, Chinese Buddhism, the Sinicization of Buddhism, and medieval Buddhist art.

教艺术的研究提供了全新的资料。

法藏敦煌资料数十年来一直吸引着法国学者，同时也引导了法国汉学的发展方向。不少在敦煌研究领域发挥关键作用的杰出学者都曾经在法国远东学院工作过。法国远东学院和敦煌研究院已有 20 多年的合作历史，通过定期的研究人员交流和科学协作，法国远东学院为敦煌研究院学者在法国查阅敦煌资料、提升学术水平提供了重要的支持。

These materials have attracted French scholars for decades and guided sinology in France. Many distinguished scholars who have played key roles in Dunhuang studies have worked at EFEO. Cooperation between EFEO and the Dunhuang Academy has continued for over 20 years, offering important support for Dunhuang researchers to access materials in France and enhance their academic abilities through regular exchanges and scientific collaboration.

## 中国敦煌石窟保护研究基金会

中国敦煌石窟保护研究基金会，是在中国国家领导人的关注、海内外有识之士和敦煌研究院的支持、资助下创办的中国全国性公募基金会。1994 年经中国人民银行批准成立，该基金会的宗旨是“在国家法律、法规和政策范围内，用公募资金从事中国敦煌石窟保护、研究、弘扬的公益活动”。

多年来，该基金会全面开展公益活动，形成了以敦煌石窟保护、敦煌石窟壁画数字化项目、敦煌学学术交流、敦煌学学术成果出版、敦煌学人才培养、敦煌石窟艺术弘扬等为主要内容的特色公益项目，持续推出“敦煌壁画精品艺术高校公益巡展”，为国际敦煌学的发展做出了重要贡献。

## China Dunhuang Grottoes Conservation Research Foundation

The China Dunhuang Grottoes Conservation Research Foundation (CDGCRF) is a national public fundraising organization established with the support and funding of national leaders, insightful individuals from home and abroad, and the Dunhuang Academy. Approved by the People's Bank of China in 1994, the CDGCRF was established with the purpose of engaging in public welfare activities for the protection, research, and promotion of the Dunhuang Caves within the framework of national laws, regulations, and policies.

Over the years, the CDGCRF has organized comprehensive public welfare activities, forming distinctive projects focused on Dunhuang cave protection, digitization of Dunhuang cave murals, academic exchanges in Dunhuang studies, publication of academic achievements, training of Dunhuang studies talents, and promotion of Dunhuang cave art. It continues to manage the CDGCRF, making significant contributions to the international development of Dunhuang studies.

## 香港敦煌之友基金会

2010 年 5 月，在国学大师饶宗颐的号召下，由热爱敦煌艺术和中华文化的人士组成、在中国香港特别行政区注册的非营利公益团体“香港敦煌之友”正式成立。该组织的创会成员包括余志明、李焯芬、李美贤、纪文凤及黄炳培等，宗旨是作为热衷敦煌文化人士的香港平台，连同香港和各方热爱敦煌文化的机构，支持敦煌研究院保护、保育敦煌石窟及培育人才；在香港推广敦煌文化及在海外弘扬敦煌文化。

“香港敦煌之友”自成立以来，通过社会力量募集的善款，用于敦煌石窟壁画的数字化、敦煌石窟的保护维修、莫高窟环境保护、人才培养、资助敦煌研究院学者赴丝绸之路沿线进行学术考察等，有力地支持了敦煌石窟的保护研究。

## Friends of Dunhuang (Hong Kong) Limited

Friends of Dunhuang (Hong Kong) Limited (FoDHK) is a non-profit organization incorporated in May 2010 in the Hong Kong Special Administrative Region, launched by Jao Tsung-I, a renowned Chinese scholar, artist, and expert in Chinese culture. Founding members included Gabriel Chi Ming Yu, Chack Fan Lee, Lee Mei Yin, Leonie Ki, and Stanley Wong, among others. FoDHK aims to provide a platform for enthusiasts of Dunhuang culture in Hong Kong to better collaborate with various organizations that cherish Dunhuang culture and support the Dunhuang Academy in protecting the Dunhuang Caves and cultivating talent. It also endeavors to promote Dunhuang culture in both Hong Kong and other parts of the world.

Since its establishment, FoDHK has raised funds through social initiatives to support various activities including the digitization of Dunhuang cave murals, maintenance and protection of the Dunhuang caves, environmental conservation at the Mogao Caves, talent training, and funding scholars from Dunhuang to conduct academic investigations along the Silk Road. These efforts have significantly bolstered the research and protection of the Dunhuang Caves.

## 国际敦煌项目

国际敦煌项目（IDP）是一项卓有成效的敦煌西域文献文物数字化合作项目。1994 年成立，其秘书处设在英国国家图书馆。1998 年，IDP 网站（http://idp.nlc.cn/）开通。

这是一个开创性的国际协作项目，目标是使敦煌及丝绸之路东段其他考古遗址出土的写本、绘画、纺织品以及艺术品的信息与图像能在互联网上自由地获取，它致力于推动文献保护修复与研究的国际合作，向全世界各层次的使用者提供优质的敦煌西域文献图像，并通过教育与研究项目鼓励用户利用这些资源。IDP 通过合作的方式，先后在北京、圣彼得堡、京都、柏林、敦煌、巴黎设立中心，包括中、英、法、俄敦煌文献四大收藏机构都设有 IDP 中心，全世界合作机构多达 20 多家。中国国家图书馆和敦煌研究院是 IDP 在中国合作的主要机构，也是 IDP 中文版的运营者。截至 2024 年 9 月，IDP 网站拥有 6 种文字版本，已成为全世界提供敦煌藏经洞文献文物图片最多、覆盖面最广的数据库。

## International Dunhuang Project

Established in 1994, the International Dunhuang Project (IDP) is a highly-effective collaboration focused on digitization of Dunhuang and Western Regions literature and artifacts. Its secretariat is located at the British Library. The IDP website (http://idp.nlc.cn/) was opened in 1998.

This pioneering international collaboration aims to make information and images of manuscripts, paintings, textiles, and artworks unearthed from Dunhuang and other archaeological sites along the eastern Silk Road freely accessible on the internet. It is dedicated to promoting international cooperation in the preservation, restoration, and research of documents, providing high-quality images of Dunhuang literature to users worldwide, and encouraging the utilization of these resources through educational and research initiatives. The IDP has established centers through partnerships in various cities including Beijing, St. Petersburg, Kyoto, Berlin, Dunhuang, and Paris. Major Dunhuang literature collections from China, the UK, France, and Russia have IDP centers, with over 20 collaborating institutions globally. The National Library of China and the Dunhuang Academy are the primary Chinese collaborators in the IDP as well as the operators of the Chinese version of the IDP website. As of September 2024, the IDP website had become the world's largest, most comprehensive database of Dunhuang cave literature and artifact images, featuring six language versions.

## 数字敦煌

敦煌研究院自20世纪80年代末开始提出“数字敦煌”的构想，并与海内外高等院校及科研机构密切合作，探索研究不可移动文物数字化保护，旨在利用计算机技术和数字图像技术，实现敦煌石窟文物的永久保存、永续利用。

“数字敦煌”项目主要包括敦煌石窟数字化、“数字敦煌”数字资产管理系统、永久存储体系和资源库四个方面。该项目利用先进的科学技术与文物保护理念，对敦煌石窟和相关文物进行全面的数字化采集、加工和存储，构建出一个多元化与智能化相结合的石窟文物数字化资源库，并通过互联网和移动互联网面向全球共享。

2016年，“数字敦煌资源库”（https://e-dunhuang.com/）上线，推出30个经典洞窟高清全景虚拟漫游；2017年，“数字敦煌资源库”英文版上线，访问用户来自全球约18个国家。2022年全球首个基于区块链的数字文化遗产开放共享平台“数字敦煌素材库”上线，2024年汇集全球范围内敦煌学研究成果与相关一手资料的“敦煌学研究文献库”上线。“数字敦煌”平台极大地促进了敦煌石窟、敦煌资料的科学保护和数据资源合理有序的利用，为科研人员提供了便捷的信息获取渠道，同时打破时间和空间的限制，满足了公众游览欣赏需求。

## Digital Dunhuang

Since the late 1980s, the Dunhuang Academy has championed the concept of "Digital Dunhuang" by collaborating with domestic and international universities and research institutions to explore the digitization and preservation of immovable cultural heritage. The aim is to utilize computer and digital imaging technologies to achieve the permanent preservation and sustainable use of Dunhuang cave relics.

The "Digital Dunhuang" project can be divided into four main realms: digitization of the Dunhuang caves, the "Digital Dunhuang" digital asset management system, a permanent storage system, and a resource repository. This project employs advanced technology and concepts of relic protection to comprehensively digitize, process, and store materials related to the Dunhuang Caves, establishing a diversified, intelligent digital resource repository for cave relics, which is shared globally through the internet and mobile internet.

The year 2016 witnessed the launch of Digital Dunhuang-Resource Library (https://e-dunhuang.com/), featuring high-definition panoramic virtual tours of 30 classic caves. In 2017, the English version of the Resource Library was launched, drawing users from 18 countries worldwide. In 2022, the world's first blockchain-based open-access platform for digital cultural heritage, the "Digital Dunhuang Resource Library," was launched. By 2024, the Dunhuang Research Archive—a comprehensive collection of global Dunhuang studies research and primary source materials—went live. This has greatly facilitated the scientific protection of the Dunhuang Caves and the rational, orderly use of data resources, providing researchers with convenient access to information while breaking the constraints of time and space, thus meeting public demand for exploration and appreciation.

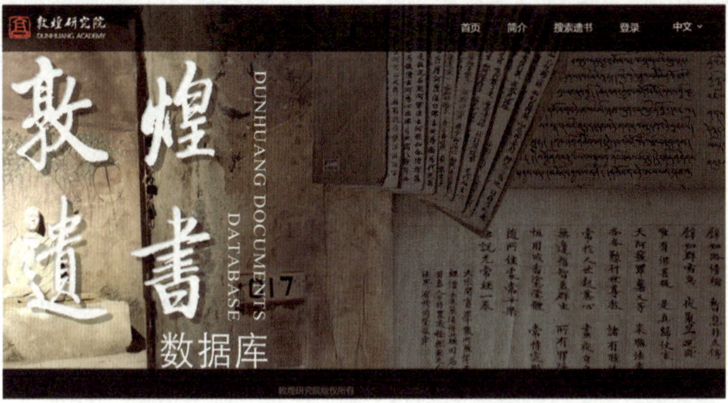


## 敦煌遗书数据库

2019年8月，习近平在敦煌研究院座谈时指出：要通过数字化、信息化等高技术手段，推动流散海外的敦煌遗书等文物的数字化回归，实现敦煌文化艺术资源在全球范围内的数字化共享。

2021年，中国敦煌研究院敦煌文献研究所承担、敦煌学专家马德主持的国家社科基金重大项目《敦煌遗书数据库建设》结项，为全世界敦煌学研究提供了一个全新的检索平台。

2022年8月，敦煌研究院宣布，“敦煌遗书数据库”（https://dhyssjk.dha.ac.cn/）正式上线。该平台已成为全球敦煌文献资源的重要共享平台，内容包括敦煌文献的基本信息、数字图像、全文录文和相关研究文献目录四个部分。截至2024年12月，已公布敦煌藏经洞出土文献和艺术品信息共计10212件，并提供汉、藏、回鹘文文献的全文检索和图文对照浏览。该数据库的上线不仅使流散于世界各地的敦煌藏经洞出土品以数字化的形式呈现给观众，而且填补了同类数据库在藏文和回鹘文录文方面的空白，使敦煌流失文物的数字化回归进程向前迈进了一大步。

## Dunhuang Documents Database

During an August 2019 meeting at the Dunhuang Academy, President Xi Jinping emphasized the need to promote the digital return of Dunhuang manuscripts and other cultural relics scattered overseas through high-tech means such as digitization and informatization, aiming for global digital sharing of Dunhuang cultural and artistic resources.

The year 2021 brought the completion of the construction of Dunhuang Documents Database project, a major project of the National Social Science Fund, led by Dunhuang studies expert Ma De and undertaken by the Academy's Dunhuang Manuscript Research Institute, providing a new search platform for Dunhuang studies worldwide.

In August 2022, the Dunhuang Academy announced the official launch of the Dunhuang Documents Database (https://dhyssjk.dha.ac.cn/), which has become an important sharing hub for global Dunhuang literature resources. This website comprises four sections: basic information on Dunhuang manuscripts, digital images, full texts, and related research literature directories. As of December 2024, a total of 10,212 pieces of information about manuscripts and artworks unearthed from the Dunhuang Mogao Caves had been published, offering full-text searches and visual comparisons for manuscripts in Chinese, Tibetan, and Uighur. The database not only presents the relics from the Dunhuang Caves in a digital format to audiences worldwide, but also fills a gap in similar databases concerning Tibetan and Uighur texts, making significant progress in the digital return process of Dunhuang cultural relics.

## 云游敦煌

为了展示敦煌文物与敦煌艺术，敦煌研究院于 2020 年 2 月推出了首个集探索、游览、保护功能于一体的敦煌主题小程序——云游敦煌。该程序应用全新的数字创意和交互形式演绎敦煌文化内涵，成为公众线上浏览敦煌文化艺术的服务窗口。小程序中包括敦煌画语、敦煌动画剧、有声敦煌、《敦煌岁时节令》等 10 余个特色板块，让海内外数字用户在线上即可了解敦煌，体悟敦煌千年的智慧与美。

截至 2024 年 6 月，“云游敦煌”小程序的阅读量超过 6262 万人次，全网新闻报道超 2 万篇。它既是文博线上游览的代表作品，也是中国乃至全球数字文保领域全新的里程碑。

“云游敦煌”小程序不仅展示了敦煌文物与敦煌艺术，还对它们进行了全新的创作，让敦煌文化以崭新的面貌融入现代社会，使古老的敦煌文化由此释放出全新的活力。科技赋能文化的组合，也成功引发了巨大的社交裂变效应，促进了敦煌文化的创新再生产，推动了传统文化在创新中普及、传播和传承。

## Cloud Tour of Dunhuang

To showcase Dunhuang artifacts and art, the Dunhuang Academy launched the first comprehensive Dunhuang-themed mini-program called "Cloud Tour of Dunhuang" in February 2020. This program integrates exploration, touring, and preservation functions, using innovative digital creativity and interactive formats to interpret the cultural connotations of Dunhuang. It serves as a window for the public to explore Dunhuang's cultural and artistic heritage online. The mini-program includes over 10 distinctive sections such as Dunhuang Painting Language, Dunhuang Animation Drama, Auditory Dunhuang, and Time and Seasons of Dunhuang, drawing digital users worldwide to learn about Dunhuang and experience its thousand-year wisdom and beauty.

By June 2024, the "Cloud Tour of Dunhuang" mini-program had recorded over 62.62 million views and inspired more than 20,000 online news reports. It is considered a representative work of online cultural heritage tourism and marks a new milestone in the field of digital cultural preservation in China and the world.

The "Cloud Tour of Dunhuang" mini-program not only displays Dunhuang artifacts and art, but also creatively re-imagines them, empowering Dunhuang culture to integrate into the modern world with a fresh perspective. This synergy of technology and culture has sparked significant social engagement, promoting innovative reproduction of Dunhuang culture and facilitating the popularization, dissemination, and inheritance of traditional culture through innovation.

# 敦煌历史纪年表

| 时代 / 王朝 | 起止时间 |
| --- | --- |
| 新石器时代 | 约公元前 2000 年—约公元前 1000 年 |
| 乌孙、月氏、匈奴争夺期 | 约公元前 2 世纪 |
| 西汉 | 元狩二年（公元前 121 年）—初始元年（8 年） |
| 新莽 | 始建国元年（9 年）—地皇四年（23 年） |
| 东汉 | 建武元年（25 年）—延康元年（220 年） |
| 三国曹魏 | 黄初元年（220 年）—咸熙二年（265 年） |
| 西晋 | 泰始元年（265 年）—建兴五年（317 年） |
| 东晋 | 建武元年（317 年）—元熙二年（420 年） |
| 前凉 | 建兴六年（318 年）—咸安六年（376 年） |
| 前秦 | 建元十二年（376 年）—太安二年（386 年） |
| 后凉 | 太安元年（386 年）—龙飞三年（398 年） |
| 北凉（段业） | 神玺二年（398 年）—天玺二年（400 年） |
| 西凉 | 庚子元年（400 年）—永建二年（421 年） |
| 北凉 | 玄始十年（421 年）—永和七年（439 年） |
| 北魏 | 太延五年（439 年）—永熙三年（534 年） |
| 西魏 | 大统元年（535 年）—恭帝三年（556 年） |
| 北周 | 宇文觉元年（557 年）—大定元年（581 年） |
| 隋 | 开皇元年（581 年）—义宁二年（618 年） |

# CHRONOLOGY OF DUNHUANG

| Period/Dynasty | Starting and ending time |
|---|---|
| Neolithic Age | circa 2000-1000 BC |
| Period of contention among Wusun, Yuezhi, and Xiongnu | around the 2nd Century BC |
| Western Han Dynasty | 121 BC-AD 8 |
| Xinmang Dynasty | 9-23 |
| Eastern Han Dynasty | 25-220 |
| Wei of the Three Kingdoms period | 220-265 |
| Western Jin Dynasty | 265-317 |
| Eastern Jin Dynasty | 317-420 |
| Former Liang Dynasty | 318-376 |
| Former Qin Dynasty | 376-386 |
| Later Liang Dynasty | 386-398 |
| Northern Liang Dynasty | 398-400 |
| Western Liang Dynasty | 400-421 |
| Northern Liang Dynasty | 421-439 |
| Northern Wei Dynasty | 439-534 |
| Western Wei Dynasty | 535-556 |
| Northern Zhou Dynasty | 557-581 |
| Sui Dynasty | 581-618 |

| | |
|---|---|
| 唐 | 武德元年（618 年）—天祐四年（907 年） |
| 初唐 | 武德元年（618 年）—长安四年（704 年） |
| 盛唐 | 神龙元年（705 年）—贞元元年（785 年） |
| 中唐（吐蕃时代） | 贞元二年（786 年）—大中元年（847 年） |
| 晚唐（张氏归义军） | 大中二年（848 年）—天祐四年（907 年） |
| 五代（西汉金山国至曹氏归义军前期） | 开平元年（907 年）—显德七年（960 年） |
| 后梁 | 开平元年（907 年）—龙德三年（923 年） |
| 后唐 | 同光元年（923 年）—清泰三年（936 年） |
| 后晋 | 天福元年（936 年）—开运四年（947 年） |
| 后汉 | 天福十二年（947 年）—乾祐三年（950 年） |
| 后周 | 广顺元年（951 年）—显德七年（960 年） |
| 北宋（曹氏归义军后期） | 建隆元年（960 年）—景祐二年（1035 年） |
| 西夏 | 大庆元年（1036 年）—宝义元年（1227 年） |
| 蒙古·元 | 成吉思汗二十二年（1227 年）—至正二十八年（1368 年） |
| 明 | 洪武元年（1368 年）—崇祯十七年（1644 年） |
| 清 | 顺治元年（1644 年）—宣统三年（1911 年） |
| 中华民国 | 1912—1949 年 |
| 中华人民共和国 | 1949 年 10 月 1 日至今 |

| | |
|---|---|
| Tang Dynasty | 618-907 |
| Early Tang | 618-704 |
| Grand Tang | 705-785 |
| Mid-Tang (Tubo period) | 786-847 |
| Late Tang (Zhang-led Guiyi Army period) | 848-907 |
| Five Dynasties period | 907-960 |
| Later Liang Dynasty | 907-923 |
| Later Tang Dynasty | 923-936 |
| Later Jin Dynasty | 936-947 |
| Later Han Dynasty | 947-950 |
| Later Zhou Dynasty | 951-960 |
| Northern Song Dynasty | 960-1035 |
| Western Xia Empire | 1036-1227 |
| Yuan Dynasty (Mongol) | 1227-1368 |
| Ming Dynasty | 1368-1644 |
| Qing Dynasty | 1644-1911 |
| Republic of China period | 1912-1949 |
| People's Republic of China | 1949 to present |

# 词条音序排列表


《案验康居王使者献驼册》 060
北宋敦煌官府的酒账 084
伯希和 048
大盛敦煌 004
东京艺术大学敦煌项目 240
敦煌壁画 114
敦煌藏经洞 110
敦煌的世界文化遗产 012
敦煌汉简 054
敦煌画派 216
敦煌纪录片 230
敦煌奖 228
《敦煌劫余录》 186
敦煌论坛 224
敦煌莫高窟 106
《敦煌石窟全集》 204
《敦煌石窟全集：莫高窟考古报告》 192
敦煌石窟群 102

《敦煌岁时节令》 210
敦煌文博会 220
敦煌仙子莫伽瑶 214
敦煌星图 070
《敦煌宣言》 222
敦煌学 016
《敦煌学大辞典》 196
敦煌研究院 174
敦煌研究院文物保护利用群体 176
敦煌研究院文物保护团队 178
敦煌遗书数据库 258
敦煌遗书与《敦煌文献全集》 190
《敦煌艺术大辞典》 198
多元文化圣殿 010
法国远东学院与敦煌学 246
反弹琵琶 136
飞天 128
国际敦煌项目 254
洪辩 038
胡商 160
胡旋舞 140

《金刚经》 074
井上靖《敦煌》 206
九层楼 122
九色鹿 132
兰州大学敦煌学研究所 182
美国盖蒂保护研究所敦煌保护项目 244
美人菩萨 144
民族融合之地 008
莫高精神 018
莫高窟的创建者 028
《秦妇吟》 078
睒子本生 148
室内第一大佛 120
数字敦煌 256
丝绸之路与丝路精神 006
丝路各民族群像 156
《丝路花雨》 234
斯坦因 044
唐代彩塑群像 124
《唐僧取经图》 168
王道士 040

《五台山图》 164
西汉生态环保墙书 058
香港敦煌之友基金会 252
《降魔变文》 092
《新修本草》 066
《行脚僧图》 096
悬泉置汉简 056
《叶净能诗》 088
《驿使图》 064
音乐窟 118
印度制糖法文献 082
元荣 032
云游敦煌 260
《张骞出使西域图》 152
张议潮 034
张芝 022
中国敦煌石窟保护研究基金会 250
中国敦煌吐鲁番学会 236
《中国石窟：敦煌莫高窟》 202
竺法护 026

# ALPHABETICAL INDEX


Academy's Team for Relics Protection and Utilization 179

*Along the Silk Road* 235

*An Analytical List of the Tun-Huang Manuscripts in the National Library of Peiping* 187

Apsaras 129

*Beauty Bodhisattva* 145

China Dunhuang Grottoes Conservation Research Foundation 251

*Chinese Grottoes: The Mogao Caves in Dunhuang* 203

Cloud Tour of Dunhuang 261

*Complete Collection of the Dunhuang Caves* 205

*Dictionary of Dunhuang Art* 199

*Dictionary of Dunhuang Studies* 197

Digital Dunhuang 257

Dunhuang Academy 175

Dunhuang Academy's Relics Protection and Utilization Team 177

Dunhuang Award 229

Dunhuang Cultural Expo 221

*Dunhuang Declaration* 223

Dunhuang Documentaries 231

Dunhuang Documents and *Complete Collection of Dunhuang Manuscripts* 191
Dunhuang Documents Database 259
Dunhuang Fairy Mo Jiayao 215
Dunhuang Forum 225
Dunhuang Han-Dynasty Bamboo Slips 055
Dunhuang Murals 115
Dunhuang School of Painting 217
Dunhuang Star Maps 071
Dunhuang Studies 017
École Française d'Extrême-Orient 247
Eco-Themed Wall Text of the Western Han Dynasty 059
Founders of Mogao Caves 029
Friends of Dunhuang (Hong Kong) Limited 253
Getty Conservation Institute: Dunhuang Preservation Project 245
Han-Dynasty Bamboo Slips, Xuanquan Posthouse Site 057
Hong Bian 039
Hu Merchants 161
Hub of Ethnic Integration 009
Inoue Yasushi's *Dunhuang* 207
Institute of Dunhuang and Turfan Studies of China 237
Institute of Dunhuang Studies, Lanzhou University 183

International Dunhuang Project 255
*Lament of the Lady of Qin* 079
Largest Indoor Buddha 121
Literature on Indian Sugar Production Methods 083
*Map of Mount Wutai* 165
Marc Aurel Stein 045
Mogao Spirit 019
Nine-Colored Deer 133
Nine-Story Building 123
Paul Pelliot 049
*Playing the* Pipa *from the Back* 137
Portrait of Ethnic Groups Along the Silk Road 157
Prosperous Dunhuang 005
Silk Road and Its Spirit 007
Sogdian Whirl Dance 141
Śyāmaka Jātaka 149
Tang-Dynasty Painted Statues Group 125
Temple of Multiculturalism 011
*The Courier* 065
*The Diamond Sutra* 075
The Dunhuang Caves Complex 103
The Dunhuang Project by Tokyo University of the Arts 241

*The General Collection of the Dunhuang Caves:*
*Archaeological Report of the Mogao Caves* 193
The Library Cave 111
The Mogao Caves at Dunhuang 107
The Music Cave 119
*The Newly-Compiled Materia Medica* 067
*The Official Document Regarding the Investigation of the*
*Camels Presented by the Kangju Envoy* 061
*The Stories of Ye Jingneng* 089
*The Transformation Text of Subjugation of Demons* 093
*The Traveling Monk* 097
*Time and Seasons of Dunhuang* 211
Wang Yuanlu 041
*Wine Accounts of the Dunhuang Government*
*During the Northern Song Dynasty* 085
World Cultural Heritage 013
*Xuanzang Going on a Pilgrimage for Buddhist Scriptures* 169
Yuan Rong 033
*Zhang Qian's Diplomatic Missions to the Western Regions* 153
Zhang Yichao 035
Zhang Zhi 023
Zhu Fahu 027

## 中国外文出版发行事业局

又称中国国际传播集团，是中国历史最悠久、规模最大的专业对外传播机构，业务涵盖翻译、出版、印刷、发行、互联网与多媒体、国际传播理论研究等多个领域，业务布局覆盖全球主要国家和地区。

## 敦煌研究院

世界最大的敦煌学研究实体，集石窟保护、学术研究、文化弘扬功能于一体的综合型文博机构，管理包括莫高窟等 3 处世界文化遗产在内的 6 座石窟，是中国管理石窟数量最多的文博机构，贯穿 1600 年历史，记录丝路东西交流；书写多民族记忆，展望“一带一路”新篇。

## 当代中国与世界研究院

国家专业智库机构，以应用研究和对策研究为特色，致力于当代中国与世界、讲好中国故事、翻译与对外话语体系、国际传播、世界舆情等研究工作，隶属中国外文出版发行事业局。

## 中国翻译研究院

国家级翻译智库平台，以翻译和对外话语体系应用研究为特色，致力于国家翻译能力研究、翻译与文明交流研究、重大对外翻译项目策划实施、高端翻译人才培养、跨文化交流合作等工作，隶属中国外文出版发行事业局。

### China International Communications Group

China International Communications Group (CICG) is China's oldest and largest publisher with an international focus. Spanning all continents, its business covers translation, publishing, printing, distribution, and internet and multimedia content. It also engages in research on issues related to cross-cultural communication.

### Dunhuang Academy

The Dunhuang Academy is the largest institution in the world dedicated to the study of Dunhuang. It is a comprehensive cultural and heritage organization that integrates cave protection, academic research, and cultural promotion. The Academy manages six caves including three World Cultural Heritage sites, such as the Mogao Caves. It is China's most prolific cave-managing institution, protecting relics and cultural heritage spanning a history of 1,600 years and documenting the exchange between the East and West along the Silk Road. It bolsters the memories of multiple ethnicities and seeks to compose a new chapter of the Belt and Road Initiative.

### Academy of Contemporary China and World Studies

As indicated by its name, the Academy of Contemporary China and World Studies (ACCWS) is a national think-tank dedicated to research and policy planning focusing on contemporary China and the rest of the world. In addition to exploring effective ways to make China's stories reach an international audience, it also studies translation and interpretation, international discourse, cross-cultural communication, and global media opinions. It is affiliated with the China International Communications Group.

### China Academy of Translation

China Academy of Translation (CATL) is a national think tank devoted to the study of translation, interpretation, and international discourse. Its mission is to conduct research on China's translation capacity and on the role of translation incultural exchanges, coordinate national translation projects, organize advanced translator training, and promote cross-cultural communication and cooperation. It is affiliated with the China International Communications Group.

**图书在版编目（CIP）数据**

中国关键词．文物与文化遗产篇．敦煌：汉英对照 / 中国外文出版发行事业局等著；赵晓星主编；王冬梅等译．-- 北京：朝华出版社，2025. 5. -- ISBN 978-7-5054-5492-7

Ⅰ. D616；G127.424

中国国家版本馆 CIP 数据核字第 20245QJ114 号

# 中国关键词

## 文物与文化遗产篇 ◆ 汉英对照

## 敦煌

# KEYWORDS TO UNDERSTAND CHINA

## Cultural Artifacts and Heritage

## Dunhuang

作　　者　中国外文出版发行事业局　敦煌研究院　当代中国与世界研究院　中国翻译研究院
主　　编　赵晓星
中文编撰　敦煌专家组
　　　　　赵晓星　张俊民　杨秀清　杜　鹃　游自勇　张善庆　牟和谛［意］
　　　　　孔令梅　张文元　神　帅　杨瀚林　殷　曦　许　莅
　　　　　当研院编辑组
　　　　　陈晓星　华光灿　江灏锋　杨超慧　赵　庆　郑华为　朱文博
英文翻译　王冬梅
英文改稿　苏　格［美］
顾　　问　林东威
英文审定　王冬梅
项目管理　朱文博
项目执行　华光灿
责任编辑　张　璇
执行编辑　陈东宁　沈羿臻　李夷白
责任印制　陆竞赢　訾　坤
书籍设计　晶　田
排版制作　创世禧图文
出版发行　朝华出版社
社　　址　北京西城区百万庄大街 24 号　邮政编码 100037
出版合作　（010）68995571
订购电话　（010）68995509
联系版权　zhbq@cicg.org.cn
网　　址　http://zhcb.cicg.org.cn
印　　刷　天津中印联印务有限公司
经　　销　全国新华书店
开　　本　880mm × 1230mm　1/32
字　　数　200 千字
印　　张　9.25
版　　次　2025 年 5 月第 1 版　2025 年 5 月第 1 次印刷
装　　别　平
书　　号　ISBN 978-7-5054-5492-7
定　　价　108.00 元